1967

THE MASTERFUL MONK

By OWEN FRANCIS DUDLEY

WILL MEN BE LIKE GODS ?
THE SHADOW ON THE EARTH
THE MASTERFUL MONK
PAGEANT OF LIFE
THE COMING OF THE MONSTER

These five books constitute the first five
of the series of which *The Tremaynes
and the Masterful Monk* is the sixth.

THE MASTERFUL MONK

BY

OWEN FRANCIS DUDLEY

Author of

Will Men be like Gods?, The Shadow on the Earth, etc.

PROBLEMS OF HUMAN HAPPINESS—III

LONGMANS, GREEN AND CO.

LONDON · NEW YORK · TORONTO

LONGMANS, GREEN AND CO., INC.
55 FIFTH AVENUE, NEW YORK 3

LONGMANS, GREEN AND CO., LTD.
6 & 7 CLIFFORD STREET, LONDON W 1

LONGMANS, GREEN AND CO.
20 CRANFIELD ROAD, TORONTO 16

Twenty-sixth printing August, 1956

AUTHOR'S NOTE

This present volume is the third of a series dealing with problems of human happiness.

The first, *Will Men be like Gods?*, is an answer to the slanderers of Religion; the second, *The Shadow on the Earth*, to the slanderers of God. In *The Masterful Monk* I have endeavoured to meet the modern attack upon Man and his moral nature launched by those who would degrade him to the level of an animal.

I would like to mention that " Julian Verrers " in this tale is neither a literary affectation nor an exaggeration. He is a spokesman delivering faithfully the ideas of certain materialistic scientists, philosophers, and leaders of thought, whose names are before the public to-day, and whose writings are everywhere on sale. He speaks as they speak and says what they say.

PART 1

CHAPTER I

SHE was in her " library " this morning, sandwiched between the recesses of an enormous leather chair and *The Times*. Her presence behind the paper was revealed by the finger-tips gripping its extremities, also by little clouds of smoke which floated up and curled about. She had been quite still for fifteen minutes.

When at length the paper was lowered, she became visible with a cigarette in a long holder between her lips, and an absorbed look on her face.

She stood up, crushed out the cigarette in an ash-tray on the mantelpiece, looked towards the window and said, " Um."

Next she said, " Julian Verrers." A minute later she said " Julian Verrers " again ; this time as if she rather liked the sound of it. " Biologist ? . . . What's a biologist ? " She went across to a bookshelf and took down a dictionary. " One skilled in biology," said the dictionary. The next word was " Biology." It was defined as " the science of life in its various forms."

The dictionary closed with a snap, and went back to its place. She picked up *The Times* again.

At the head of one of the columns stood in bold letters —" A Plea for Freedom," and beneath it—" Speech by Mr. Julian Verrers." Then came half a dozen lines in italics, in which Mr. Julian Verrers was referred to as " the biologist." Underneath began a verbatim report of the speech.

She turned to the illustrated page muttering, " *The* biologist." Amongst the photographs was one subscribed, " Mr. Julian Verrers, whose speech of yesterday is reported elsewhere."

She studied it.

It was a very clear portrait ; the face of a man of about forty. The eyes were deep-set and straight-lidded, and appeared to be jet-black. The hair was swept sideways over a broad forehead, the photograph indicating slight greyness above the ears. She guessed the nose would be very straight in profile. Beneath a short upper lip, the mouth, though shapely, showed a peculiar, cynical twist.

" Julian Verrers."

She put down the sheets and stood there, thinking. Suddenly she went across to her writing-desk in the corner, pulled up a chair, fiddled about for paper and envelope, found them and began to write :—

" MAGGIE,—I want to meet Julian Verrers—this biologist person. See *Times* to-day, if you don't know him. But, of course you *do*. ' *The* biologist.' I'm hugely intrigued with this speech of his. And his face (illustrated page). You *will* work it, won't you, Maggie ?—Yours, BEAUTY.

" P.S.—For preference, at one of your ' very, very ' dinners."

The envelope she addressed to a Mrs. Sands-Woodford, of Eccleston Square.

She was called " Beauty " by her intimates.

It pleased her. It proclaimed that, physically, she was a complete success. It was true. She knew it. The blue depths in her eyes, the pure gold of her shingled head, the white of her skin, the very poise of her chal-lenged you to deny her right to the name.

It pleased her, too, to be considered intellectual. And she was, fairly so. What she lacked in experience, at twenty-three, she culled from books and clever people.

Books interested her. Clever people interested her. Life interested her. The bookshelves in her " library," as she chose to call it, shouted half the philosophies of the twentieth century. When friends came to tea at the flat, books would be lying about. She liked them to pick them up with, " I wish *I* could read these things." She would murmur : " Oh, well, they interest me, you see."

Books helped.

For it pleased her also to talk well, with the right men and right women. It was gratifying. She had once noticed a well-known author, a psychologist, talking-down to some brainless butterfly from mere politeness ; and had mentally resolved never to be talked-down-to herself. The incident had stimulated her to study the great man's writings. She happened to be introduced to him a few weeks later, and straightway tackled him on one of his own arguments. He did not talk-down to her. He deliberately drowned her with technical terms. He even asked her technical questions with a patronizing smile. Having courteously exhibited her ignorance of his science, he bowed and left.

The humiliation had rankled, but taught her to temper daring with discretion. After that she had kept within her range, or, if in danger, manœuvred into safer waters.

Yet, despite limitations, she maintained a reputation for being clever. And it pleased her.

Her flat was in Curzon Street.

She lived there alone, save for her maid and the necessary servants. To live alone, away from her people, was one of Beauty's whims. It symbolized her independence. It was not a pose. She enjoyed living alone. Whenever she went down to Dorsetshire to her people they protested. She merely kissed her mother and smacked her father, and went back to her flat in London.

She loved her flat.

It was all her own ; from the enormous leathern chair

in the library to the exquisite crockery in the kitchen.
The curtains and the carpets were unquestionably dis-
tinctive. All the curtains in all the rooms were deep,
clear orange, and all the carpets in all the rooms were
deep, clear green. These two colours throughout gave
the deliberate, daring note that she intended. And she
liked the mysterious, warm light that filtered through the
orange curtains half-drawn on a sunny day. It emphasized her own bold splendour. Very few women
could stand up against those orange curtains. Beauty
could—and did.

She had written to Mrs. Sands-Woodford on Monday.
On Tuesday the reply came.

Yes, said Mrs. Sands-Woodford, she knew Julian
Verrers. On receiving Beauty's letter she had telephoned,
asking him to her next " very, very " dinner, on Friday.
He had accepted. Would Beauty come ? She would
put her with him.

Beauty wrote straight back—" Maggie, you're a brick.
Of course I shall come. Exactly what I wanted. Ta,
tremendously.—Yours, BEAUTY."

She lunched that day at a house in Kensington Palace
Gardens.

It was a dull affair, and the customary half-hour in
the drawing-room afterwards was duller. She sustained a
bromide conversation with a semi-deaf barrister, who
rumbled on in a soporific monotone until somebody's
watch-case clicked, giving the signal, and people began
to rise with relief to express their regrets at leaving.

She started to walk back along Kensington Gore,
wondering why it was demanded of rational beings that
they should spend an hour and a half of the best part of
the day talking about nothing at one another.

" Dowds and frumps ! "

She disliked these people. They were inexpressibly flat. The sort of people who went out to lunch and ate and talked solely because it was done. They would probably do it all over again this evening at dinner some-where else, and to-morrow and the day after. They said the same thing in the same way to the same kind of people day after day. They were perfectly correct. They did exactly what they were expected to do. They never enthused. They just existed and went on.

It was not merely their conventions that irritated her ; Beauty was quite honest with herself. These people gave her no opportunity of shining. She liked shining. Her instinct scented their disapproval of anything like shining. You had to keep to a rut. If you became excited or earnest or controversial you were promptly refrigerated.

At lunch to-day she had so far forgotten herself as to talk with considerable heat about Julian Verrers' speech. A remark from her hostess about the King's visit some-where had cut her off. She had been refrigerated. A row of expressionless faces opposite had completed the process.

" Mugwumps ! I wish I'd smacked them."

Her mind turned to Mrs. Sands-Woodford's " very, very " people. They, at any rate, were never dull. They were alive. Many of them were brilliant men and women who had made their mark in life.

She stopped to look at Kensington Gardens, glittering in the sunshine of early spring. At the gates further down she turned in and sauntered along until she came to the bridge. The Serpentine was one long sparkle. Over the bridge she quickened her pace and started to walk the whole way round. By the time she reached the gates again the "Mugwumps" had vanished, ousted by somebody else. She was wondering what Julian Verrers would be like.

CHAPTER II

THE pagan notions of most of her friends disturbed Beauty very little nowadays.

Their morals, in practice, she found difficult. It had come as an unpleasant shock once to find that a man, with whom she had been particularly friendly, danced and ridden in the Row, was living with somebody else's wife, and his wife with the latter's husband, apparently by agreement. She had refused to believe it, when told; but, all the same, had challenged him with it next time they were riding. He had pulled up, laughed at her judicatory air, and answered: "Why not?" She had halted, sat there for a moment with the blood mounting to her face, and then wheeled round, lashed her horse furiously from him and galloped away with his parting imprecation in her ears: "Damn you, Beauty! Damn you, my little prig!"

No, she found their morals difficult. But she found it more difficult to answer that "Why not?" She could have fallen back on her religion for an answer, of course. That, however, did not suit her. She was dispensing with religion.

Beyond occasionally attending Mass at the Oratory, she had practically discarded her duties as a Catholic. Lately she had been asking herself why she was a Catholic at all; she had been given no choice in the matter; she had grown up·to find herself saddled with a set of beliefs utterly incompatible with the paganisms of the world in which she lived. With people like Mrs. Sands-Woodford and her "very, verys" she was silent about herself. She frankly preferred their liberty of outlook to what she mentally dubbed the bondage of her childhood.

*   *   *   *   *   *

" Maggie, let me have a look first. . . . The one in the middle ? "

Mrs. Sands-Woodford waited while Beauty scrutinized a group of three men talking together in the corner, and in particular the one who had been pointed out as Julian Verrers.

" Beauty, you're the limit. Come on ! " And her hostess led her by the hand through groups of two's and three's, at whom Beauty threw, " Hullo ! " and " Oh, there you are ! " in her passage.

Julian Verrers' back was towards them and had to be tapped.

" Mr. Verrers, this is Miss Dethier. You're with her at dinner."

He turned round, apologized for his back and bowed.

"Mr. Verrers, I'm enormously excited about you," began Beauty. " The ' Plea for Freedom ' was too entrancing. I simply had to meet you." She smiled expectantly.

He did not react, however, to her carefully rehearsed spontaneities, but merely nodded. With an " Excuse me, one moment," he turned to the two men with whom he had been talking, to finish the conversation.

Mrs. Sands-Woodford caught Beauty's eye. " Don't try effusiveness," she whispered. Beauty had coloured up. She stood there self-consciously, like a child waiting for attention.

" Forgive me, Miss Dethier. We were discussing something."

Verrers had turned back to her. The two men joined another group, and Mrs. Sands-Woodford sailed away. They were left alone.

" So we're to be together."

" Yes. I hope you didn't——"

" Oh, that's all right," he said. They had been talking

about the Labour scene in the House that day, he informed her. He proceeded to enlarge on it.

Beauty began to perceive how she had approached him wrongly. He was a very much " bigger " person than she had imagined. She had noted the deferential manner of the two men, and the furtive looks being directed at him from others in the drawing-room.

The Times photograph, she realized, had not done him justice ; it had given no indication of the impressiveness he conveyed ; or of his true appearance. He was startlingly handsome.

A gong boomed from down below. The door was flung open and dinner announced. People paired and began streaming out. Verrers offered her his arm ; and they were being swept down the stairs into the diningroom.

" Yes," she thought, as Verrers was placed with herself at the right of his hostess, " he's the guest of the evening."

She looked down the long dinner-table at the array of white arms and white fronts. There must have been quite twenty present. Maggie's dinners were always on a large scale. She knew most of them quite well ; some she had met only occasionally. There was one man whom she had not seen before. He was sitting exactly opposite, talking rather earnestly to his partner.

Verrers began to divide his attention between Mrs. Sands-Woodford and herself.

It was not until fish that she sensed an atmosphere of restraint over things. Usually these " very, very " dinners went with a terrific swing ; these people were anything but reserved. They were not at their ease to-night somehow. Instinctively she perceived that it had to do with the presence of Julian Verrers. There was something overpowering about him. She could feel it congealing the frivolities and witticisms that should have been flowing over the candle-flames.

The meat came round. As it was being handed to her, she remembered it was Friday. At the same moment Verrers turned to speak. She hesitated, and then accepted it. The man opposite, she noticed, refused.

" Mr. Verrers, I want you to talk shop." Mrs. Sands-Woodford's voice cut into a pause. " We break all the rules here."

" What kind of shop ? " Verrers looked at her questioningly.

" I want you," his hostess took the bull by the horns, " I mean, will you tell us whether you really believed what you said in your ' Plea for Freedom ' ? " She had raised her voice.

Beauty plunged in : " Yes, Mr. Verrers, I wish you would."

He leaned back and laughed, quite pleasantly.

" I've been asked that question at least fifty times in the last few days. People seem to doubt my sincerity." He straightened himself and looked down the table : " I don't know whether—— ? " The look suggested willingness to talk on condition of undivided attention.

All in a moment the ice was breaking. " Yes, *please* do." " Oh, yes, *do*." " Yes, tell us "—came in a volley from all directions. Beauty thrilled to their eagerness. She observed the man opposite looking interested, but doubtful.

" Yes, Mrs. Sands-Woodford, I certainly believe what I said." Verrers spoke the words slowly and then looked down the table again. " I imagine you want me to say something about the views I expressed in that speech ? If it interests you, I will do so. But I warn you beforehand that susceptibilities are liable to be shocked by them, especially those of religious people."

Beauty, watching his face, recognized the cynical twist about his mouth that she had noticed in *The Times* photograph.

"There are no religious susceptibilities here," said a woman's voice from the far end of the table.

The man opposite stirred, and looked in the direction from which it had come.

"Are you quite sure ? " he remarked quietly.

There was an uncomfortable pause. Verrers did not appear to notice the remark.

"I never water down my convictions either in public or private. What I said in that speech was to this effect. If men are to attain freedom they must deliberately break the chains of their own making. I pointed out that far and away the larger proportion of human unhappiness was self-inflicted, and that it was due to craven fear. Mainly the fear of inherited superstitions."

He fingered his wineglass.

"I said that the oldest and most depraving of these superstitions was the religious one, the idea of responsibility to some Being outside the universe for whose existence there is no scientific proof. No man can be free who lives by the notion that he is accountable for his actions to a God. Such an attitude means servility, slavery ; it produces a further notion called ' sin '—the idea that certain actions are punishable by this Being. No man can be free unless he acts according to the dictates of his nature, which very often means ' sinning,' in religious parlance."

He turned to Mrs. Sands-Woodford as if seeking her permission to continue. She smiled. A footman handed sweets to the man opposite. The fingers with which he took up a fork were trembling.

"My ' Plea for Freedom ' was intended as a challenge to all who allow themselves to be ruled by the theological dogmatism of the past. It has fostered this notion of moral responsibility. I maintained that there is no such thing as morality, except as a social convenience. I went further still ; I charged all those who talk so glibly about

the progress of humanity with cowardice, for refusing to
act on the consequences of what every reputable scientist
now knows—that man is evolved from some mammalian
stock resembling the modern ape.

" This fact involves, not a re-casting of theology, as
religious modernists say, but an entire rejection of
Christian dogmas. The Christian system rests on the
assumption of ' sin.' It is sheer cowardice for educated
men to cling to it, when, presumably, they know that
' sin ' consists in no more than tendencies inherited from
ape-ancestry."

He paused. Mrs. Sands-Woodford leaned towards
him :

" You said more than that in the speech ? "

" I did," he replied.

" About the consequences ? "

" Yes. About the consequences of our new knowledge."

Beauty, a little uncomfortable, was aware of the strained
attention around.

" Are you going to tell us ? " she asked, rather tremulously.

" Certainly. If you wish."

" Yes, please. No ladies will mind," called the same
woman's voice from the far end.

" There may be gentlemen present."

The remark produced a general start. It had come from
the man opposite. He was regarding Julian Verrers with
an unmistakable challenge in his look.

Verrers remained silent and completely self-possessed.

Nothing further came.

" The consequences," he resumed, as if nothing had
happened, " the inevitable consequences of our new
knowledge are these. Things formerly considered
immoral are now seen to be merely natural. The chains
which held men in the past from the release of their
instincts are now recognized as mere ecclesiastical shackles.

The days of subservience to a traditional authority are over. Modern science has taught us that man is not what religion has made him—a being apart. He is the product of a vast evolutionary process. He must take the consequences of this discovery about himself."

" Yes ? " Mrs. Sands-Woodford murmured.

" There can be no fixed standard of morality in an evolutionary system. Morality must progress with the system. A fixed code is harmful to society. Why, for instance, are the law-courts clogged with unsavoury divorce cases ? Merely because men and women submit to a fixed notion of permanence attached to the marriage union two thousand years ago by the Christian religion. Love, the most sacred thing in human life, still allows itself to be blindly fettered by an *un*sacred marriage-bond. And why ? Because of certain loathsome injunctions originally imposed by the Catholic Church, and still enforced. Further——"

" Thank you ! " It was from the man opposite.

Verrers looked quickly at him over the candle flames.

This time the remark was addressed directly to himself and could scarcely be ignored. Yet he did ignore it. And at that moment Beauty understood something—that there was a set purpose in what Verrers was saying. He was not merely talking. He intended to enforce his ideas upon his audience. He would not brook opposition.

" Further——"

" Thank you ! " It was snapped at him now. There was anger in the tone.

Verrers stared coldly at the interrupter ; and then, with a slight lift of the eyebrows, indicated amused surprise.

Mrs. Sands-Woodford took the cue from him, and smiled reassuringly at her guests.

" Mr. Raynor," she said to the angry-looking man on her left, " you're taking Mr. Verrers too seriously." She had said the wrong thing, however.

"Excuse me, Mrs. Sands-Woodford," said Verrers, "but I prefer to be taken seriously."

His hostess sat back and looked from left to right.

"Come, come," she laughed, "this is not a political meeting. Mr. Verrers, you're neglecting that *soufflé*."

He did not respond to her attempt.

"Mrs. Sands-Woodford, you asked me to discuss these matters. Do you wish me to continue or not?"

She was spared an answer by the man Raynor himself: "Perhaps Mrs. Sands-Woodford did not know that one of her guests was a Catholic."

"That," returned Verrers quickly, "may be of interest to one of her guests; but it hardly concerns the rest of us."

Mrs. Sands-Woodford looked rather helplessly at "the rest," seeking inspiration. They returned glances of sympathy.

"Really, you know, you two men *are* placing me in a difficult position. Er—Mr. Raynor, would you mind very much if Mr. Verrers were to finish what he was saying?"

"Yes, I should mind very much."

Verrers cleared his throat:

"A minority of one can scarcely expect to dictate to the dinner-table. Shall I continue?"

Mrs. Sands-Woodford looked undecided. Beauty experienced a sudden wave of anger against the man opposite, and exclaimed warmly: "Yes, Mr. Verrers, please go on." A murmur of approval decided the matter.

Verrers bowed.

"I was speaking of the marriage-bond, and how it fettered human love. With its removal, which is merely a matter of time, there will be a drastic change in the relations of the sexes. For example——"

"I must say good evening, Mrs. Sands-Woodford."

Raynor stood up—white and resolute. The movement was sudden, and his shoulder caught a footman unawares.

There was a shattering crash on the parquet floor, followed by the slither of broken china and glass.

" I must also apologize for my clumsiness."

He pushed back his chair, bowed to Mrs. Sands-Woodford, and walked towards the door. One of the footmen, recollecting himself, opened it smartly. Raynor passed out. The door closed again.

No one spoke. . . .

" You may bring the ices."

Mrs. Sands-Woodford signalled to a footman standing there stupidly. A minute later the clink of the débris being swept into a dust-pan, mysteriously smuggled into the room, broke the spell. The tension relaxed. Beauty looked at Julian Verrers. He was eating an ice.

" When we're smoking, perhaps ? " his hostess whispered.

Verrers understood and smiled.

Subdued conversation began to flow.

CHAPTER III

BEAUTY took a cigarette, lit it, inhaled deeply, blew a long trail of smoke, lay back against the pillows and watched the cloud eddying about the light above her head.

On the little table at the side of her bed there was a silver tray with tea; her maid had just placed it there and withdrawn. She looked at her watch. It was a quarter to twelve.

She began to think.

It had been a bewildering evening. A series of mental jolts.

Uppermost in her mind loomed Julian Verrers; the sense of his dominating personality was still upon her; an overwhelming personality. At the dinner-party no one else had counted. He was disconcertingly outspoken. He had fascinated her. As a specimen of virility he was magnificent—from the black intensity of eyes to the whole physical Greek-god perfection.

His ideas had certainly not been veiled.

Some of them had been familiar. The consequences of those ideas, that he had put before them, had come as a shock, however.

Was it her conscience that had been shocked? She doubted it. Her conventions? Hardly; she had not many left. And yet something within her had been thrown out of gear. He had been so horribly thorough. The thought came to her—If her people had been there? No, she could not see them there at all. She simply could not picture them listening to Julian Verrers. But then they were devout Catholics.

Of course, it was a matter of outlook really.

The others had listened without the slightest qualms.

17

She knew that quite well. She had watched their faces. Their interest was purely intellectual. They had no moral sense to shock. Ah !—moral sense ? It was her moral sense that had been thrown out. " I suppose one's moral sense *is* one's conscience."

Beauty sipped her tea, and went on thinking furiously.

" No, it is *not*. I haven't a conscience. I haven't the slightest compunction about that meat. . . . That fool Raynor !—refusing meat, telling that crowd he was a Catholic, walking out ! Good heavens ! If Catholics are expected to make asses of themselves in public——" She stopped, conscious of the fact that she was talking aloud. " No," she thought, " and I haven't any conscience about listening to Julian Verrers. It's just one's moral notions getting jarred. One's moral sense is simply one's training. I've been trained as a Catholic."

She was sensible of a growing irritation.

" It's utterly absurd for a woman of twenty-three to be tied down. I've a right to think for myself. It's what he said—I'm the slave of a code. No, I'm not. I won't be. Why should—— Oh, damn it all ! . . ."

Her mind went back to the events following Raynor's embarrassing exit.

With the arrival of coffee Mrs. Sands-Woodford had invited Julian Verrers to continue from where he had been interrupted by " Mr. Raynor's unmannerly behaviour." Verrers had shrugged his shoulders, conveying the impression that the incident was unworthy of notice, and then begun to talk again. Beauty had wondered at the instant attention accorded. His first sentence had silenced every chatterer's tongue.

It was now that he had spoken out so boldly, without any restraint. He had re-emphasized the folly of fear. " Freedom, freedom for humanity, that is all I am fighting for." He had said that two or three times. He had explained what freedom meant—freedom to follow instincts, to experience, freedom for nature to express itself.

" But wouldn't it be rather disastrous socially ? " Mrs. Sands-Woodford had put in. " Not if laws were framed on a frank recognition of the findings of biology," he had replied. And then he had told them what the exercise of moral freedom would involve.

First, marriage, as hitherto understood, would cease. The marriage-bond would b'e abolished ; the tragedies and cruelties consequent upon it would disappear. Instead, temporary unions would be legalized.

" In other words—free-love," from Mrs. Sands-Woodford.

" Precisely."

He had broken off at the approach of liqueurs and waited until they had been served. Beauty had taken the opportunity of scrutinizing some of the party. As far as she could judge they were in agreement. One or two had looked doubtful. There had been sipping and cigarette-lighting. The door had closed.

He had broached the matter of birth-control. " Free-love also means freedom to reproduce or not, at choice." Temporary unions must not be hampered by undesired children. Love and parenthood would have to be separated. Selective breeding—yes. For the " herd " to breed indiscriminately was socially unsound. Reproduction would have to be controlled by the State. Clinics would have to be established in which birth-control could be officially taught.

At this juncture some man had ventured : " But doesn't this merely strike at freedom from another angle ? " Verrers had replied : " No, not if the necessary laws were scientifically framed." Applied scientific knowledge could never be the enemy of freedom. The man had not seemed satisfied. Instead he had queried whether the axiom were valid, and rather astutely remarked that the State had applied scientific knowledge during the Great War, but hardly for the freedom of the millions who were slaughtered.

Julian Verrers had not appreciated the thrust, a slight frown manifesting his dislike of the interruption.

The rest of what he had said centred on Christian as opposed to Natural ideals. " Christian ideals have clogged humanity with its own waste-products." Why were values placed on human life in direct contravention to the dictates of Nature ? Merely because Christianity had traded on fairy-tales of eternal life. Why was the individual preserved to the detriment of the community ? Why were the diseased and maimed condemned to drag out their miserable existence to the bitter end ? Solely because Christianity had laid down a spurious obligation to preserve life. Why was euthanasia still opposed ? Because of a sneaking fear of suicide and murder ; because Christianity had warped the human mind. " The notion that men's lives belong to a Deity and not to themselves has entailed pain and agony untold." He had added, with a glance in the direction of his recent doubter, that the Deity had evinced remarkably little interest in human lives during the Great Carnage.

" Before we leave you men to your port," his hostess had suggested, " tell us what ' Natural ideals ' are." And he had explained how Nature always eliminated the unfit as a biological necessity, by natural selection. The survival of the strong supplied a life-giving principle. Any animal species secured dominancy at the expense of its weaker kind. Primitive tribes, living closest to Nature, followed her precepts. Their incurable sick were abandoned or put to death, or their end accelerated ; the same with the insane, or the aged.

Beauty had winced at this, partly at his callous tone and partly at the idea. He had noticed it and said : " Miss Dethier, I know all this is harrowing to sentiment ; but if we want freedom from false values we must take

Nature as our guide. We are the products of Nature.
Nothing that is natural is wrong."

And with that he had ended.

Mrs. Sands-Woodford had risen with : " Mr. Verrers,
you've absorbed us ! Positively absorbed us ! " She had
asked him whether he would be making any further
speeches, and he had told them that there would be a
second one at the Queen's Hall shortly.

" How splendid ! Now, Beauty and you others, come
along ! "

And the men had been left to themselves.

Upstairs in the drawing-room she had planted herself
at Beauty's side, and expressed herself freely on " that
Raynor man."

After that :

" You were a little bit shocked with Julian Verrers ?
Confess it."

" I don't know about ' shocked,' " Beauty had answered.
" But—well, it wants thinking over."

" You like him ? "

She had pondered.

" Er—he fascinates me. Yes, he's horribly fascinating,
and he's appallingly good-looking. And I suppose he's
brilliant. But—Maggie, he *is* rather frightening."

" Forceful ? Overbearing ? "

" Y-es . . . I suppose it's that, partly. Maggie, was I
desperately dull ? "

" My dear, nobody can shine with Julian Verrers
present. It's his personality. He expects to hold the
floor."

Beauty had thought.

" He's a coming man, I suppose."

" My dear, he's come ! "

" But he's come so suddenly ; I never heard of him
until his speech."

"Before the public? Yes. Specializing for years though. Biology, of course."

Mrs. Sands-Woodford had prattled on about him: He had served in the War, and had a leg broken.

"Now, my dear, here are the men. And here's our Julian. And don't let him frighten you, Beauty."

Julian Verrers had strolled up to them. Mrs. Sands-Woodford had given him her place on the divan beside Beauty, and moved off to chatter elsewhere.

Beauty had found her tongue now. She had also found that he could be human when he chose. He had listened and even drawn her out, apparently anxious to discover her interests. She had told him about her flat in Curzon Street, and her books and authors. He had jested about some of them. At the end, when the others were making a movement to depart, he had risen with genuine reluctance to say good night, and thrilled her with: "I wonder if we shall meet again. I hope so."

"I—I hope so, too," she had stammered.

And then, suddenly, for some unknown reason, she had felt afraid.

From the foot of the staircase in the hall a few minutes later, with Mrs. Sands-Woodford's arm in her own, she had watched a footman assisting him into his coat. He had turned and smiled. The double-doors had been flung wide by two inclined automata, and he had passed down the steps to a large car waiting alongside the pavement. After a direction to the chauffeur, also inclined, he had stepped inside. The click of the door, a soft purr, and the car had glided out of the stream of light.

"And that's that," from Mrs. Sands-Woodford, who had then kissed her good-bye: "Beauty, you're a golden goddess to-night with that hair and dress. Gold sheen ? Cunning, Beauty, very cunning ! "

She had laughed and run down the steps to her own car, which had drawn up next.

Beauty sat up in bed.

She looked at her watch again. It was nearly one o'clock. She removed a silken covering from her shoulders, rolled it up into a ball and threw it in the direction of an arm-chair by the window. Then she re-arranged the pillows, flung back the eiderdown over the foot of the bed and touched a switch behind her head.

In the darkness there was a rustling of linen sheets, and finally silence.

About an hour later the moon crept up above the houses opposite, ventured through the uncurtained window and discovered Beauty lying on her back with her hands behind her head, looking out into the night.

" Whew ! ' A blanket followed the eiderdown.

No sound for a time.

" Oh, stop thinking ! "

No sound for a time.

" Oh, hang it all ! I'm not a child. . . . He was only putting it scientifically. . . . The rest was nerves. Nerves ! Nerves ! Nerves ! . . . Go to sleep, you ass ! "

CHAPTER IV

MAJOR BRANDRETH crossed over the Bayswater
Road, passed into Kensington Gardens, and then
sauntered slowly along the Serpentine.

He stopped on his way to watch Peter Pan piping in
the sun of the May morning to his bronzed admirers
swarming up from the green beneath his perch.

" Cheeky little devil ! " And he went on.

At the elm-avenue he left the Serpentine and walked
over the grass sward between the trees up to where Watts'
statue stood at the farther end. " Physical Energy " was
exuding its title to-day, horse and rider burnished and
radiant as the spring life around. Another few hundred
yards, and the Round Pond came into view, and beyond it
Kensington Palace, with the spire behind lightly veiled in
London haze.

The Major selected a chair under the trees and sat
there flicking with his stick at the grass, scattering dew-
drops. He took a cigarette out of his case, lit it, put the
case back, and from another pocket drew out an envelope.
From the envelope he took a letter.

This he read from beginning to end. It was signed—
" Eric Esterton." He replaced it and the envelope in his
pocket, and looked away over the Round Pond.

" Wonder what it is. I'll go, though."

He took out a note-book and consulted it. The jottings
revealed engagements for the next few days. There came
an empty space at " Saturday, May 12th." He removed a
pencil from the back of the note-book and wrote in the space
opposite the date—" Week-end at Hendringham Park."

That over, the Major settled down to a reverie.

The letter had awakened certain memories. They were memories of this time a year ago—of a garden set amidst the glories of Nature, a great monastery looming in the background, the white Alps towering beyond. In the garden amongst the trees lay a young man on his back in an ambulance, his face emaciated and marked with pain. The Major had found him there like that—Eric Esterton ; he had been broken for life on the Alps. Last autumn he had brought him back to England, and delivered to Lord and Lady Esterton their son—a helpless cripple.

The Major had not seen him since that day. He had not even been asked to Hendringham: Lord and Lady Esterton, though grateful for what he had done, had connected him in some way with what had happened to Eric at that monastery in the Alps. The accident on the mountains had been followed later by his reception into the Catholic Church in spite of his parents' violent opposition. Eric, with his shattered body, had been brought back to them a Catholic. Lord Esterton, during the short stay at Hendringham after his arrival with Eric, had hinted to the Major, more by manner than by word, that he should have done something to prevent the " outrageous occurrence." Actually, he had not even been at the monastery at the time. Though not a religious man himself, the Major had heartily disliked their attitude.

They had seemed to regard Eric's religion almost as a greater evil than the accident. Particularly, they had been embittered against Brother Anselm, the monk who had received him into the Church. The Major had remonstrated that a man's religion was his own look-out, and warmly defended Brother Anselm as a man of scrupulous honour and a personal friend of his own.

It had been useless, though. They had refused to consider the matter in any other light than that of an underhand business ; the monk had taken advantage of Eric's helpless condition. The Honourable Eric Esterton had been baited for his name and, of course, for the coffers of Rome. It was an insult to the family honour. " I'll alter my will," had been Lord Esterton's final fling.

That was eight months ago. Eric had written fairly frequently, each time informing him that there was no change in the situation.

But now, this morning had come a letter asking him down to Hendringham. He gathered that something had happened. It evidently had to do with Lord Esterton himself : " The Dad wants you to come. I'll tell you all about it when you are here," wrote Eric.

The Major roused himself, and came back to Kensington Gardens and the Round Pond. Children were playing there now. He could hear their clear voices. Sailing-boats were being launched gleefully, and scudding about to the fitful spring breezes over the water. He could detect its lapping.

As he watched, he became aware of a girl sitting on a chair a little distance to his left, also looking at the children. She was smartly dressed. He could only catch her side-face half hidden under a close-fitting hat. There was something familiar about it, though. Next moment he had recognized her :

" Beauty ! I'm damned ! "

The Major hesitated ; he saw an opportunity. He crept in a half-circuit from his own chair to behind where she was sitting ; then advanced boldly with—" Ticket. Twopence, please ! " He watched a charming young lady feeling mechanically for twopence in a hand-bag, and presenting it to him without looking up. The Major took the twopence and also her hand. . . .

" What—— ! "

"Morning, Beauty ! Holding a park-keeper's hand, eh ? "

" Major Brandreth ! . . ."

Beauty sat back and laughed delightfully. She kicked at his shin.

" You appalling person ! What are you doing here ? "

He drew up another chair and planted himself beside her, handing back the twopence. " I'm soaking my soul in Nature."

" Same here. Isn't it gorgeous ? "

The Major studied her.

" How's life ? "

" So, so."

" When did I see you last ? "

" You ought to have seen me last night. Why weren't you there ? "

" Where ? "

" At Mrs. Sands-Woodford's."

" Oh, that high-brow show. Not in my line."

" Maggie said she'd asked you."

" She did."

Beauty turned round.

" Julian Verrers was there. Have you met him ? "

" No. Heard about him. What's he like ? "

Beauty entered on a description which ended with : " And there's a sort of cynical something about his mouth."

She looked at the Major. He was suddenly sitting bolt upright.

' What do you know of Julian Verrers ? "

" Very little. Why ? I never met him until last night," replied Beauty.

" How old is he ? "

" About forty, I should say."

The Major thought.

" Do you happen to know whether he was out in France during the War—with the Gunners, shall we say ? "

" I don't know about the Gunners, but he certainly served in the War. Maggie said so. He had a leg broken."

The Major turned towards her. His eyes had lighted curiously.

" Do you know anything more ? "

" Not much. But why ? "

The other watched her. At length he said :

" Yes, Beauty. I *do* know Julian Verrers."

" You do ? But you said you didn't."

" I didn't know Julian Verrers was the Verrers *I* knew. Apparently he is. I hadn't put the two together. I only knew Captain Verrers' surname in the Army."

There was a pause.

" Pity you didn't meet him again, at Maggie's," said Beauty.

The Major did not reply. She prodded at a worm with the toe of her shoe.

" Major, what's up ? You're mysterious."

He looked up enigmatically.

" I think, perhaps, we won't talk about Julian Verrers."

He switched off deliberately : " Look here, Beauty, have you ever come across the Estertons ? "

She laughed in a puzzled way.

" You weird person ! Oh, very well. The Estertons ? I don't think so. You mean the Hendringham crowd ? "

" Yes. Did you ever meet Eric—the son, eldest one ? "

" No, not that I'm aware of. Eric ? Didn't something happen to him ? "

" Something did," said the Major. " Smashed himself, climbing, last year."

" Oh, I remember now. Yes, I heard about it."

The Major laid his hand on the back of her chair.

" Beauty, I'd like you to meet Eric Esterton."

" Me ? Why me in particular ? "

" Dunno quite. But I'd like you to. Er—aren't you a Catholic ? "

She moved.

" Why ? What's that to do with it ? "

" Well, he became an R.C. after it."

" Yes ? " Indifferently.

" Thought it might help him—same religion and all that. Not many Catholics knocking about at Hendringham. Hell of a row with his people over it, at first."

" Yes ? " Still indifferently.

" Heard from him this morning. Wants me to go there. Rather think his people have climbed down. Supposing things are all right, would you like me to run you down sometime ? "

Beauty uncrossed her legs.

" Oh, I don't know."

The Major experienced a sense of disappointment. It was unlike her.

" But you'd like Eric. He's—so darned fine, the way he's taken it and all that. Anyway, wouldn't hurt you, would it ? "

" I daresay not."

Which meant that she did not want to be pressed further. This unresponsive Beauty was new to him.

" Beauty, what's up ? You're mysterious." It was the phrase she had applied to himself.

" That's what I said of you just now," she answered. " Let's both be mysterious, then. You dried up over Julian Verrers. I dry up over Eric Esterton. Quits."

The Major laughed. They changed the subject.

§ 2

On Saturday he went down to Hendringham Park.

At Windern station, two miles from the house, a chauffeur was waiting on the platform and a car outside. He sped through the Sussex hedge-rows wondering what Eric's " The Dad wants you to come " portended. There was another thing in the letter that had puzzled him : " Somebody will be here in June. So will you, when you know *who*."

At the lodge gates the car slowed up. A man came out in response to the horn and opened them. They passed up the drive at a lessened pace, rabbits darting across from the woods on either side, and over a bridge crossing the river that ran at the bottom of the Hendringham grounds. Beyond that, the great Georgian house appeared, and sunny lawns sloping up to the southern front. The car came to a standstill opposite the terrace steps.

At the same moment the front doors opened and some-one came out. The Major recognized Lord Esterton. Half a minute later he was being genially grasped by the hand.

The grasp revealed immediately the truth of " The Dad wants you to come." Lord Esterton linked his arm as he led him into the hall. He brushed aside a footman to attend upon him himself, manifesting, in every gesture, genuine delight. In the drawing-room it was the same. Lady Esterton came forward, wafting an aroma of tea, kindliness in her eyes, the warmth of her manner un-mistakable. He exchanged courtesies and sat down, astonished.

What on earth had happened ? The cold, haughty couple he remembered had vanished. Here were two simple people welcoming him with unfeigned pleasure.

He pulled himself together.

" And how's our Eric ? " His own question surprised him.

Last time it would have been, " And how's your son ? "

" Eric's coming now," said Lady Esterton.

Through the open glass-doors, following her glance, he saw an ambulance being wheeled across the terrace by a male nurse. Lord Esterton opened the doors wider and went outside. " All right, Spence." The Major watched the father taking over the ambulance and then wheeling it towards the drawing-room. He forestalled Lady Esterton in clearing the gangway of an arm-chair.

" All clear ! " came a familiar voice.

Then :

" Dear old Major ! "

He found a hand stretching out from the ambulance,
and himself grasping it.

" Well, Eric, my boy ? "

The ambulance was manœuvred into position near the
tea-table : " Getting on the Dad. Barged over the hot-
cakes yesterday." Lord Esterton smiled.

And in that smile and Eric's chaff the Major perceived
a new relationship between the father and son.

At tea he did most of the talking, the others listening.
As he related happenings since their last meeting he took
stock of Eric. His appearance was much the same as last
year, emaciated and fragile. The same unbroken spirit
and boyish eagerness animated him. There were still the
undeniable good looks, in spite of his crippled condition—
the fair, curly hair, the peculiar radiance in the eyes that
had always puzzled him.

Afterwards, when tea had been removed, Lord Esterton
strolled on to the terrace and Lady Esterton murmured
an excuse. They were left together for a few moments.

" Well ? " said the Major.

" Dear old Major ! " Eric's eyes were bright. " The
Dad's going to tell you all about it himself. He wants to.
But you've seen it already ? "

" Couldn't help it. Astounding ! "

" You're not to let the Dad tell you the other thing.
That's mine."

" What, who's coming in June ? Who the devil is it ? "

Eric laughed : " I'll tell you this evening. The Dad's
waiting for you now."

The Major had to allay his curiosity.

Lord Esterton reappeared.

They went off together, across the lawns and down to the river. There, along the path at its side, came what the Major was expecting.

"Major Brandreth, I want to tell you something."

He found himself listening to what was virtually a confession. Lord Esterton hid nothing.

The tale was this.

One evening, a month ago, Eric had undergone one of his recurrent attacks of pain. Lord Esterton had been in his room at the time. Usually the male nurse, Spence, administered a drug before the pain reached its crisis. On this occasion Eric deliberately and repeatedly refused it, and endured the agony unalleviated. Afterwards, when the attack had subsided, the father had questioned him on this strange insistence, intimating that it was senseless.

"Not so senseless as you think," Eric had replied. And then he had given him the reason.

That night the father had lain awake in the throes of a mental struggle; for, dimly though he understood it, he had learnt this much—Eric had endured that unnecessary pain for *his* sake. He had of set purpose offered up that agony as a kind of expiatory act to break down the estrangement between them. And he would do it again, unless . . .

Eric had not said it in so many words, but Lord Esterton had known well enough that this "madness" (he had called it) would continue as the price of his own intolerance, and as long as that intolerance remained. "You hate my religion, and you've made Mother hate it," the boy had declared, and that he was making things impossible between them.

All through the night he had wrestled, Eric's clear gaze searching his soul in the darkness. A dozen times or more he had resolved against that appeal, impelled by the bigotry of generations.

In the early dawn, restless and sleepless, he had paced about his room, cursing his stubborn pride.

After breakfast a broken man was kneeling by his son's bed, the son's hand in his own. . . .

" Damned good of you to tell me, Lord Esterton."
They gripped.

Later he learned how Lady Esterton, amazed at the change in her husband, had questioned him. He had told her everything. Her own antipathy had been largely borrowed. She had gone straight to Eric, gladly, willingly, her mother's heart aching for reconciliation. The barrier of a year had been swept down with one touch of his hand upon her cheek : " Dear old Mater, you didn't understand ; that was all."

After dinner the Major went to Eric's room. It was on the ground-floor.

As he entered, the same impression was borne upon him, as before, of its pathetic bravery—the walls hung with football and cricket teams. On mantelpiece and tables stood silver cups and trophies. There were a couple of guns in a corner with a battered tin-hat above. The Major remembered them all—and their mute witness.

The cripple was in bed, a look of expectancy on his face.

" The Dad's told you ? "

" Everything," he said, and sat down.

" What do you think of it ? "

" Darned queer thing your religion," he replied, grinning.

And then they discussed the great happening.

" Did the Dad tell you they were not going up for the season ? " Eric was asking later.

" No. Didn't tell me that," the Major answered:

" Basil's representing the noble family." Basil was his younger brother.

" Good boy." This was not the mysterious news that Eric had promised to divulge, though.

" Have you guessed yet who's coming here in June ? " from the bed.

The Major sat up.

" Can't imagine."

" Would you like me to tell you ? "

" I would."

Eric waited a moment.

" Brother Anselm's coming here in June."

The Major stared.

" What ? "

" Brother Anselm's coming here in June."

" Just say that again, will you ? "

" Brother Anselm's coming here in June."

The Major stood up, seized a chair, and did a fox-trot round the room.

" The *Doc* at Hendringham ! "

" Yes."

" How the devil did you work it ? "

" I didn't work it. The Dad suggested it."

" No ? "

" He asked me whether I'd like him to come. I think he wants to make a sort of personal apology for the things he wrote. I'd told him, of course, again and again, that Brother Anselm hadn't ' got hold ' of me. I don't think he ever really believed it. He just wanted to, that was all. Anyway, he doesn't now. I told him all about Brother Anselm, when things came right. Major, it simply pulverized him. He'd never understood a monk being like that. I told him about the Verrers part of it, the What is it ? "

The Major had started at the name.

" No, go on, Eric. Go on. I'll tell you afterwards "

The other looked momentarily puzzled. He continued, however :

"Well, when he heard about that thing at the Front, it just thrilled him. The Dad's an old soldier himself, you know. And Brother Anselm at the monastery, too—what he did for me. It bowled him over. I was to write straight off and ask him to come and stop with us, if ever he got the chance. I did, you bet. And——" Eric switched on a light, hunted and produced a letter. "And that's his reply. Read it."

The Major took the letter. It was headed :—

> "Il Monastero, Issano sott' Alpi,
> "Italia.

"MY DEAR ERIC,—Your news came as a great surprise. Your letter came first, and then one from your father by the next post, telling me everything.

"*Deo gratias*. It has made me very happy. I had hardly dared to hope for this.

"For more, wait until we meet. For we are going to. I have just been ordered to return to England, and have permission to stay with you. Expect to arrive at the beginning of June. It will be great, and I am looking forward more than I can say. It is very good of you to have asked me. Is it really a year since you left us ?

"About yourself——"

"Whoa !" The Major looked up. "Not for me, this."

"Oh, yes, sorry ; I'd forgotten. Turn to the last page."

The Major found it :—

"How's the Major getting on ? I gather he will be with you shortly. Ask him from me whether he remembers that hiding I gave him for sitting on the end of your pram. Throw something at his head for me—and tell him to be at Hendringham in June.—Good-bye, Ever Yours, ANSELM."

"Great lad, the Doc !" said the Major, grinning. He handed back the letter.

" Well, what do you think of it ? " from Eric.

" Let us pray," he replied.

" Let us—— ? "

" Don't disturb me. I'm praying—that this great event may be worthily celebrated. . . . No, don't trouble ! "

Eric pressed a button at the side of his bed.

" Of course, if you insist—— " said the Major.

A manservant appeared.

And reappeared with whisky and a siphon.

" I like that man," said the Major, getting to work. " He's a man of God. He answered my prayer."

He lit a cigarette.

" Yes, that's great ! Will he come in that, what do you call it—habit ? "

" Ordinary clothes, I should think," replied Eric. " They wear short coat and trousers in England."

" Shorts ? Don't like it."

" Owl, Major ! "

They talked on about the monk, until :

" Major," Eric's tone changed, " what were you going to say about Verrers just now ? "

At the question the Major put down his glass. He raised himself in the arm-chair.

" I was hoping you'd forgotten that."

" Why ? Tell me."

The Major rose, went slowly across to the window, and stood with his hands plunged in his trousers pockets. " Like those twilight effects in the garden."

" Tell me," repeated Eric.

The other turned round.

" Your mention of Verrers reminded me of something. But I don't know that I want to bring it up."

" About what ? Verrers ? We both know pretty well the same about him, don't we ? "

" We both know about him and the Doc at the Front, and we both know about him and the Doc at the Monastery. But I rather think we don't *both* know what he's doing now."

" I've no notion. Have you ? "

" I hadn't—until this week." The Major traced a pattern with his finger on the window-sill. " Oh, well, I suppose it won't do any harm." He turned again and regarded Eric fixedly.

" You've seen in the papers about this *Julian* Verrers ? "

He watched the other mentally fumbling : " *Julian* Verrers, yes. But—— ? "

" Ever connected him with our Verrers ? "

He saw perplexity giving way to amazement.

" Major ! He's *not* ? "

" He is, my boy, I'm afraid. Look there."

And Eric found himself staring at a photograph which the Major had produced from his notecase.

It had been cut out of a paper.

He drew in his breath with a low whistle.

The Major, coming down next morning, found Spence and one of the menservants busy in the hall with a kind of stretcher. There was a car in readiness outside.

" Trotting him round early, Spence ? "

" Mr. Eric's going to church, sir."

" Church ? Sunday, is it ? "

" Yes, sir."

" Of course," said the Major.

He went in to breakfast. In answer to an enquiry of Lord Esterton he learned that it was Eric's custom to be driven over to Windern on Sunday mornings for Mass at the Catholic Church. " We haven't got as far as going with him, yet," said Lady Esterton with humour in her eyes. As the father left the breakfast-room to see Eric off, the Major remarked : " I'll walk over there. Come back with him."

He ascertained the way, and half an hour after, set out.

From the bottom of the drive he took a short cut across the fields, leading off from the main road opposite the lodge-gates. The dew lay on the grass unlapped by the morning sun, buttercups and daisies peeping through the glitter and patterning the green.

A mile of this, including stiles, brought him to Windern. He found the little Catholic Church and the Hendringham car outside, Spence and the chauffeur strolling up and down.

He hovered uncertainly by the door ; then pushed it open and went inside, to find a concentrated hush of kneeling people. He decided for an available chair near by. As he knelt the hush intensified.

A bell rang. It was the Consecration, he guessed ; having been at Mass before. The bell rang again, accompanied by movements of the priest at the altar. As the tension relaxed he looked about. Eric's ambulance was in the corner to his left. Eric was lying there, very still.

The Mass continued until people began to rise and walk with bowed heads towards the altar-rail.

There was a movement at his left, and he saw a man approach Eric and, then, wheel him up the aisle in front of the sanctuary. The priest came through the gates at the centre of the rail, and bent over Eric . . . and returned to the altar. Then the ambulance was being wheeled back.

Outside, when Mass was over, the Major felt rather out of it.

The Honourable Eric Esterton speedily became a centre of attraction, people surrounding him to talk. He seemed thoroughly at home with them, especially with the children. He was holding two little pairs of hands together, while their owners, a small boy and girl, chattered away. As the circle broke up, Spence came forward,

He turned the ambulance towards the pathway leading to the road. The two children, claiming a privilege, wheeled Eric slowly, with mutual admonishments of caution, to the gates, before which stood the car.

The Major followed and waited while Spence and the chauffeur lifted the cripple inside on the stretcher, after unstrapping it from the wheels. They fixed the wheels to an attachment at the back of the car.

" Travelling circus," said Eric as the Major stepped in and sat alongside. He waved good-bye to the children as they moved off.

" Topping kids," the other remarked. He studied Eric's stretcher.

" The Dad had it made," the cripple explained. It was certainly ingenious, with springs beneath the canvas to take jolts—an evidence of the father's care.

As they entered the Hendringham drive, Eric, for the first time since the previous evening, referred to the discovery made known by the Major :

" I'm wondering whether I'd better write and tell Brother Anselm—about Verrers. What do you think ? "

The Major played with the window-strap.

" Ought to know, I should say. Especially as he's coming to England."

" So it seems to me." He added : " I'll do so."

There was no need, however.

For in the hall, when they were back, a letter was waiting for Eric. It was addressed in Brother Anselm's handwriting. He opened and read it through, and then looked up at the Major, who was concealing his curiosity examining a golf club.

" Yes ? " He put down the club.

" Brother Anselm knows," said Eric, his usually pale face flushed with colour. " In fact, the reason for his coming to England is—Julian Verrers ! "

CHAPTER V

§ 1

THE policeman on duty in front of Brompton Oratory was fond of " observing."

This particular Sunday morning in June he was observing two men. They had just met. They were standing and talking on the pavement by the railings that guarded the church. It was the taller of the two who interested the policeman ; for he knew who it was.

" Julian Verrers, that is. Know 'is photer."

While he was looking, his eye caught the vanguard of what speedily became a crowd streaming down the steps out of the Oratory. He smartened up and began to get busy. Holding up the traffic, he managed to achieve a further observation.

Julian Verrers' head was turned towards the Oratory. He appeared to be staring at someone. On the steps stood an exquisitely dressed girl, talking to some men.

When next the policeman's eye was disengaged, the little group was raising hats and dispersing. The girl walked down the steps and towards the exit at the left of the railings. At the same time Julian Verrers, after hurriedly dismissing his friend, threaded his way to the exit also.

Dutifully, but with an inward expletive, the policeman released his eye from this interesting development and also the traffic from east and west. The ensuing swirl blotted out any chances of immediate reconnaissance. The road normal again, he swung carelessly up the centre for a distance. When he returned, it was along the pavement, where Julian Verrers and the exquisitely dressed girl were now engaged in conversation.

He passed them. They were expressing surprise at meeting. The girl was not only exquisitely dressed, but exquisitely beautiful. He stood at ease about five yards away, sideways to the two, studying intently the buildings opposite. . . .

" You won't think me impertinent if I ask a personal question ? "

" Oh dear, no." A delightful trilling laugh. " I love impertinent questions."

" All the easier for me. Are you a Catholic, Miss Dethier ? "

Pause.

" Why do you ask ? "

" You didn't give me a hint of it at Mrs. Sands-Woodford's. I said things a Catholic would hardly appreciate. Are you one ? You go to Mass apparently."

A throat was cleared.

" Mr. Verrers, I'll answer your question if you'll answer mine. Is it true that you left the Church ? Mrs. Sands-Woodford says so."

" That is very obliging of Mrs. Sands-Woodford."

A moment's hesitation.

" Supposing I admit it, will you admit my interpretation of your presence at the Oratory on a Sunday morning ? "

" That I am a Catholic ? "

" Yes."

An uneasy little laugh.

" I really don't know whether I am or not. Will that satisfy you ? "

After an interval :

" For the present, yes. You'll forgive my curiosity ? "

" If you'll forgive mine. Call it quits, shall we ? "

A relieved laugh. Movement of feet.

" Well, good-bye, Mr. Verrers."

" Good-bye. . . . Oh, will you be at Lady Derringham's by any chance ? "

" To-morrow night ? Yes, indeed. Why, will you ? "

" I'm due there, yes."

" We shall meet, then. Lestroi is playing, you know."

" So I understand. But I shall be more interested in you."

" Poor me ! . . . To-morrow, then."

The policeman pulled himself together and began to pace unconcernedly away from the Oratory. The sharp tap of heels came behind him, and their owner alongside and past him. He caught her side face. She was flushed and smiling to herself.

" Gawd, ain't she lovely ! "

The space increased between them. She disappeared, a tiny figure in the distance, up Queen's Gate.

The policeman stood at ease facing the road, surveyed right and left, and spat.

" Wouldn't moind bein' there meself."

§ 2

It was the first time Beauty had been asked to one of Lady Derringham's receptions. The invitation had pleased her. It intimated that Lady Derringham had jotted her amongst the " right people."

Her dress also pleased her. Mrs. Sands-Woodford's " Golden goddess " remark had suggested its scheme. Her dressmaker, approached on the matter, had found a shade of gold exactly the gold of Beauty's hair.

She stood now, her maid admiring, before the long glass in her bedroom, surveying the effect—stockinged and shoed, too, in the same golden hue. No jewellery. The unadorned white of skin, the sapphire brilliancy of eyes ; she knew their value.

" Now, Marie," to her maid, " none of your French complexions."

Marie deftly obeyed with a minimum of powder.

One or two supple movements before the mirror, and Beauty was satisfied.

Mrs. Sands-Woodford was waiting for her by arrangement in the hall at the great Queen's Gate house. Together they merged with the throng surging up the staircase. On the landing the congestion became a queue, in which they moved slowly towards the reception-room. At the entrance names were being announced. Their turn came. Beauty shook hands with Lady Derringham and Sir Henry, and passed on into a roar of conversation and strains of band mingled.

It was a brilliant scene.

She became pleasurably conscious, whilst sighting acquaintances and exchanging greetings, of heads turning in her direction. The golden scheme was producing the anticipated effect. Mrs. Sands-Woodford assimilated herself into the buzz and was lost to view.

Warily, she began to search. Julian Verrers was not visible, as yet.

" Golden glory ! " said a voice. She turned to find Major Brandreth at her side.

" You appalling person ! How are you ? Come and talk to me." And she led him by the hand out of the swarm to a divan, the thought flashing—did he know who would be here this evening ?

" Major, tell me about Hendringham. You were going down there."

" You're holding the hand of an eligible bachelor. You're compromising me."

Beauty dropped it.

" That's my ankle, thanks ! Why does Hendringham suddenly interest you ? "

" The Esterton crowd have an interesting reputation," she replied. " For rapidity."

The Major rested his arm on the back of the divan.

" That's all finished. Hunting set doesn't come now."

" Oh ? Why ? "

" Girls getting married, partly. Not wanted, anyhow. Remember what I told you about Eric—his religion ? "

" Oh, that ! " Beauty broke him off : " Tell me about the place itself."

The Major experienced a sense of disappointment. He showed nothing, but began describing Hendringham.

At the end he ventured :

" One of the Estertons is here to-night."

" Really ? Which is that ? "

" Basil. Second boy. Just been with him over there." He indicated the next room.

" What's he like ? "

The Major played with the scrub of his moustache.

" Why not be introduced ? Shall I find him ? "

" Yes, do," said Beauty. Julian Verrers was seemingly in no hurry. Basil Esterton might fill a gap.

The Major had scarcely left to pick his way through the crush when a stir near by drew her attention to the door.

Julian Verrers was shaking hands with Lady Derringham.

The stir became a hush ; people staring and making no attempt to disguise their interest. After a marked extension of the usual formalities at the door, he was moving into the room. People made way. A man came forward effusively and engaged him in conversation.

Beauty watched.

" Got him," said the Major's voice.

She started, recovered herself and rose.

" May I introduce you ? Miss Dethier —The Honourable Basil Esterton." She returned the bow of an attractive-looking young man. The Major stayed for a moment only. " Beauty, I'm going to leave you two. See you later." He went off again.

" Have you heard Lestoir ? " she began at random, as

they settled on the divan. He had not. The question served, however. Lestroi led to music. She talked it, forcedly, glancing at times to where the tall, erect figure was moving from group to group. She noticed that, while he talked, the black eyes were looking about.

Suddenly he saw her.

Beauty smiled.

" I beg your pardon," to the young man at her side. He repeated some remark. She made an attempt to attend. Julian Verrers was coming towards them. . . .

" Will you think me abominably rude if—— Shall we talk again later ? "

Her partner did not quite comprehend until Julian Verrers' presence before them supplied the clue. He was on his feet immediately, embarrassed and flushing like a schoolboy.

" Later, then ? " said Beauty sweetly.

He bowed confusedly and walked away.

" Rather shabby, wasn't it ? " she said, taking Verrers' hand and conscious of her pulse quickening. He shrugged slightly, appearing to take the other's dismissal as a matter of course, and remarked :

" Shall we find a quieter place ? "

" Certainly, if we can."

She allowed him to lead the way through to the next room, followed by curious eyes. It was fuller than the first. Lestroi was preparing to play.

" Come this way."

" This way " was away from the piano, whose first notes rang out challengingly as they gained a door at the further side. Beyond it :

" This really is rather nice," said Beauty. They were in a glass palm-house, hung with colours and fairy-lamps, and fragrant of lily and hyacinth. Among the palms nestled cunningly contrived sitting-places. Verrers motioned her to one of them. They sat down.

" Do you prefer this ? " he asked.

" To the scrum ? "

" I meant to Lestroi, too."

" It's certainly peaceful," she answered.

Subdued chords from the piano stole in. So Lestroi was not to claim her attention.

He began without any preliminaries : " I asked you a question yesterday, and I'm going to ask you a second one now. You agreed with what I said at Mrs. Sands-Wood-ford's, didn't you ? "

It took Beauty aback. But she laughed.

" You very abrupt person ! What makes you think that ? "

" Because you did not disagree."

She studied the toe of her shoe.

" I did not resent the expression of your ideas, like Mr. Raynor. Do you assume my agreement from that ? "

" Silence gives consent," he answered.

" My silence may have meant merely that I was listen-ing."

He turned towards her.

" I think it meant more. Had you resented my ideas, you would have resented my expressing them. Surely ? "

She did not reply. He added :

" I assume you would agree, if——" He did not finish.

" If what ? "

" If you were not a Catholic."

It was plainly a challenge, to draw from her more than she had said yesterday. " You want me to declare myself, Mr. Verrers, isn't that it ? "

" Quite candidly, I do."

" Tell me why, first."

It was Verrers' turn to laugh.

" You have a way of demanding prices for your answers. Very well ; I want to know what you meant yesterday, because I'm interested in you."

" I've gathered that already." Her boldness astonished herself.

He laughed again.

" Shall I risk offending you ? "

" You may chance it."

" Miss Dethier, I'm interested in you because the other night you listened to me as few women would. Most women listen from curiosity. You were vitally concerned. Isn't that so ? "

" Go on, please."

" May I ? You were wondering how far you could go with me ? You were afraid of committing yourself whole-heartedly ? "

." Perhaps."

" Why were you afraid ? "

She did not answer for a moment.

" What are you leading to, Mr. Verrers ? "

He moved nearer, a little.

" I have been thinking of making a—suggestion. If you were not nominally a Catholic, I should not hesitate. Before I go any further, will you tell me what you meant yesterday ? You didn't know whether you were a Catholic or not."

" A suggestion ? Will you make the suggestion, what-ever it is, if my answer is not satisfactory ? "

" Yes."

Beauty thought.

" Mr. Verrers, I'm beginning to doubt religion alto-gether. I'm not sure that I believe in the Catholic Faith at all ; although I was brought up in it. Some of the things you said the other night were things I'd already been thinking ; they merely confirmed my doubts. I don't know that I'm prepared to deny everything yet and give up the Church. But I can see it may come to that." She halted. " Will that do ? "

" I understand exactly," said Verrers.

She met his eyes.

" And your suggestion ? "

" I'll be frank. What I'm going to suggest would

involve giving up your religion. You may know it, or you may not, but there is a movement in progress for the cause of reason over religion; for freedom. It will narrow down before long to a struggle with the Catholic Church—the only formidable enemy of freedom left."

" That I can believe."

He waited.

" What has this to do with me, personally ? " she asked.

" This. At present we are limited, for the main work of the movement, to men. Many of them, like myself, are scientists by profession. If we are to advance we must draw from a wider circle. As well as men we want——"

" Why do you say ' we ' ? Who are ' we ' ? "

" You are meticulous of words as well as answers." He said it with a slight frown. " Shall we let ' we ' stand for those who are working for freedom ? "

" As you wish," she replied. The frown puzzled her. It seemed to convey that he had used the term unwittingly and was annoyed with himself.

" We want not only men," he resumed in a level tone, " we want women. We want women like you, Miss Dethier."

" Oh ? "

" If you were free you could share in the work of this movement. You could do work of immense value."

" Oh ? " she repeated.

" You have qualifications. You are intellectual. You've a personality. You have social standing. These things count. You are beautiful, too, if I may so say—no mean asset, as you would find."

" My beauty is obvious, I believe. I'm called Beauty." It slipped out flippantly. She felt suddenly piqued at the impersonal way in which he was summing her up. His interest in her was utilitarian, apparently. " How do you know all this about me ? We've only met three times."

" I read people rather quickly. Also I've been told about you ; by Mrs. Sands-Woodford, for instance."

" Really ?   Maggie's been retailing my points ? "   She moved round.   " Er—what exactly would this work be ? *My* work ? "

" It would be both public and private.   In public, mainly lecturing.   Writing, possibly, too.   In private, using your influence.   You would have to specialize first in subjects like sociology, the apologetics of reason as opposed to religion, the fallacies underlying Christianity, and so on.   This preliminary preparation would not be dull ;   it would be intensely interesting once you had the work at heart.   It would be worth it ;   assuming, of course, that you were to consecrate yourself to the cause of humanity."

It sounded like the formal recital of a programme.

" Lecturing, writing, influencing ? " she murmured, more to herself than to him.

Suddenly she turned.

" Your suggestion, then, is this.   I am to apostatize from my religion, as you have done, Mr. Verrers ;   to hate it, and devote my life to destroying its influence.   Is that it ? "

Her flippancy had gone.   She had spoken rapidly, under an uncanny sensation of fear that had come.

" Rather a violent way of putting it, but——"

" I couldn't possibly do what you suggest."   She continued quickly :   " I should have to hate it, just as you hate it.   No, please let me speak.   You've been personal ; quite nicely, I know.   May I be personal, too ?   You are not just a biologist by profession, are you ?   Your profession is also to work against religion.   You've implied that, at Mrs. Sands-Woodford's, and now, too.   Your next speech is to be against Christianity, I hear.   It is *your* work you are asking of me, isn't that it ? "

" I am."

" Well.   If I did leave the Church, it would be because I no longer believed in religion.   If I did, I might come to accept your doctrines ;   although at present some of them sound rather disgusting. That, however, may be my Catholic instinct—what's left of it. It's one thing to accept them, though. It's another thing altogether to work in the way you suggest. It would mean a tremendous conviction, a literal hatred of religion before I could bring myself to robbing other people of it."

She paused.

"It comes to this. I cannot imagine myself capable of doing what you ask. Now, may we change the subject ?"

He had remained still throughout. His face was impassive. The fingers that rested on his knee had closed tightly, though.

"Mr. Verrers, do you know a Major Brandreth ?"

The quiet gaze of the man watching her flickered for an instant. Instead of replying to her question, he asked :

"You wish me to say nothing more ?"

"About your proposal ? No. At any rate, not now. I don't think there's anything more to be said."

She waited.

"Major Brandreth ?" he remarked indifferently. "Do you mean the Major Brandreth who is here to-night ?"

"He is here, yes. He introduced me to the person you supplanted just now."

"I recognized him."

"You've known him some time, haven't you ?" And instantly she saw her mistake.

"Why did you ask if I knew him ?"

She bit her lip in vexation. It was too late, so she faced him with :

"Major Brandreth was mysterious about you the other day, that is all. I'm curious to know why."

"Oh ? And what did he say ?"

"Nothing. Except that he had known you during the War—you were in the Gunners with him. I wanted him to tell me more, but he dried up."

" More about me ? Do I interest you ? "

He was warding her off.

" All mysterious people interest me. You *are* rather mysterious, Mr. Verrers. You're being mysterious now."

He laughed quite pleasantly, but in a way to intimate that nothing further would be gained from him.

" Who was the attractive young man he introduced to you ? " he asked.

" Basil Esterton. One of the Hendringham Estertons."

" Basil Esterton ? . . . Esterton ? " He played with the name as if it might be familiar.

" Why, do you know him too ? "

His eyes had left hers.

" No, I don't know Basil Esterton," he answered slowly. " Is he the only son ? "

" The second. The eldest's a cripple. He smashed himself ; on the Alps, I believe."

" Do you know his name ? "

" Er—Eric. Yes, Eric."

He nodded. She noticed that he did not remark on the fact of his being a cripple.

" Perhaps you know Eric, then ? "

" I asked his name, that was all," Verrers replied.

The evasion was so uncalled for that she felt nettled. For the second time he had become inscrutable, for no apparent reason. He knew Major Brandreth without a doubt, and, from his manner, Eric Esterton, too.

" This could hardly be described as a very satisfactory conversation," she remarked at his averted head. " We seem to arrive at deadlocks. I'd rather like to hear Lestroi, I think. Shall we go back ? "

" As you wish." There was a decided hardness in the tone. Either he had not liked her remark or, more probably, he was dissatisfied with the way she had treated his suggestion to her.

They rose and walked from the palm-house without saying more. As he opened the door of the salon, a burst

of applause announced the reappearance of Lestroi at the
piano. Verrers bowed to her, and she made her way
to where she descried Mrs. Sands-Woodford sitting with
others at the far side.

" Did the golden goddess weave her spells ? " whispered
that lady, squeezing in Beauty beside her.

" Maggie, I'll murder you ! "

Lestroi, seated at the piano, was waiting for silence.
His hands poised over the notes and dropped impatiently
to his knees instead of striking, as some disturbing sound
caught his ear. He looked round. Julian Verrers was
walking across the floor, frowning heavily to himself.
The pianist delayed uncomfortably until the distinguished
disturber had passed into the next room, and then began.

Afterwards, under cover of clapping, Mrs. Sands-
Woodford asked : " Beauty, what *did* you do ? Did you
put him out about something ? "

" I put him off about something, if you want to know,"
she answered sharply.

And that was all Mrs. Sands-Woodford could elicit.

CHAPTER VI

§ 1

ERIC lay in his ambulance under the elms beyond the tennis-court, watching the white figures at play.

"Thirty all," "Forty-thirty," "Deuce," travelled across the hot glare, and finally, "Game, and." He saw the couples on either side sauntering up to the net, tapping it with rackets, confabbing, adjourning to the chairs outside the court, and flopping into them perspiringly. All except Basil, who strolled through the gate in the wire-netting and into the shade under the elms.

"Hullo, Eric! How's life?"

"Hullo, Basil! When did you arrive?"

"An hour ago. Only seen the Dad and Mater for a second. How are they?"

"Going strong. What's it like in town?"

"Hot as hell. Fearful frowst at the Derringhams' last night. Major Brandreth was there. He introduced me to a topping girl."

"Oh?" said Eric. "Who's the topping girl this time?"

"Somebody called Miss Dethier—'Beauty,' the Major called her."

"And how did you get on with the topping girl?"

"All right. In the end. But she's appallingly popular. I only got five minutes, first time. Some long-legged chap collared her, after that—walked up as if she belonged to him."

"Hard luck, Youngster," said Eric. He cast a glance at the Youngster's charming person, clad in "whites," arms bared. Most men would find it difficult to cut

53

Basil out. They were alike, these two—the same fair
hair and eyes, with their mother's sensitive mouth. Basil's
six feet of lithe muscle had been Eric's before his accident.

The Youngster received his sympathy merrily, with a
wave of his racket.

" You wait. I got a second innings ; after the long one.
They went off to the palm-house. Left me blasting every
girl under the sun. I spotted them coming back, though ;
and I don't believe they'd got on too well. The long one
looked off his feed—walked across the salon just as some
piano-man was getting to biz. Polite consternation.
Anyway, down in the supper-room she came up. Said
she was awfully sorry, frightfully rude of her going off
like that, et cetera. I bagged a table and—I say, Eric,
we got on magnificently. She's perfectly gorgeous.
Dressed in sort of gold all over."

Eric laughed. The younger brother hastened to
assure :

" Oh no, she's quite different."

" They're all different, Lothario."

" You wait ! I say, Eric, I'm going to get the Mater
to ask her down here. I told her so."

" Oh ? What did she say ? "

" Said she'd like to come." Basil hesitated. " Eric,
she asked about *you* in a funny way. You won't think me
rude, old man ? But she's a bit afraid of meeting you, I
think. The Major said it was—your religion. He'd told
her about you. Anyway, she'll come, I'm certain. I'm
going to get round the Mater."

Eric wondered why she should be afraid of his religion.

" Don't let the long one get another look-in first," he
cautioned the Youngster.

" Be damned to the long one ! He's only a chap who
makes speeches."

" Get his name ? "

" Yes. Julian Verrers."

Eric started. His smiled vanished.

" Julian Verrers ? Basil, are you sure ? "

" Yes. What's up ? "

Eric did not answer. He was thinking. After a time he remarked :

" Never mind. Unless—— Did Major Brandreth say anything to you about—Julian Verrers ? "

" Only that he knew him. Didn't like him, I think. Oh ! . . . We were saying good-bye to Miss Dethier and he whispered something in her ear about him. She didn't like it, because she flushed up. My hat, Eric, she's stunning when she colours ! "

" Why do you think it was about Julian Verrers ? "

" Heard her answer. "

" What was it ? "

" That Julian Verrers was her affair. " He asked curiously : " Why are you so keen ? "

" Perhaps I'll tell you some time," Eric replied. " That was the tea-bell, wasn't it ? Do you mind shoving this old pram back ? Give a yell to the others to go up to the house. "

Basil gave a yell. The " others," consisting of two girls and a man, waved their rackets in answer and began wending their way up to the terrace.

As he was being wheeled along the path, Eric turned his head :

" Youngster, I'll persuade the Mater to have Miss Dethier down. "

" Sportsman ! I say, Eric, you don't think me a blithering fool ? But she is topping, you know. "

" So was the last one," said Eric. " Do you mind keeping off the arum lilies ? By the way, you know who's coming to-morrow, don't you ? "

" Yes, they told me—your Brother Anselm. "

" Like the idea ? "

" Hardly got used to it. Bit alarming, a monk ? Here?"

" Ass ! The Dad asked him. "

" So I gathered. I say, Eric, *aren't* they different ? "

It was the first time Basil had referred to the change in his parents towards Eric.

" Are you glad ? " his brother asked.

" Rather ! " he replied simply.

As they neared the house he asked : " Is he—is Brother Anselm stopping long ? "

A chuckle from the ambulance brought the blood mounting to his cheeks.

" Transparent one ! " said Eric. " Brother Anselm is stopping a week or two. But it won't interfere with Miss Dethier. He's quite civilized. Washes and shaves."

" Sorry, old man."

Basil wheeled him into a clatter of tea-things on the terrace.

Eric worked it that evening, when Lady Esterton came to his room for the customary good night.

" She's the Dorsetshire Dethiers, I expect," his mother said, after he had put the case. " It's not the usual thing to ask a young lady down when you've only met her once."

" Basil is smitten," said Eric.

" My dear boy, he's smitten every week. I could ask her, of course, as a friend of Major Brandreth. Is he coming on Friday or Saturday ? "

" Saturday."

" I'd better ask her to come down with him for the week-end. It won't look so bad as——"

" Mater, you're a brick ! " called Basil through the door, and rushed in on them. " It's all right ; I only got that last bit."

He proceeded to do the Charleston in front of her.

" Basil ! "

When he had become static, Lady Esterton remarked drily : " She's not here yet, young man. She may have the grace to refuse. Have you your divinity's address ? "

He had.

§ 2

Six o'clock, Wednesday evening, found Hendringham awaiting Brother Anselm. The train from London was due at Windern at five-thirty. The car should be here with him by now.

Eric, lying on the terrace and watching the bend of the drive, was unashamedly excited.

"Bit late," said Basil's voice behind him, almost simultaneously with his own, "Here we are!" as the Hendringham car swept into view. A lump came into his throat.

A minute later a big, familiar figure, unfamiliarly dressed, was stepping out of the car at the bottom of the terrace steps, and coming up them.

"I say, what a whacking big chap!" escaped from Basil. Remembering himself, he went forward.

"I'm Eric's brother. How do you do?" reached Eric as they met, and the big person's, "I thought so."

They came towards him.

"Well, Eric?"

"Brother Anselm!"

And a rough hand was holding his own.

"Yes, you're just the same," said Eric at last. "Can't quite get the hang of you in these clothes, though. You've got a figure."

The deep, vibrant laugh that followed brought Lady Esterton outside from the drawing-room, Lord Esterton in her wake.

"Here he is, Mater," said Eric.

There were the usual courtesies.

And then they were talking, naturally and easily, to an extremely human being, quite different from their preconception of a monk. Basil stood by, studying him in silence.

" Now, you'd like to know your room. Basil, take **Mr.**—
er——" Lady Esterton hovered.

" Brother Anselm," helped the monk.

" Basil, take Brother Anselm up to his room."

" When you've done gaping, Youngster," from the
ambulance. It was a tennis-racket, strapped to one of
the suit-cases being carried up the steps, on which Basil's
eyes were glued. He removed them, screwed up the left
one at Eric, and led Brother Anselm in through the front
doors.

At dinner, Basil continued to take in the monk.

Eric's description had been inadequate. He had been
unprepared for the well-groomed, obviously English
gentleman sitting opposite, talking easily with his father
and mother and completely at home. At the best he had
imagined the monk polished up for the occasion, hastily
recovering 'dropped aitches and watching not to mix up
knives and forks. This was a person of inherent breeding.
There was no ill-fitting, greasy frock-coat, but a dinner-
jacket, well cut as his own, the waistcoat beneath but-
toning up to an immaculate clerical collar. There was
not even the water-brushed hair ; just a close, brown crop,
tinged with grey. He liked the monk's face with its
massive strength and the straight-set eyes of grey—pene-
trating eyes. Getting on for forty he decided him to be.

The conversation was mainly about his brother. Lord
and Lady Esterton dropped all restraint and drew from
Brother Anselm an account of Eric's life at the monastery
of Issano. The monk told them many things—of the
accident itself, the terrible days of slow realization, the
triumph over despair. He did not refer, however, to the
reception into the Church.

Basil listened. At the end of it Lady Esterton, partly
to cover her feelings, said :

" You've told us nothing about yourself, Brother Anselm."

" There's nothing to tell," he replied, " except that it was my privilege to look after him." He put in quickly : " You've a very wonderful son, Lady Esterton."

" So I am beginning to understand," she said quietly.

In the cool of the evening, when dinner was over, Lord Esterton led Brother Anselm outside.

They strolled down the drive.

And there, shortly, the monk was listening to the sincere apology of a proud man who had steeled himself to the acknowledgment of a mistake. It was embarrassingly personal, and offered in a painfully humble way. He did not interrupt, however, but let the other finish. Then he said :

" You no longer think I took advantage of Eric's condition, or entrapped him into the Church ? You believe it was his own sincere conviction ? "

" I do."

" Thank you very much."

The monk stretched out his hand. Lord Esterton grasped it.

Eric, propped up on pillows, was dismissing Spence as Brother Anselm entered.

" At last," he said, as the door closed.

" Oh, monk, it's very good to see your face again. Pull that chair up."

Brother Anselm did, and sat down. Eric turned on the light above the bed, and examined him. " Yes, you're the same, really. It's the clothes, though. Give that old chuckle, will you ? "

Brother Anselm chuckled, deeply.

" How do you like us all ? " And Eric insisted on first
impressions. The monk responded with humour.

" And Basil ? "

" Basil's very like you. Absurdly like you."

" Is he ? I suppose he is, really. Has he talked to
you yet ? "

" Hardly a word. He's trying to size me up."

" Yes, that's Basil," said Eric. " Bit suspicious ? "

" More puzzled. He expected something different,"
replied Brother Anselm.

" Holmes, how did you know ? "

" Observation, Watson."

And so on. Until Eric halted from his fire of questions
and they turned to more intimate things, the days at the
monastery still vivid to them both.

With those days the name of Julian Verrers was connected. It cropped up inevitably and gave Eric his
chance. He seized it, unable any longer to suppress his
curiosity.

" May I ask you something ? "

" You may. You've held yourself in quite well."

" Uncanny monk ! What was I going to ask ? "

" You want me to tell you what I meant in my letter."

" Will you ? "

" There's no reason why I should not. I have been
called to England, as I told you in the letter, on account
of Julian Verrers."

" I'm awfully sorry," put in Eric, " but I showed that
letter to Major Brandreth. It came when he was here.
Does it matter ? "

" Not in the least. I knew you had. The Major came
to see me in town this morning, and spoke of it. He told
me things I wanted to know about Verrers, also that he'd
informed you. He's coming for the week-end, isn't he ? "

" That's right."

" Well now, I'll tell you. I learned three weeks ago
that Julian Verrers had been making a speech in London:

It did not altogether surprise me. He was not likely to
remain in oblivion. He is the kind of man who would be
sure of a public hearing if he sought it. As you know,
the speech itself attracted unusual attention. A verbatim
report of it was sent out to me from our house in London.
There came with it an invitation from ecclesiastical
authority asking me to make some sort of public answer
to Verrers. That is why I have been recalled to
England."

"I say, this is magnificent!" exclaimed Eric.
" *You!* "

"I used to lecture in biology."

"Is it going to be a speech, or what ? "

"At the Queen's Hall, yes. Julian Verrers is speaking
there again next Monday—against Christianity directly,
this time."

"Oh ? . . . When's yours ? "

"Thursday. To-morrow week."

"This is positively thrilling. Does he know ? "

"He can hardly help discovering that ' Father Thornton ' is myself. I shall be that in the papers, of course."

"What does the Major think ? "

"About all this ? " Brother Anselm smiled. "I had
to try and make him see that I couldn't ' get that snake
in the neck,' as he put it, in a public speech. It couldn't
be, of course. The personal side will have to be eliminated.
Julian Verrers must be taken solely on the grounds of his
public utterances. There will be no mention of the
past."

"What will Verrers do ? Will he come and listen ? "

"Listen-in, I expect."

"Why, are you to be broadcast ? "

"I believe so."

"This is super-thrilling. Aren't you feeling nervy ?
You seem to take it very calmly. But then you would."

Brother Anselm gave his deep laugh. Eric was silent
for a moment.

" Really ! "

He was silent again.

" Did the Major say anything to you about a Miss Dethier ? "

" He did. Quite a lot."

" In connection with Verrers ? "

" Verrers was a friend of hers. He was trying to influence Miss Dethier, he thought. He was vehement about it. She's a Catholic, I understand."

" Oh ? " said Eric. " Oh ? That explains . . . There's something about Miss Dethier which may amuse you," he went on. " Basil was introduced to her by the Major at a reception on Monday. He could talk of nothing else when he came down yesterday. The Mater has yielded to his persuasions, and mine ; she's been invited for the week-end with the Major."

" Indeed ? " The monk pondered. " This is becoming interesting. She's coming ? "

" Not heard yet. She may not. For some reason she's afraid of myself. Possibly she's uncomfortable over her religion and doesn't like meeting Catholics. If so, it certainly looks like Verrers."

" Why did *you* want her invited ? " asked Brother Anselm. " You saw a chance ? "

" Precisely. Basil might act as an antidote."

" You wily young man ! Hullo ! . . ."

The door flew open suddenly, and Basil himself burst in. " Eric, she's coming ! " He stopped short, seeing the monk. " I'm awfully sorry ; I didn't know you were here." The letter he was waving at arm's length dropped doubtfully to half-mast.

" Don't mind me," said Brother Anselm.

" It's Miss Dethier—a friend of Major Brandreth," apologized Basil. " She's coming for the week-end. Good, isn't it, Eric ? "

" Splendid," replied his brother. " Let's have a look at her letter. Come here . . . How beautifully oiled your hair is ! Let me hide your confusion over the Major's friend ! " And he ruffled Basil's hair over his face.

" Bounder ! " came grinningly out of the fiasco.

§ 3

Saturday came, a day of summer glory.

And with it Major Brandreth and Beauty. They reached Hendringham in time for tea, the Major motoring her down.

She was sitting now with the others under the cedars on the lawn, gracefully posed with a tea-cup in a deck-chair, chatting lightly to Lord Esterton.

Lady Esterton was deciding that, for once at any rate, Basil was right ; her loveliness was beyond dispute.

The monk was marking a forceful character expectant of attention, also unusual self-possession. She had covered her start at the introduction to " Brother Anselm " remarkably well. She had taken Eric in his ambulance as if she met people in ambulances every day.

Basil was handing about cakes, usually in her vicinity, and sparring with the Major.

After cigarettes he decreed tennis, having ascertained already that Beauty played. Brother Anselm, approached tentatively, had promised to make a fourth with a " Molly Turner," who was coming over.

They went into the house to change, and reappeared after an interval, three figures in white, just as a car drove up and unloaded a fourth. There were introductions, and then they crossed over the lawns and down to the court at the bottom of the grounds. The Major followed, wheeling Eric, and stationed him and himself on the bank outside the wire-netting. He made some preliminary remarks at Brother Anselm to the effect that he was pained beyond words to see a monk playing tennis.

Basil paired with Beauty, and Brother Anselm with Molly Turner.

As the set advanced it became painfully evident that Brother Anselm was making a very poor show. Eric, whose game had been tennis, guessed that it was lack of practice. Basil, less observant, concluded that he could not play. A slight frown was betraying his annoyance at the set being spoilt for Beauty, who was showing as good as himself. The Major became taciturn and refrained from gibing.

It ended in a " Love " set for Basil and Beauty. Brother Anselm apologized neither to his partner nor to his opponents.

They changed over, Basil looking bored at the prospect of a repetition. He began sulkily hitting back balls, treating them with scarcely concealed contempt.

" Try and be a gentleman, Basil," said Eric quietly, as he came near the netting. Basil did not answer, but reddened.

The next moment there came an unexpectedly swift return into his corner. It was from Brother Anselm's racket, and he missed it. He pulled himself together. Another came shortly from the same quarter, and he realized that the monk was either having some luck or . . . " Damn ! " He had missed again in the same place. Beauty laughed. He laughed back good-naturedly and became taut and leaning forward. It might be a game, after all.

In five minutes' time two evenly matched couples were contesting fiercely at " Two all, Deuce." Twenty minutes later, Brother Anselm and Molly Turner had won at " Six-five."

They changed over, Basil wiping his forehead and smiling again.

The third set saw Basil and Beauty on the back line, just holding their own against continued hard drives from Brother Anselm.   They came low and fast with deadly precision, just skimming the net—the full arm strokes of a first-class player who had found his form.   The game settled down into a grim silence, save for the ping of rackets and thud of the ball.   Basil and Beauty were on their mettle now ;   on the defensive, too—compelled repeatedly to play into Molly Turner at the net.   There were " Deuces," but they failed to pull off the games. The score crept up to " Five-love " for their opponents, and finally a " Love " set, and victory.

The couples, panting and laughing, met at the net for mutual congratulations on the game.   An exodus was made for drinks, just brought down.   The Major served, in charge of the bar.

Basil, taking advantage of the others' backs, drew Brother Anselm away.

" Sorry if I was a bit rude."

A brawny arm was laid on his shoulder.   That was all. But it was enough.   And it banished the reserve of four days.

" Didn't know you could play like that."

" Monks are dark horses," said Brother Anselm.

It was not until well after dinner that Brother Anselm and the Major had an opportunity of being alone with Eric.

Basil secured Beauty for himself to show her the river and woods by moonlight.   " The moon hath raised her lamp above," sang the Major after their departing figures.   Basil threw gravel and told him to go to his kennel.

He adjourned with Brother Anselm to Eric's room, where the three of them could discuss, together for the first time, the absorbing matter of Julian Verrers. There, the Major proceeded to reveal a thing which indicated a new drift of relations between Beauty and Verrers.

Dining at the Carlton the night before he had discovered them together at a table near his own. Beyond bowing to Beauty he had taken no notice. He had referred to it, very unsuccessfully, on their drive down in the afternoon. She had refused to listen. There was only one construction : the trouble between them at Lady Derringham's, if any, had been of the slightest, and was over. The glamour of the man was upon her.

"Verrers is making for that girl." The Major finished his narration, almost angrily. "And, damn it all, she's not averse to it, either—looks at him like a fascinated rabbit ! That snake wants her. And it's not for platonic reasons."

"So she won't take a hint from you ? " asked Brother Anselm.

"Tried twice. She's not in the mood. Says she can look after herself."

"With anybody else she probably could," remarked the monk.

After breakfast next morning an incident occurred. It confirmed what the monk already guessed from Beauty's obvious avoidance of both himself and Eric.

Being Sunday, at nine o'clock the car drove up to the front doors to take Eric down to Windern. The monk was accompanying him to say the nine-thirty Mass. After letting Spence and a manservant lift Eric in, he was about to step in himself, when a groom came round the corner from the stables, leading a couple of horses saddled and bridled. They stood there champing and jingling their steel.

Eric and Brother Anselm looked at one another—the

same thought in both minds. Beauty and Basil were
going to ride. Beauty was not going to Mass.

At the same moment the voices of the two could be
heard in the hall. Next they were coming through the
doors, both dressed for riding, swinging their crops.

It was a bold thing. But the monk did it.

" May I speak to you—inside ? " he said to Basil,
without noticing Beauty.

" Yes, rather ! " Basil led him into the hall. " Anything wrong ? "

" Yes, something is wrong. Basil, do you know Miss
Dethier is a Catholic ? "

" Er—yes, I believe she is."

" Do you know that Catholics are bound by their
Church to attend Mass on Sundays ? I don't ask you to
agree with it ; but only if you know it."

" Oh yes, I do."

Basil began to see something. He was colouring and
looking haughty.

" Basil, I am not interfering to spoil your pleasure.
Will you trust me without understanding my motive ?
Will you ? Can you do a big thing ? "

Basil remembered yesterday, after tennis.

" What do you want me to do ? "

" Tell Miss Dethier you are not riding with her this
morning."

A flash of anger lit his eyes.

" Basil, will you trust me ? "

The boy's face softened.

" Sorry. Yes, I'll try."

" Thank you," said the monk.

" It won't make her go to Mass, you know, if I do,"
said Basil. " She suggested riding herself."

" Very likely. And I don't suppose for a moment she'll
go in any case."

" What's the point of not riding with her, then ? "
Basil clung on.

" If you ride with her, it will mean your approval of what she knows, or ought to know, is wrong. Do you see what I mean ? "

Basil hesitated still.

" I suppose I do. But she'll be furious."

" Probably she will," replied the monk. " But there's a bigger thing at stake than her temper."

" How ? "

" That's where I want you to trust me. I can tell you this, however. No man who panders to a girl, spoilt like Miss Dethier, will ever win her respect. And I think it's charitable to tell you so."

Basil straightened.

" Shall I tell her myself ? "

" Yes," said Brother Anselm. " But leave the rest to me."

He saw Basil's lip tremble. The boy walked across the hall and through the doors, outside. He followed.

Eric, in the car, caught his eye as they came out. Beauty was standing at the edge of the drive with her back to them, tapping a riding-boot with her crop. Basil approached her.

" I say, Miss Dethier, would you mind very much if we were to ride another time ? "

Beauty turned round, slowly.

" Oh ? . . . Why ? "

" Well—er—it would give you a chance——"

" Of what ? "

" Of going to Mass."

" Really ? How *very* thoughtful of you ! "

Basil winced. There was a tense pause.

" And who put you up to this ? "

Brother Anselm came across.

" You know that already, Miss Dethier. I did."

Beauty stared the monk up and down. The colour left her face. . . .

" Thank you for your impertinent interference ! "

The chauffeur, on his seat, coughed. The monk leaned his elbow on the back of the car, and regarded her.

" You . . . silly . . . little . . . girl." Each word came slowly.

She looked uncomprehending, unable to grasp it.

" Wh—what ? "

" You silly little girl. That is what I said. Shall I say it again ? "

" How dare you ! . . . I won't stay here to be insulted ! "

" Just as you wish," said the monk as she swept past them. At the doors she turned and made a step towards him, blazing with fury.

" You insolent person ! "

The monk smiled : " You'll snap your riding-crop."

It rendered her speechless. She stood gasping for a moment, whipped round and flung into the house. . . .

" It's a quarter past nine," remarked Brother Anselm, consulting his wrist-watch. " Can we get to Windern in ten minutes ? "

The chauffeur, petrified, roused himself to action.

" Yes, sir."

There was a whirr.

" May I come too ? I simply can't stop here."

It was Basil, terribly agitated.

" Hop in ! " said the monk.

CHAPTER VII

BROTHER ANSELM lay upon his back looking up into the blue. Three yards away lay Basil, also looking up into the blue.

To their left two horses were stamping impatiently, tethered to a stump. All round, the moorlands stretched away, sweep upon sweep of brown expanse, heather and gorse, purple and gold, until lost afar in the haze.

They had ridden up here, seven miles from Hendringham, at Basil's suggestion. The monk had been working at his speech for the coming Thursday, ever since Mass yesterday morning. It would occupy most of his time for the next two days ; and he was allowing himself a break. Basil, highly strung and sensitive, had not easily shaken off the effects of the incident with Beauty. The monk guessed that an afternoon on horseback would restore his balance. The long gallop over the moors through the keen air had already dispelled the boy's gloom.

Beauty had come down to lunch yesterday and addressed herself throughout, with remarkable self-possession considering, to Lord and Lady Esterton, and occasionally to the Major. Her marked ignoring of the others had necessitated a brief explanation of affairs. Their hostess had been gracious about it, if bewildered. Lord Esterton had grunted. Until her departure this morning with the Major, Beauty had spoken neither to the monk nor Basil.

While, however, the Major was fetching his car from the garage, she walked out on to the terrace, where Basil was hanging about moodily. Brother Anselm, who had come out also to see the Major off, saw her go up to him and hold out her hand :

" Good-bye, Mr. Esterton. It was nice of you to ask me down. Please don't imagine I blame you for what happened yesterday. I'm only sorry that you allowed our morning to be interfered with by a priest." It was spoken loud enough for him to hear.

He noticed Basil drop her hand.

" Brother Anselm asked me not to ride with you, that was all. You know why."

" Oh, well, if you prefer to be dictated to by—a monk." And with that she turned away, as the Major drew up with the car.

Brother Anselm came out from the doors for a last word with him. Beauty waited, and then stepped in.

In the act of doing so her hand chanced to strike against the door. A little leather case she was carrying dropped, the contents scattering on the gravel. The monk stooped to collect them, a few letters and such. He handed them to her.

" Thanks." But she did not look at him. " Got a cigarette, Major ? "

While she was lighting up, something under the car caught the monk's eye. He picked it up. It was a blue printed card.

" This must be yours, too."

" Oh yes. Thanks."

She took it and put it in the case, observing carelessly : " Yes, it's for the Queen's Hall to-night. Thanks."

" So I noticed," said the monk.

" Well, cheerio ! " cried the Major. " Cheerio, Basil."

" Good-bye," called Beauty airily.

As the car moved off she glanced at Brother Anselm. And the monk knew why. The " Queen's Hall " had been a chance shot. The glance was a challenge, and a question. It was to defy him—if he knew.

That was this morning.

" This is very gorgeous," said Brother Anselm, sitting up and surveying the vastness before him. " Do you often come up here ? "

" When I've time," replied Basil, struggling to his elbow. " I'm taking on the estate now, you know."

" So Eric tells me. Do you like it ? "

" Very much." And he started describing what the " taking on " entailed. He had manifestly been at pains to acquaint himself with the details of estate work already. He explained the extent of the Hendringham lands.

A chance reference to Windern occurred. It led him to ask rather an abrupt question.

" By the way, I went inside yesterday while your service was on. What's it all about—Mass, I mean ? "

Brother Anselm picked a stalk of grass.

" Eric asked me a question like that once." It was partly to himself.

" Oh ? . . . Rather interested me, that's all. Used to wonder what Eric did on Sunday mornings."

Clipping sentences with Basil meant shyness.

" Have you ever heard of Calvary ? " asked the monk.

" Calvary ? Yes, I think so."

" Well, if you understand Calvary, you understand the Mass."

" Oh ? " said Basil again, and stuck.

" Were you brought up a Protestant, Basil ? "

" I suppose so. I wasn't brought up to any religion much. The Dad and Mater don't go anywhere, you know."

" Do you know anything about Christianity ? "

" Christianity ? Yes, of course."

" What is it ? " asked the monk.

" Well, it's—— I don't know. It's doing the decent thing and all that, isn't it ? "

" My dear boy, it's more than that—very much more. It's believing something, and ' doing the decent thing and all that ' because you believe it."

The monk sucked the stalk of grass.

" Do you want me to go on ? "

" I wish you would," said Basil.

" Right. Listen."

And Basil listened for ten minutes.

When Brother Anselm had finished, Basil was sitting upright.

" Rather terrific," was his comment.

" It is. Christianity's the most terrific thing that has ever happened."

" Do you really believe it all—all that ? " Basil turned to him an engagingly innocent face.

" As I believe that you are sitting here."

" Really ? "

He ruminated.

" Does Beauty Dethier believe all this ? "

" She believes it, yes. But she's trying not to, I fancy."

Basil remembered the Major saying that she was " up against her religion."

" Are Catholics bound to believe all this ? " he asked.

" Bound to."

He thought.

" Why doesn't she want to, then ? "

" I can't tell you. I've only known her for two days ; and circumstances were not propitious for confidences."

Basil thought again.

" Isn't it rather rough, being bound to believe things ? "

" Not if they're true. It's not very rough on you being bound to believe there was a Great War, is it ? "

" Of course not. But that's a fact."

" So are the dogmas of Christianity facts."

" How do you know they are ? "

" Because the Almighty has said so. He ought to know."

" When ? "

"When did He say so ? When He came down to this earth, two thousand years ago."

Basil was held up for a moment.

"He didn't tell *you*," he persisted.

"No, but He told some fishermen and others, who happened to be His Church, and His Church happens to have told me."

"What, the Catholic Church ? "

"Exactly."

"Supposing it told you wrong ? "

"It couldn't. The Almighty sees to that. He made it so that it couldn't."

There was an interval.

"And that's why Catholics are bound to believe it all ? "

"That is why Catholics are bound to believe it all. Because the Almighty has said so."

Basil studied his riding-gaiters.

"Sort of ends matters, that."

"It does."

Another interval.

"Um."

Basil lay on his back again.

"Is this how you made Eric a Catholic ? "

"I didn't make Eric a Catholic."

The curly, fair head revolved at him :

"Who did, then ? "

"The Person we've been talking about."

There was another "Um."

"Basil," Brother Anselm switched off, "I'd rather like you to know something about Miss Dethier. Have you heard of a man called Julian Verrers ? "

The recumbent figure jerked itself to the upright.

"Heard of him ? I've seen him. Saw him at a reception in town last week. *Heard* of him ? Hang it all, he cut me out with Beauty Dethier for nearly an hour."

"Indeed ? " said the monk. "Indeed ? Then this

will interest you all the more. It is Julian Verrers who is responsible for her present attitude ; partly, at any rate."

" How ? " asked the other.

" By trying to undermine her belief. Miss Dethier is a girl of sterling character underneath, I should say. But she's worldly and she's modern, very ; and she finds her religion in the way. Probably she's on the verge of giving it up altogether, now that she's come under the attraction of a man who openly hates all religion. There are men like that. Julian Verrers is one of them."

Basil was all ears.

" Can you see now why I asked you what I did, yesterday ? "

He began to comprehend.

" If she sticks to her Mass, there's a chance for her. If that goes, it will mean good-bye to everything. As one of her own priests, I had to remind her. If I hadn't, it would have encouraged her still further."

" But won't she chuck things, now that her back's up ? " asked Basil.

" Not necessarily. I think she's too strong a character to be swayed like that. When she calms down, she may find her conscience at work, too. In any case, it's her reason that will decide ultimately, unless I'm very much mistaken. The young lady's no fool. I know this ; it's upon her reason that Julian Verrers is exerting his pull. He'll be exerting it to-night, I'm afraid."

" To-night ? "

" He's speaking at the Queen's Hall to-night—against Christianity. That ticket I picked up was for his meeting."

" No ? Was it really ? . . . Bl—t him ! " exclaimed Basil.

The monk studied him.

" I thought I'd let you know how things stand. You're a friend of Miss Dethier. I'll tell you something more, if you like ? "

" What's that ? "

" I am answering him on Thursday night, at the Queen's Hall."

Basil regarded him, astounded.

" You ? . . . Are you really ? "

" I am."

A light dawned.

" Then that's what all this swotting up's about ? "

" It is."

" Eric said it was work."

" Eric was right. Hard work."

Basil asked :

" Er—will Beauty Dethier be there, I wonder ? Do you think she'll know ? "

" She *will* know, almost certainly. She may know already. It was in the papers this morning. In any case, the Major will tell her. Whether she will come is another matter."

" May I come ? "

" Certainly, if you bring her with you."

" If—— ? "

" If you bring her with you. She would come for you. The Major's probably brought her to her senses by now. I don't suppose he'll succeed in bringing her on Thursday, though. You would, I believe."

" What, after this row ? "

" Yes. She will like you better than before, for standing up to her. Why not talk nicely to her on the phone to-morrow morning, say ? "

" Shall I ? . . . Oh, but is she on the phone ? "

" She is. I have her number, from the Major."

Basil gaped.

" You—— So you planned this ? "

" I thought the number might be useful," said the monk. " Anyway, think about it. Now, look here, it's six o'clock."

Basil jumped up. There was a glitter of excitement in

his eyes. He went across to the horses and began to untether them, plunging and dancing to be off.

Brother Anselm stood watching him at work with bits and buckles, the superb young strength grappling with the tossing heads, the thought suddenly striking him that Eric must have been like that. It made him look away over the brown spaces.

"Can you do this?" called Basil. He turned to see him vaulting with a wild whoop into the saddle.

"Whoa! . . . Sorry. Collar her, can you?"

Brother Anselm's mare, a big chestnut, startled by the jumping figure, was pirouetting on her hind legs, front hoofs pawing the air.

The monk walked over. "Coom, coom. Silly old girl. Come down." The mare dropped gracefully, and began curvetting sideways. "Come on." Her nostrils quivered, blowing agitated puffs at the approaching hand. "Good old girl." She drew back with a jerk and then steadied at the touch on her glossy neck.

"Anything more to show me?" asked the monk, as he swung himself into the saddle.

"Yes, watch that gorse bush!" cried Basil, unrepressed. "Come on! Let the mare rip! Stables!"

Two pairs of ears pricked up. There was a champing of bits and jingle of steel, as they wheeled their horses into position. A little prancing, some mincing steps, spur-pricks, and then the thud of hoofs . . .

"Lift!" shouted Basil.

The gleaming bodies rose and sailed gloriously over the blaze of yellow beneath. And then, at a gallop, they swept away towards Hendringham.

CHAPTER VIII

FIVE and twenty minutes past eight.
Brother Anselm sat, tapping a pencil between his
teeth. In front of him was a small table on which a note-
book lay. Beyond the table was a loud-speaker projecting
an ominous mouth in his direction. He was alone in this
little room, next Eric's, set apart for listeners-in.

He had dressed for dinner quickly after the ride,
securing a few minutes with Eric first. When dinner was
over he had excused himself for the evening, explaining
to Lady Esterton as much as was necessary. He had
already told Lord Esterton the main facts concerning
Julian Verrers and himself. Basil, understanding that he
wanted to listen-in alone, had first seen that the wireless
was in order and then gone out into the garden. The
monk could see him there now through the open window
standing on the terrace, a hand in his pocket, between his
father and mother. Wispy rings from Lord Esterton's
cigar were curling upwards, mingling with the spirals from
Basil's cigarette.

Half-past eight.

He glanced at the loud-speaker. A throat was clearing
itself at the other end. And then the announcer's voice
came :

" We shall now go over to the Queen's Hall, London.
Listeners-in will be aware already of the address to be
delivered there to-night by Mr. Julian Verrers, the
biologist. Contrary to our usual custom of not broadcasting controversial matter, it has been decided on this
occasion to do so in view of the extreme interest aroused
by Mr. Julian Verrers' previous speech. The decision was
made subject to the condition of broadcasting another

address from the same hall on Thursday night next by Father Anselm Thornton, a Roman Catholic priest, who will answer Mr. Julian Verrers . . . The Queen's Hall, London."

The announcer's throat scraped apologetically.

There was a momentary interval ; and then another voice was speaking, rather haltingly. This would be the chairman of the meeting. He was introducing the speaker. The monk drew his note-book nearer, opened and flattened it out.

The chairman was brief. There was mild applause as he finished. It died down and suddenly revived. It grew, crescendoed swiftly into a tumultuous sea of sound, reverberating into the little room.

" What a hell of a row ! " It was Basil with his head through the window. " Is that——"

" Yes, he's just beginning. Clear off ! " replied the monk.

A voice that he recognized at once was coming through now. The microphone had been well placed. He could hear every word. This voice rang out clear and compellingly in contrast to the former. He began to feel, even at that distance, the personality of the man exerting itself at the outset ; he could almost see him standing there, strong and self-possessed. In measured, resonant tones it came. He was giving a résumé of his previous address, briefly recapitulating point by point his " Plea for Freedom." Brother Anselm made no notes yet ; he had the verbatim of that speech in his possession.

The points came in concise order.

From a picture of man as the product of an evolutionary process and a descendant from some mammalian stock, Julian Verrers passed on to the " evolution of the Deity." He had previously pointed out, he said, how freedom for humanity meant freedom from the notion of responsibility to a Being outside the universe. This notion had its origin in the personification of natural phenomena by primitive man. In his mind they assumed the character of dangerous spirits, propitiation of whom was to his interest. From this primitive philosophy, known as animism, man had slowly passed, by a process of de-spiritualizing the universe of endless spirit-gods, to a conception of a limited number of deities who divided among themselves the sway of the world. From these conflicting gods of polytheism he had, by an instinct for simplification, evolved the idea of one solitary deity.

At first this one God had been conceived as regulating the world by arbitrary acts of will, as a Being whose anger when offended must be appeased—an anthropomorphic god. Hence the idea of sin. By the gradual recognition of the uniformity of nature and the immutability of natural law it had been found necessary to relieve the deity of His multifarious duties and relegate Him to the position of a Creator alone . . .

The monk ran his hand over his head ; and then jotted down : " Terms from Frazer."

In recent times this Creator had receded further and further into the background until He had become little more than a name. With the vanishing from man's mental horizon of a God, except as a mystical unreality, his sense of responsibility to the same was quickly vanishing too. The day was coming when humanity would finally shoulder for itself the responsibility for its own conduct and affairs. With the fading out of his childhood's notions had come man's discovery about himself—that he was not a being apart from the animal world, but part with it and akin with it, and merely of a higher mental development.

It was this new knowledge, declared Julian Verrers, or rather its consequences, upon which he had based the proposals contained in his " Plea for Freedom."

En passant, he had noted a certain vehement, if limited, opposition to these proposals. Why ? Simply and solely because they conflicted with an outworn code of morality. From what quarter had the opposition come ? Almost entirely from the religious quarter. From any particular religious quarter ? Yes, in the main, without any question, from the one religious body which consistently and doggedly refused the advance of modern thought. He referred to the Catholic Church. He had sufficient faith, however, to believe that the intimidations of a few Roman ecclesiastics would carry no weight with the common sense and enlightenment of the modern British public. There could be no progress or freedom for humanity if men stagnated in the superstitions of the past . . .

Brother Anselm made another note ; and then leaned back and listened as Julian Verrers repeated the proposals which, if put into practice, were to free humanity from its " chains."

First, there would be the elimination of all religion from the conduct of human affairs. Religion would be relegated to the realm of private concerns, entirely segregated from public matters, having no contact with the laws that govern social life. Human affairs would no longer be referred to an exploded God, but to the bar of man's reason. Moral responsibilities to a supposed out-side Being would be replaced by such utilitarian regula-tions as were socially necessary. All the traditional taboos, sprung from man's past misconceptions, would be banished, and with them the fictitious restraints he had imposed upon himself. Behaviour would be moulded by social convenience, not by imaginary prohibitions, not by a " sin obsession "—the most damnable delusion ever endured by the human race, and fostered by its priests. Upon this obsession, now happily vanishing, lay the onus of half the world's past miseries and the stunting of its moral freedom. Did Nature " sin " ? Did animals " sin " ? Man was part and parcel of Nature and the animal world, with just such responsibilities as animals. As a higher animal he had naturally higher responsibilities, but only of degree, not of kind. Animal responsibilities were limited to the welfare of the species ; so also those of man to the welfare of his species, the human race . . .

Again the monk made a note.

The speaker paused.

And then he passed in quick review the further scheme included in his proposals, the scheme that Brother Anselm had studied closely during the past two weeks.

It included the abolition of marriage as hitherto understood, and, instead, temporary unions terminable at will ; birth control, to be taught in official clinics ; love divorced from parenthood ; selective breeding superintended by a scientific department of the State ; euthanasia for the old, permanently sick, and insane. The summary concluded with, " I am pleading, in the name of science, for man's freedom, for a new life untrammelled by craven fears or embargoes from above upon the dictates of his nature.

" And now . . ."

He waited for close attention.

" It is these outlets to freedom that the Christian religion has persistently closed for two thousand years under the plea of a code of moral law which forbids them. That code has rested on the assumed sanctions of a Christian Deity. That code has been exploited by a priestly despotism, maintaining power by threats of hell for those who disobey. That code has for centuries reduced men to a state of abject fear. Its influence has even permeated beyond its own borders. It has influenced governments and laws ; ruled our very homes. And that code rests on phantoms of the human imagination . . ."

Brother Anselm was writing steadily now.

" Why is it that, although these phantoms are passing, in fact have passed for educated men, yet the code still

holds its sway ? What is maintaining its sway ? Why is
it maintained here in England, where seventy per cent.
of the people are now indifferent to the dogmas of
Christianity ? How are we to account for this anomalous
situation, for the folly of clinging blindly to a system of
morality while rejecting the grounds on which it rests ?

" The answer is this.

" It is due, first, to sheer human stupidity—to the
amazing notion that respectability of life is somehow
bound up with this morality of the past. There are sane,
intelligent English men and women to-day who allow
themselves to be bludgeoned by their susceptibilities
into ostracising those who refuse to conform to a fetish.

" My only reply is : If you value the future of this
nation, put an end to your folly. If you have not the
courage to break from your own chains, do not hinder
those who have. Your prudish respectability will yet be
ousted by something far nobler and higher—the right of
Nature's way.

" There is another reason for this folly, more potent.

" I said the Christian religion was closing the outlets
to freedom. And when I speak of the Christian religion I
am not referring to that form of it which arose at the
Reformation. The Protestant religion has not, and never
had, the power to inflict on its adherents a binding code.
For that we may be grateful. No, I am referring to that
vast religious body which, for twenty centuries, has held
in its grip millions and millions of the human race, and
which holds them in its grip to-day. Its name is the
Roman Catholic Church.

" You may be surprised when I say that the Roman
Church is largely responsible for what I have called your
folly. Yet it is true. Though repudiating the dogmas,
you have not yet shaken off the moral traditions of your
Catholic past. You may be still further surprised when
I add that many of you are at this moment, unconsciously,
borrowing the morals by which you consider yourselves

bound. Does the Protestant religion bind you to them ?
It does not ; and you know it does not. It leaves you
your private judgment. Do your natural instincts and
desires ? They do not. No, it is an alien voice to which
you unwittingly listen. It is the voice of the Latin Church
still sounding powerfully in your midst.

"Let me put it to you in this way. If the Roman
Catholic Church were to be swept out of existence to-
morrow, if her voice were to be heard no more, how much
longer would you cling to the morality you now endorse ?
I venture to suggest that the voice of reason would very
speedily be heard.

"Do you realize that you are clinging to a man-made,
mediæval morality, to the morality of a Church that
enchains men in intellectual slavery, in subservience to
unalterable traditions ? In doing so you are subsidizing
the power of the Roman Church, the one enemy of
human freedom left."

Brother Anselm jotted in the margin to his notes :
Argumentum ad populum.

"May I digress for a moment ?" continued the
voice.

"I doubt if any members of that Church are present
in this hall ; but in case some of them are listening-in,
which is possible, I will add this for their benefit : Do
not imagine that you can serve two masters. The master
of the future is Science, not Christianity. Do not bolster
up fond hopes of your present master coming to some
truce with modern Science. The Catholic Church stands
or falls by the fixed dogmas of an assumed revelation.
Those fixed dogmas are in open conflict with the findings
of biology. You will have to choose. You will have to
choose between cringing to a theological tyranny, or
walking boldly through the gates that lead to a wider life,
a life of intellectual and moral freedom. In the latter case
you will be placing yourselves on the side of humanity in
the war that is coming. And a war *is* coming. In fact

has come—a war for the world between Science and
Religion. And it is war to the death . . ."

A volley of clapping, and some cheering, interrupted
the speaker. It was apparently from a section of the
audience only, as a certain lack of volume indicated.

Brother Anselm put down his pencil and switched on
an electric lamp at his side. He remained gazing into the
half-lights of the evening outside, while Julian Verrers
touched on a more general note—the gain to the world
already from the discoveries and inventions of science,
as compared with the gain from Christianity. The monk
was waiting for the renewal of the attack.

It came at length.

" To return. In appealing to you, as I did just now, I
laid upon myself the onus of explaining how the Catholic
Church debars men from the natural life of full enjoy-
ment. I will do so.

" The first essential in my scheme for freedom was the
abolition of what is called Christian marriage, one of the
most heinous inventions ever foisted on mankind. By
its means the Catholic Church has for centuries held
family life in her keeping. By claiming a monopoly on
marriage she has, more or less successfully, determined
the conditions under which human love shall express
itself. By her iron law of an indissoluble bond she has
laid a veto upon any attempt to rectify mistakes of choice ;
tied men and women for life to what is often an irksome
and odious union. She has even dared to regulate the
workings of human passion within the marriage state.
And, incredible though it may be, the State has frequently supported these monstrous claims by framing its
laws in accordance with them. How is it that millions
have submitted, almost without protest, to such a tyranny ?

" I can offer a key to the situation, I think.

" Certain social factors have, in the past, relegated
women to a position of dependence. Women have
yielded to the servitude of a permanent union for the

simple reason that by so doing they could secure life-long maintenance ; also, owing to perverted public opinion, temporary unions have placed them outside the pale of what is called decent society. Now that women can earn their own living, and temporary unions are no longer censured by the enlightened sections of the community, the excuse of dependence and the fear of a stupid stigma should carry little weight. I believe myself that the majority of men would welcome legalized unions terminable by mutual consent, without the obligation of maintaining the woman for life.

" If you ask me whether such an arrangement would prove beneficial to the happiness of humanity, I answer unhesitatingly that it would.

" First, the example of men and women freely express-ing their love, as instinct led, would be followed speedily by multitudes of those who still submit to the Christian yoke.

" It would help to break that yoke. Freedom witnessed creates the desire for freedom.

" Again, free-love is love freely given and freely re-ceived. Love amongst humans should be as free as in the animal kingdom. Love cannot be limited to fixed channels, as the science of Nature amply proves. With the removal of the marriage-bond the necessity of miserable pretences between men and women, whose love has expired, would cease. Love would assume a new grandeur, a new unfettered strength, with the knowledge that it need no longer die, but feed itself in other pastures.

" Again, the immense advantage of temporary unions is seen when we realize that, owing to the present system, our youth of both sexes are continually condemned to a restraint upon their passions which is unnatural and psychologically bad. Conditions of existence and slender means forbid them embarking on life-long matrimony. Temporary relations, openly recognized by the com-munity, would solve this problem. It has been shelved far too long, out of deference to a fastidious minority.

" These are but a few of the gains that would accrue to society if its more advanced sections were to strike boldly against the bondage of Christian marriage."

There was a pause.

" The next essential for freedom is to regulate and standardize the reproductive activities of the human species by a universal system of birth control.

" Against this also the Catholic Church inveighs, and somewhat illogically. I say illogically, because this champion of morals condemns the practice of birth control as a violation of Nature, while itself upholding another violation of Nature. I allude to celibacy ; the celibacy enforced upon its priests and monks and nuns— a violent violation of Nature.

" If these protagonists of pseudo-chastity could offer us some rational argument against birth control we might be prepared to listen. Such arguments as they do put forward are based, not on reason, but dictated by the Christian veto. The practice is said to be displeasing to a Deity who invented intercourse between men and women for the propagation of children. How much value need be attached to the interdicts of a mediæval God I have already indicated. If you tell me that in many cases the State opposes birth control, or, at any rate, refuses its official sanction, I answer : Certainly. And why ?

" For two reasons. First, to conciliate the Catholic vote ; secondly, lest the supply of cannon fodder for future wars should be diminished.

" It is scarcely a pleasing spectacle to see governments pandering to the power responsible for a world over-crowded with the unhealthy products of indiscriminate breeding. As for the provision of cannon fodder, the nations could apply the principles of the limitation of armaments to the limitation of population without in any way endangering national security in time of war.

" And if you ask me why the present system of repro-duction is harmful to the happiness of humanity, my answer is : The system is a purely haphazard one. It brings into the world a multitude of diseased and insane, inflicting a life of torture upon millions who should never have existed, and encumbering an already over-populated surface.

" Now that Catholic moralists alone frown upon what has clearly come to stay, the time is ripe for State-established clinics in which medical means of preventing conception may be taught systematically. In this way, and by the restriction of breeding to scientifically selected parents, and children under State care, the race will be thinned out to a healthy and happier few. The incubus of teeming hordes struggling for overstocked professions and trades, as well as the accumulation of undesirable degenerates upon a dole or the rates, will be lifted for ever.

" There has been a wearisome surfeit of thinking and talking and writing by eugenists already. The time for action has come. The *coup de grâce* must be given to Christian sentiment. One courageous act by the eugenists and scientists of all nations, one concerted demand on humanity's behalf—and a new world will be in sight.

" There would undoubtedly be an upcry from Rome ; for the new system would necessarily be universal and therefore enforced upon her adherents too. If so, it will afford an opportunity of tendering to her the information that the populace is ours, not hers. I can conceive of no more powerful weapon with which to unloosen her grip on humanity. Take away Christian marriage and substitute free-love, take over parenthood and weed out her decadent millions, and I venture to prophesy that very soon the day of Rome will wane.

" It may be objected that the removal of ancient barriers would precipitate a welter of unbridled licence. Is that fear valid ?

" No. Continence and constancy are, within reason,

natural to human beings. It is the idea of certain things being ' sinful ' which has encouraged undue attention to them. Remove taboos, and they will revert to their natural position of comparative unimportance, as in the animal world. The natural impulses of self-respect and moderation, the sense of what is fitting implanted in the human species, will check men far more surely than artificial inhibitions."

The voice halted for a moment.

" The third wide road to freedom is that of escape from useless existence.

" It is a road which Rome will also strive to block. Christianity preserves life at all costs, and preserves it to the detriment of the race. On what ground ?

" That life belongs to its mythical Deity, and therefore cannot be released from the human body by man. The fact that the Deity in question takes singularly little interest in human life does not appear to matter. This particular superstition has weighted humanity for nigh upon twenty centuries with a load of diseased ; of incurably sick, aged, crippled, and insane. A humane, scientific system of euthanasia, voluntary for some and compulsory for others, would remove this evil and relieve the world of an intolerable burden. It would also release millions from a life of prolonged torture.

" What more virtuous course could be taken ?

" The inhuman injunctions of Christianity chain life's victims to a living hell, and that at the expenditure of colossal sums of money perpetually poured down a waste sink. And sane men submit to this insanity ! Sane men fling at the advocates of euthanasia accusations of brutality for suggesting a merciful system in place of a merciless one !

" It is one more example of the immense harm done by Christianity to the intelligence and common sense of the race.

" What more merciful sight could there be than great

euthanasic homes standing in every city and town, in which life could be painlessly liberated from bodies broken on its wheel, or worn by disease ? What more glorious symbol of human progress than the destruction of those futilities known as hospitals ; such of them, at any rate, as stand for the preservation of hopeless cases ? What more magnificent renunciation of Christian folly than the command to humanity to march on unhampered by its wounded ? "

The speaker waited. There was a vociferous approval from the hall. It came thinly, though, from only a part of the audience again, Brother Anselm gathered. It was nothing like the strong, sustained cannonade at the beginning. A sudden desire possessed the monk to penetrate the minds of those listening hundreds, who were refraining from outward expression. Were they merely indifferent ? Hardly. That challenging appeal could not leave them unmoved, let alone the personality of the speaker. Was their silence significant of disapproval ; of hostility ?

He wondered.

Julian Verrers continued in a milder strain, suggesting a method of co-operation between eugenists and scientists throughout the world to issue in an international demand for action on the lines he had indicated. There was not, however, the same assured confidence in his tone. His consciousness of the half-hearted response to his declamation was conveyed even at that distance.

The monk looked at his watch. Half-past nine. Julian Verrers was to speak for an hour. The end must be near. Yes . . .

" And now I have this left to say:

" To some of you the measures I have suggested may sound drastic. If so, I make no apology. There has been enough temporizing on these matters ; a tendency to dream and a reluctance to act. Many who agree theoretically with rational schemes for the future hesitate when it comes to actualizing them. The reason is not far to seek.

" They have not succeeded in shaking off a lingering sentiment for Christianity and a foolish fear of its vetoes. It is understandable. A superstition which has permeated the very marrow of man's mind is hard to kill. It still lingers here in England, a phantom of the past. It means nothing to you in practical life, and yet you are afraid of it, as of a ghost. Rise and dispel your foolish fears ! Flood in the light of common sense and the phantom will vanish in its beams !

" Place yourselves boldly on the side of reason. Spread the ideas that have been laid before you ; show men what freedom means ! Once those ideas have coalesced into one universal conviction, the future is assured. Demand release from the insane restrictions of the past, intolerable to the modern mind. Let the voice of science be heard ! Replace your timorous politicians with true servants of humanity !—and victory is won.

" Most surely of all, understand this:

" Freedom and Christianity cannot exist together. There is no room in the world for the two. The dogmas and laws of the Christian religion stand for a perpetual menace, for fear and slavery. Freedom stands for release from their tyranny. The world will have to choose. It cannot have both.

" Which is it to be—freedom or Christianity ?

" If freedom, then Christianity is a deadly enemy, to be dealt with as such. Its stronghold you know. Do I make myself clear ?

" *Freedom will be won when, and only when, Christianity has been destroyed !* " . . . . . .

It was over.

There was a momentary silence. And then the clapping came, mingled with cheers. It continued for some time.

The monk listened carefully, and detected the same thin-
ness of volume as before. The crowd in that great hall
were, to a large extent, keeping silent ; he was morally
certain of it. The applause faltered, became spasmodic,
and died down. . . .

" You Judas ! . . . You vile Judas ! "

The microphone had caught the shout of fury, coming
from somewhere in the audience. The monk leaned
forward quickly in strained attention.

He could hear a commotion, coming through confusedly ; then the sound of hissing ; then cheering again.
Then an uproar. What happened next he could only
guess. The chairman was trying to speak, apparently, to
be drowned at each attempt by jeers and hissing. The
man who had shouted had supporters with him.

The efforts to quiet them must have failed ; for a
shuffle of feet moving over the stage began—the occupants
of the platform seats leaving. The noise in the hall
diminished, and finally reduced itself to single voices.
At the same time he could hear an undercurrent of
rustling, the Queen's Hall emptying itself.

The monk went round the table, and switched off the
wireless. He came back, sat down again and rested his
chin on his hand, staring into the blackness of the garden.

" So Verrers is an apostate. And that Catholic knew it."

*   *   *   *   *   *

" Come in ! " called two voices in unison.

Brother Anselm found Eric in bed and Basil in an arm-
chair with a pipe.

" Well ? What happened ? "

" What did he say ? "

He gave them a short summary.

They both listened intently. At the end Basil said
nothing, but Eric asked :

" And didn't he say anything about *you* ? "

" Not a word," replied the monk.

" Does he know about Thursday ? "

" He could hardly help knowing by now. Possibly, though, he has not connected ' Father Thornton ' with ' Brother Anselm ' of Issano."

Basil looked puzzled.

" I'll explain that some time," said the monk to him.

" Rather curious his not referring to it at all ? " persisted Eric.

" I should have been surprised if Julian Verrers had," replied Brother Anselm.

The following morning Basil did as the monk had suggested, and telephoned to Beauty.

When, after the preliminaries of a trunk-call, he heard her voice at the other end and put his invitation, it sounded more daring than ever.

" Brother Anselm's speaking, you know, at the meeting."

He waited in suspense.

" Can you hear me ? "

" Yes," came through. " I knew your monk was speaking. I'm thinking."

Basil waited again, nervously fingering the receiver.

" He put you up to this, I suppose ? "

Basil hesitated. He wasn't quite sure, but he thought he caught a laugh.

" Quite honestly, he did. But I want you to come myself."

" All right. I'll come. Call for me at Curzon Street, then. What time ? "

" Eight o'clock. Right, I will. . . . Good-bye."

CHAPTER IX

BEAUTY was waiting.

It was cool here in the library after the heat outside. She had returned from a lunch about an hour ago, changed into a light dress of Madonna blue which became her exceedingly, and now—was waiting.

It was Wednesday afternoon. Julian Verrers was coming to tea at the flat.

There had been no opportunity of talking with him after the Queen's Hall meeting. Even had there, she would not have known whether to congratulate him. Somehow she had felt a secret sympathy with the man who had shouted, vulgar though the incident was. And that touch of sympathy had revealed her own antipathy to some of the things Verrers had said.

The papers of yesterday, reporting and commenting on the speech, deplored the unseemly ending to the meeting ; but some of them suggested that Julian Verrers had gone too far. They noted that the crowd, waiting outside to see him come out of the Hall, was singularly silent, neither applauding nor manifesting hostility. They merely stared as he was conducted to his car.

At the Carlton last week, when she dined with him, Verrers had refrained from religion entirely, exhibiting no sign of annoyance over her attitude to his suggestion at Lady Derringham's. Instead, they had struck a new note of intimacy. He had been clearly interested in herself now ; he had not broached again her possibilities for his work. She had encouraged this personal strain.

She wanted things to continue from that point. It was

exciting, and it pleased her. She had determined to avoid, as far as possible this afternoon, the subject of his speech. She had also determined not to mention her visit to Hendringham. Should she tell him that Basil Esterton was taking her to-morrow night, and where ?

It was this she was deliberating now.

Why had she accepted the invitation ? She was not quite sure. It would be an interesting meeting, engrossingly so, perhaps, in view of its nature ; the papers were discussing it already. Also she liked Basil. She had quite forgiven him for the Sunday morning episode at Hendringham. And she had almost forgiven the monk. When her anger had cooled off she had admitted to herself that, under the circumstances, a priest could hardly have acted otherwise. It was more her religion that had stung her—the reminder of it. If she could have disavowed it openly before them, she would have done so ; but it was that exactly which she could not do.

She was going to-morrow night, not merely because of Basil, but because she wanted to hear the monk's answer to Julian Verrers. Curiously enough the latter's antagonism had aroused a deeper interest in these things than she had experienced for years. Her indifference had changed to a desire to face her present position. One way or other the matter had to be settled, if . . .

She shivered slightly.

If what ?

She rose restlessly and stood by the open window, the same unaccountable fear upon her again. Had she been a fool to ask him to the flat ? But why ? Other men had been to tea here.

Julian Verrers, though ? Should she——

The sharp ring of the electric bell startled her. She went quickly across the room and glanced in the mirror over the mantelpiece. " Don't be an idiot ! " She was actually trembling. With a strong effort of will she controlled herself, picked up a book and returned to the arm-chair. The door was opened.

" Mr. Verrers."

He came in, tall and dominating. Beauty jumped up.

" This is very nice of you. How do you do ? Bring in tea, Marie."

The maid retired. Verrers sat down, smiling :

" You've a delightful flat, if I may say so. Is the scheme your own ? "

" What, the green and orange ? Yes. It's the same all over. Do you like the idea ? "

" Very much, I think," he replied. " One wants to get used to it, though. Is this the ' library ' ? "

" I dignify it by that name."

" May I look at the books ? "

" Do."

She was fairly easy after all, helped by his matter-of-fact manner. He strolled about, examining the shelves and making occasional comments. Beauty followed his movements with remarks in answer. Marie brought in tea.

At first, as they talked lightly over cakes and delicacies, her courage began to return and the fears seem stupid. It was not until after the maid had removed the things, and they were left to themselves, that she became aware of Verrers growing silent and watching her with a peculiar light in his eyes.

The manner of the cold scientist was falling from him. He was looking at her as other men had looked at her, sometimes. He was slowly conveying, without saying so, that he had come here for a purpose. With all the pre-occupation of his work and public life upon him he had yet come here to see her.

It had been homage at the Carlton. There was more than homage now looking out of the blackness of those compelling eyes. Rather breathlessly, as if to ward something off, even at the risk of her resolution, she asked :

" Did Monday night tire you ? "

He removed his gaze.

" The meeting ? Oh yes, I was rather tired afterwards."

" Did that man annoy you ? You seemed to take him
more calmly than your chairman."

He smiled cynically.

" My chairman was too precipitous. If he had ignored
the imbecile and sat still there would not have been much
trouble."

Beauty stuck. His eyes had returned to her again.
She began to feel a sense of helplessness and an increasing
fear.

" Still, it was decidedly exciting." It was a stupid
remark, but she was trying to keep him at bay. He made
no reply. Instead he leaned forward. . . .

" Mr. Verrers, what's the matter ? " Unknowingly she
moved back, really afraid now.

" There is nothing the matter," he replied. " Why are
you frightened ? I want you to listen to me, that is all."

" What is it you want to say ? "

He stood up with his back to the mantelpiece, towering
strongly above her. Then he spoke slowly, watching her
all the time.

" Miss Dethier, I've known you for a few weeks only ;
but we have met a good deal during that time. We've
met enough, I think, to form a fairly accurate estimate of
each other ; at any rate, enough for me to know you
better, I suppose, than any other woman of my acquaintance. It may sound strange, but you are one of the few
women who have ever seriously interested me in themselves. I have seldom, if ever, wanted a woman for
herself. You——"

" Oh, please, won't you sit down ? I'd rather you
didn't stand over me."

He did so, quite leisurely.

There was a delay.

" Miss Dethier, you know my views on marriage. Would you be willing to tell me how far you agree with them ? "

Beauty fingered the leather of her arm-chair.

" Why do you want to know ? "

" Because, until I do, it is not very easy for me to go further."

" Further ?   How do you mean ? "   She was breathing quickly.

" I wonder if you can guess ? " said Verrers.

She felt a sense of shrinking.

" No, I can't.   At least——   Tell me what you mean ! "

" Very well.   Do you agree with what I hold about the love of men and women ? "

She fumbled for an answer.

" I really don't know.   But what does it matter, whether I do or not ? "

" It matters very much," he said.

" Why ? "

He replied slowly :

" Because if you do, then——"

" Oh, what do you want ? "

There was a pause.

" I want *you*, Beauty."

She lowered her head, trying to avoid his eyes.   The hot crimson flooded into her cheeks.

" You want *me* ?   I don't quite——"

Before she could prevent it, he was on his knee, gripping her hand :

" Yes, Beauty, you do understand."

She unloosened his hold and sprang up ; then stood away from him, shaking from head to foot.   He rose and faced her.

" You are afraid of me ? "

" Yes, I am."

She steadied herself, resting a hand on the back of the chair.   A wave of burning anger swept through her as the full realization came. It submerged her fear, and with it her courage returned.

" Yes, I do understand. You want me in—your way. Is that it ? "

" Yes, Beauty, I do. Why not ? Is the love of a man for a woman so terrible ? "

" This is *not* love ! "

" It *is* love. Do you think I've come here to make a fool of you ? "

" You've come here to insult me !—No, please, let me speak. You asked whether I agreed with your views on— love. No, I don't. I think they're disgusting. I've implied that before. And yet you've come here—— Oh, how dare you ! "

He leaned an elbow on the mantelpiece. Outwardly he was composed.

" Shall we discuss the matter reasonably ? "

" There's nothing to discuss. I know exactly what you mean."

He remained thinking.

" Supposing I had asked you to be my wife, to marry me in the ordinary way, what would you have said then ? "

" Since you asked nothing of the kind, I refuse to answer."

Verrers continued deliberately :

" You say ' nothing of the kind.' You mean that I didn't suggest what is commonly called holy matrimony. I certainly did not. You know quite well these religious pretences mean nothing to me. May I ask why they should mean anything to you, if, as I understand, you have practically rejected your religion ? "

It pulled her up, as he intended. And it left her at a loss for an answer. She began to trace a pattern with the point of her shoe.

" Beauty, cannot you see ? You are afraid ; that is all. Why should you be bound by these ideas ? Why should they bind human love ? "

She was listening.

"Please understand me when I say that I can fully sympathize with your feelings. Your sentiments are shocked, because they haven't yet changed. It was clumsy of me not to allow for that, and I apologize."

She looked hesitating.

And then she helped herself to a cigarette with fingers that still trembled slightly. Rather doubtfully she pushed the silver box along the mantelpiece towards him. He struck a match, lit hers and next his own.

For a time neither spoke.

"I suppose," she said at last, "you're logical. And I suppose it's unreasonable to blame you for acting on your own principles. My instinct, though, is against your principles ; and a woman cannot stifle her instincts. If you had asked me to marry you in the ordinary way, as you put it, I should have—taken it differently. To what you want, I can only say no."

"Beauty, do you love me ? " It came passionately.

She met his look. He made no attempt to come near, though she knew he would do so at the slightest sign of yielding. The appeal of the man was returning. She could feel the magnetism of his presence, the spell of the dark eyes. A moment's weakness on her part, and——

"You don't answer me."

Still she did not reply, but lowered her head, lest he should read the reason for her delay. She had intimated the terms on which he might approach her.

"If I offered you marriage in the usual sense and you accepted, would it be because you love me ? "

"That's not quite fair," she answered.

"I think it is, under the circumstances," he said. "The main thing is whether you love me or not, surely ? If you don't, then this is finished."

She thought rapidly.

"Shall we leave out that word—love, for the present ? Can you be patient to that extent ? "

" Very well," said Verrers.

He deliberated. Then :

" May I be quite frank ? If I were a Catholic I should ask you to marry me according to the rites of the Catholic Church. Since I am not, and, as you know, am utterly opposed to marriage in the Catholic sense, that way of offering my love to you is closed. Why should this prove a barrier, though ? If you were a devout believer, it would. But you are not ; the religious side cannot weigh much. It is not your religious instinct which is against my principles ; it is your sense of propriety, the fear of social stigma. And it means a good deal to you, that, although it means nothing to me. Social taboos are so many stupidities."

" Social taboos involve women far more than men, remember that," said Beauty.

" They do ; and so I can sympathize with you. Will you listen if I put my—offer in another way, so that there would be no question of compromising you ? "

" Er—yes, I will listen."

" Thank you. Well, I take it that ecclesiastical censures would not bother you much ; you would assert your independence where your own happiness was concerned ? Am I right ? "

" Oh yes, I suppose so." It was not spoken very assuredly.

" It's a question of propriety, then. I don't see any serious difficulty there. Why couldn't we compromise ? For my part I should be quite prepared to go through the formalities of a registrar's office, if you would dispense with religious rites."

He was watching her closely.

" What do you think ? "

She toyed with an ornament on the mantelpiece.

It would mean final severance from her religion, she saw that. Socially it would not affect her, beyond ostracism by a few Catholic friends. A rupture with her people, certainly. In the eyes of the world she would be the wife of Julian Verrers. At least——

"What am I to understand by 'going through the formalities of a registrar's office'?"

It put him on his guard, she noticed.

"Surely that is clear?" he answered.

"Civil marriage is clear enough, yes. But is it in keeping with your own principles? I thought one of them was 'temporary unions terminable at will'?"

"Civil marriage is merely a legal form. Circumstances can always arise to terminate a union."

So he was safeguarding. It flashed upon her that this was only a legalized edition of his first suggestion. He wanted her passionately; but he wanted her on his own terms, the whole time. With equal clearness it came to her at this moment that a mere continuance of their friendship would never satisfy him. It was to be all or nothing.

She shivered.

"What's the matter, Beauty?"

"Oh, I don't know; but—Mr. Verrers, will you be patient again? Will you give me a little time to think?"

"How long?"

She hesitated.

"Give me a week."

"If you will give me a definite answer then, yes."

"I will write to you," she said. "I think perhaps we'd better not meet until I've done so. Do you mind?"

"Since you ask me, yes, I do. I've a box for to-morrow night and was hoping you'd share it."

"I couldn't come in any case to-morrow night. I've promised—I'm booked."

She pulled herself up just in time.

"Anything very important? Couldn't you cut it?"

"I'm sorry, no, I can't. And I'd really rather we didn't meet until the week is over."

"Couldn't the week start a day later?"

" No, from now, please."

It was his persistence which brought the intuition to her ; he knew what was happening at the Queen's Hall to-morrow night, and he had taken the box to ensure her not being there. If he had taken it ? Had he guessed something, too, from her slip ? . . .

" As you wish."

But a frown accompanied the concession. He stood there furrowing the carpet with his foot. The question she expected did not come, though.

" I shall hear from you ? "

" Yes, I promise," she answered.

He drew himself up, came nearer and gave her his hand. She took it.

" Good-bye, Beauty, for a week."

" Good-bye." And she tried to withdraw her hand. He held it though.

" Beauty——" He was drawing her towards him. Only when the dark head was perilously near did she release herself with an effort, and step back.

" No, Mr. Verrers ! "

" I must wait for that, too, then."

He was very certain of her.

The next moment he was walking across the room towards the door. She recollected herself to press a button in the wall. The door closed behind him. After a time she heard the front-door do the same, and Marie's step returning.

Then silence.

* * * * * *

That evening she dined at Mrs. Sands-Woodford's. It was only a small affair of people she knew well, but it taxed her to tune in with them. Julian Verrers' speech cropped up inevitably, two or three times ; but she refrained from contributing any opinion.

" What's up, Beauty ? You're not at your best," asked Mrs. Sands-Woodford afterwards.

" Tired," she answered. " Fag-end of season, Maggie." She excused herself on the same score from accompanying them to a night-club later. Instead, she said good-bye hurriedly and escaped further inquisition from that lynx-eyed lady.

She drove back, barely aware of the streets passing by.

At the flat the chauffeur of her hired car was absently dismissed without the customary tip. The lift-boy, whose wont it was to land the object of his secret adoration at the third floor each night, wondered at the complete ignoring of his existence. Marie, assisting at her toilet in the bedroom, found her unresponsive to all questions. Usually she talked freely. To-night it was monosyllables.

Left to herself, Beauty lit a cigarette. There was a peculiar intensity about her.

After a few minutes she rose, opened the window wider and began to wander about restlessly. Then she stood motionless, staring before her. Once she muttered impatiently, fiercely, as if driving off some apprehension. Next her expression was hardening.

She looked about the room, noting various objects.

A few quick steps took her to a table in the corner, on which lay a small pile of books. From among them she picked up one entitled *The Garden of the Soul*. There was a sound of ripping and the cover was off. She flung it into a waste-paper basket under the table. The naked pages were separated hurriedly into sections, and her fingers began to tear them across and drop them in after the cover.

She went to the head of her bed and detached, from

the knob on which they hung, a chain of rosary-beads. Stretching them to their length she tugged until the chain gave. The beads still remained in position. She pulled at them, detaching as many as she could ; returned towards the waste-paper basket, but changed her mind and flung them with the chain out of the window.

A faint clatter came as they bounced on a roof beneath. Her eyes rested on the mantelpiece.

In the centre stood an ivory crucifix, the figure of the Christus hanging twistedly from the cross-piece. She approached, her hand to her cheek. Within arm's-length she stopped and regarded it. A sudden deathly silence pervaded the room.

A dog barked in the distance.

She stretched out her arm, slowly. It wavered and dropped to her side. She shuddered.

A terror came, uncannily, as of some presence urging her on. She wheeled round, trembling violently, half expecting to see——

In a frenzy she reached out her hands and clutched wildly at the crucifix. . . .

What happened she never knew clearly. It may have been the illusion of a scared imagination. But, as her fingers closed upon the figure to break it in two, a monk's grey eyes were looking into hers. . . .

Her grasp unloosened.

She moved back, swaying ; and then stumbled blindly towards the sofa.

CHAPTER X

BROTHER ANSELM looked at his watch.
A quarter-past eight. In fifteen minutes he would
be facing his audience.

The stage-porter had just informed him that the
Queen's Hall had been filled throughout by eight o'clock.
Outside, his car had been delayed for a while from reaching
the platform door, the road being blocked with those
unable to gain entrance.

He was pacing to and fro now in one of the little green-
rooms behind the scenes, reflecting that many of the world's
great singers must have waited in this room, too, listening
to a murmur like that of a distant sea—of an audience on
the leash of expectation. The bishop and two priests,
who had come with him in the car, had departed to their
seats. At his own express wish he was to be alone on the
platform, without even a chairman.

He had journeyed up from Hendringham yesterday
morning and spent the day quietly at the London house
of his Order, going through the notes of his speech.
To-day something had happened. A lay-brother had
entered his room with a note, saying that the bearer was
waiting for an answer. The contents had puzzled him
for a moment, and he had asked the lay-brother to return
in five minutes' time.

It was from Miss Dethier. She had managed to discover
his address. First she apologized, very humbly, for the
incident of Sunday, then for troubling him at a busy time
with a question which would seem extremely curious.
Would he be willing to tell her what he was doing about
eleven o'clock on the previous night ? He had considered, and then scribbled an answer : " I was in our

106

Chapel here at the time you mention. Something con-
strained me to pray for you." He had added : " Sunday
morning is quite forgotten. I, too, apologize, if I was
rather brutal." The lay-brother had departed with this
in a sealed envelope.

*   *   *   *   *   *

Beauty dined early, at her flat, to be ready for Basil
Esterton when he came.

She had passed a restless night after her experience.
In the morning Marie, calling her, had handed with the
letters a little golden object, like a locket ; it had been
found on the floor of the library. She recognized it
immediately as an ornament that Julian Verrers carried
on his watch-chain.

After Marie had left the room, she examined it. The
tiny gold case opened easily. It contained a thin disc,
also of gold, about the size of a sovereign, quite plain,
except for four incised words—*Contra Fidem et Ecclesiam.*
The meaning of the Latin, *Against the Faith and the
Church*, she understood at once ; but why should Julian
Verrers wear such an inscription upon his person ?

She had almost given it up when something came to
her mind.

At Lady Derringham's, in referring to his work, he
had inadvertently used the term " we "—" *We* want not
only men, *we* want women." She had asked him what
he meant by " we," and he had evaded the question.
Did the unintended term stand for some organization ?
And was this inscribed disc the symbol of its membership ?
If so, his urgent effort to enlist herself in his cause could
have only one interpretation ; he had intended, if possible,
to secure her for this organization, whatever it was.

She had returned the little gold case to him after
breakfast by registered post without any comment.

The theory had simmered in her mind all the morning

and had opened out an ugly vista. If it were true, and if she said yes to him, she would be united to a man whose profession it was to work *Contra Fidem et Ecclesiam*. He wanted her ravenously for himself, she knew that; but he also wanted her for "their" work—the work that she could never do. Once she was with him, he would use his power to the utmost, morally, to try and force her to his will—the power that since last night she had begun to dread.

Until then it had fascinated her. Now it had become haunting and repelling. Last night she had virtually surrendered. The glamour of being his wife in the eyes of the world had swept aside all other considerations.

Then had come that strange experience !

The clinging memory of mingled terror and shame had worked upon her steadily. By the end of the morning she had reached a final and irrevocable decision.

Under no conditions, under no terms whatever would she accept Julian Verrers.

After lunch she had dispatched the note to Brother Anselm, and received his reply.

She was waiting now for Basil Esterton.

His ring came at five to eight. As he entered the room and she greeted him, the fresh youthfulness of his presence came like a tonic to her overstrained nerves. " Your monk and I have made it up ; but you're not to ask questions," she told him straight away.

" I'm awfully glad." Basil looked wonderingly at her, and enormously pleased.

He was unashamedly delighted with the prospect of taking her to the Queen's Hall. The car was below in Curzon Street, his own new one. He had driven it up from Hendringham especially for her. He told her so. She found herself contrasting his open candour with the hidden manner of Julian Verrers.

Sitting in front beside him on the way she felt glad, with a healthier kind of happiness than she had known for weeks. Once, while he was intent upon the traffic, she glanced at his profile and then at the strong, easy hands upon the wheel.

"My hat!" exclaimed Basil. They had crossed Oxford Circus into Upper Regent Street. "Look at the crowd!"

Before the Queen's Hall there seethed a mass of humanity. Beauty gasped at the sight. It had been nothing like this on Monday night.

"They must be Catholics," said Basil.

He slowed down. A policeman was motioning cars up the street to the right. He followed in the stream, parked at the appointed place; then, with Beauty, walked back. At the corner they fell in with a line of seat-holders, moving slowly towards the Queen's Hall. The police were doing their best to make a passage through the block for those with tickets. As they neared the main doors the jam grew worse.

"Take my arm," said Basil. Beauty did.

Gaining entrance was no easy matter. The vestibule was surging with those who still hoped for unclaimed seats at the last moment. Three minutes before time they were inside and passing through to their block-entrance. The interior of the great hall appeared, and a sea of faces sweeping up to the roof. An attendant led them to their seats in the area stalls.

"I say, it's great, isn't it?" said Basil, turning round and taking stock. "Hullo!"

He had discovered Major Brandreth a couple of rows behind them. The Major waved.

In front, beneath the platform, a long row of reporters were sharpening pencils and whispering. Above hung great shaded lights, shedding circles of radiance on the scene.

The audience began to stir.

It was the half-hour.

Then, at the far left of the platform, a curtain was drawn aside. A figure came through, and walked slowly towards the centre. Basil stared, hardly recognizing Brother Anselm in his monk's habit.

The murmur that had greeted his appearance increased, then changed into clapping which swelled to a steady thunder, a large section of the audience, evidently Catholics, rising to their feet. The monk stood immovable to the ovation, singularly calm, the long lines of his habit accentuated in the stream of light from above. He glanced at the microphone in front, moved the table before him slightly forward, and waited. The thunder abated. There was a rustling as people resumed their seats. The long row of reporters' heads bent in readiness.

Beauty met Basil's eyes. They were sparkling.

Into the expectant hush the monk's voice broke, deep and easy and powerful. He began by remarking on the presence of others than those of his own Faith ; he understood that something like a third of his audience were non-Catholics. He took it as a sign that those outside the Catholic Church were desirous to hear whether an answer could be given to the challenge issued from the same platform by Mr. Julian Verrers the previous Monday evening—a challenge not merely to Catholics, but to all who respected and valued Christianity.

He must apologize for the choice of himself, an obscure monk, to reply to a brilliant orator like Mr. Verrers ; the blame lay with his superiors, not himself. He must also thank the broadcasting authorities for the immense pains they had taken to secure for him the fairest and widest hearing possible. Not only had they interfered with other programmes to enable people to listen-in to the Queen's Hall from all parts of England, but they had also arranged the instalment of loud-speakers outside for the benefit of those who would be unable to gain entrance :

" In speaking, as I am, to such a vast unseen audience,

as well as seen, to men and women of every kind, I must necessarily put my answer as simply as possible. I have no desire to impress you with rhetoric or a flood of technical terms ; I want you to understand me, that is all. You, who are Catholics, the majority in this hall and perhaps of listeners-in, know the answer already in a general way ; but you may not know all the facts or the grounds on which the answer rests. When you have heard them, I want you to remember them. We Catholics take our Faith and morality for granted ; we sometimes forget that those outside do not. It is some of our first principles that I shall enunciate to-night, principles which are almost forgotten by the masses of England to-day— if I may be forgiven for saying so."

He looked to left and right, and then up at the tiers of heads craning from the balcony and above.

" I shall begin by examining the main assertions on which Mr. Julian Verrers has based his ' Plea for Freedom ' and his contention that Christianity is the enemy of freedom. I say ' assertions ' because I can find no other word for the theses he has advanced.

" First and foremost, in both his speeches, he endeavours to strike at the root of all religion by advancing certain arguments against the existence of a Supreme Being. Very wisely he does not claim to prove His nonexistence. Mr. Verrers knows enough to know that he cannot. He intends to convey the impression, however, of demolishing a Supreme Being. He invites us to shake off the notion of responsibility to a Creator.

" Together with the evolutionary anthropologists whom he follows, he would have us believe that man invented God ; that the religious idea of God arose out of the superstitions of man's savage state ; that it began with a belief in spirits animating natural phenomena, passed to a conception of a limited number of deities, and finally became monotheistic. That is the notion which Mr. Verrers developed at some length.

" How far he believes it, I do not know. His frequent use of terms and phrases from Frazer leads me to suspect that, like others, he borrows from a well-worn stock.

" Now, what are the facts ?

" The idea of God did not evolve. The existence of God is a primary conclusion of the human reason. It is not a development of the imagination. It is common to all races, whatever their stage of culture. We have to judge the primitives of the past by the primitives of to-day. When we do, we find that the evolutionary notion of God is pure guesswork, and extremely bad guesswork, totally at variance with attested facts. Research into the mental habits of unadvanced races now living proves their belief in a Supreme Being, in a Maker of all things, in a Guardian of morality. This belief, it is true, frequently accompanies spirit-worship and magic and mythical deities. These, however, do not lead to the God-idea as assumed, but away from it. In the early stages we find God's supreme dominion and man's obligations to Him more clearly recognized. Gradually these truths become obscured under the influence of superstition ; primitive monotheism may lapse into polytheism.

" Animism, the theory put forward by Mr. Verrers, reverses the process. It supposes that the cult of spirits evolves into polytheism and finally monotheism. In other words, that ghosts lead to gods and God. On the contrary, ghosts lead to nothing of the kind. The notions of ghost and God have nothing in common in the primitive mind. To a native, to connect the Supreme Being with a fetish would be the height of folly !

" And yet Mr. Verrers would have us believe that the God-idea arose out of superstition !

" Now why does a man, who is a scientist by profession and should therefore know the value of evidence, try to force upon us a theory which conflicts with ascertainable facts ? He does so because the whole of his scheme falls to pieces if he admits a Supreme Being to Whom we are responsible. He dare not acknowledge the fact that all races, civilized and uncivilized, have been compelled by *reason* to affirm the existence of God, and that atheists are decidedly in the minority. He wants God to be a superstition invented by superstition. He intends us to draw the conclusion that all religion rests on superstition, and that those who dismiss it as such are the enlightened ones of to-day.

" Has it ever occurred to him that the last thing man would do would be to invent God ?

" Would man invent a Being Who imposes on him an urgent moral law ? Would men be such fools as to invent a moral responsibility for themselves ? Would men invent sin—and its consequences ?

" For this is what we are to understand.

" Now, I am not going to give you the proofs from reason for the existence of God—I am merely taking Mr. Verrers on his own grounds and answering what he has said. When he states that there is no scientific proof for His existence, he means that God cannot be *directly* observed. Have we ever claimed such folly ? How could a purely spiritual Being come under scientific observation ? I might quite validly put it to him that even the laws of Nature, which he is so fond of quoting, are not objects of direct observation ; that they are deductions from observed effects. Are the laws of Nature superstitions, too ?

" May I assure him that, if in modern times God recedes into the background, as he puts it, with the advance of civilization and science, it is not because He is a superstition, but an inconvenience."

The monk picked up his notes from the table.

Basil glanced at Beauty. She was leaning forward. Her face told him nothing except that she was listening closely.

" The second prop on which Mr. Verrers leans is his assumption that man, though ' of a higher mental d●

velopment,' is not distinct from the animal, but ' evolved from some mammalian stock resembling the modern ape,' as ' every reputable scientist now knows.' I use his own words."

He put down the notes and smiled.

" I rather like that ' now knows.' I also like ' reputable scientist.' So the reputable scientist *knows* that we are mere glorified monkeys ! The implication is that no scientist is reputable who does not know it ; who does not affirm what Mr. Verrers affirms.

" May I affirm that no reputable scientist knows any such thing. A scientist, who ' knows ' it, is not reputable, but disreputable. To affirm what cannot be proved is disreputable and unscientific. To know a thing means that you can prove it.

" What scientist living can prove that man is evolved from the ape ?

" Will Mr. Verrers forgive me if I say that there are scientists of greater standing than himself who would laugh his dogmatism out of court ; that those who really know are the ones who admit they do not know. If by ' reputable ' he means those who prostitute their science in the service of materialism, then let him change his term to—' reputed.'

" What proof can science offer that man is evolved from the ape ? By man, I mean a being possessed of a rational soul and body.

" It can offer none.

" At the best it can offer an hypothesis for the evolution of man's *body*—moreover, an hypothesis with a shifting base. Formerly the motto was—Nature does not make leaps ; now it is—Nature does make leaps. The failure to discover missing-links has necessitated jumping the gaps. The evolution of the human body is only guess-work. It has yet to be proved.

" It is a further matter, however, when we are told that *man* is evolved from the ape. Man is not a body. He is a rational soul and body; and it is his rational soul which makes him a man, and distinct from the ape. An ape is not rational. An ape could never evolve a spiritual substance like the human soul. It could never evolve the power to abstract ideas, to control with the will, to reflect. It could never evolve human self-consciousness. In a word, an ape could never spiritualize itself as man is spiritualized.

"I might add that the direct creation and infusion of the human soul into the body is easier to suppose psychologically than the hypothetical modifications of brain-cells assumed by materialists to account for human intelligence. We, at any rate, can offer reason and revelation for what we hold. They, however, cannot offer one shred of evidence for the organic evolution of the human intellect!

"I shall not enlarge upon this : I am merely answering Mr. Verrers' assumptions. I only want you to understand that the whole of his scheme for freedom depends upon the abolition of God and the relegation of man to the apes, and that both these notions involve intellectual suicide.

"Now.

"We will examine the constituents of his scheme—what he calls the ' consequences of man's new knowledge.' "

There was a stir in the audience. The girl at Basil's side changed her position.

"First, he would like to see all religion eliminated from the conduct of human affairs. Listening-in to his speech last Monday, I wondered whether he quite knew what religion was.

"It is not a mere ethical system imposed by the God he denies upon human conduct. Religion is primarily an acknowledgment by the creature of his Creator, of his relation to the Being to Whom he owes his existence. Ethics, or morality, are the consequence of that relation. Religion is the first rational act of a human being, not a

hobby for the ' servile victims ' of a ' priestly despotism.'
Its elimination would not rationalize, but irrationalize
man. Neither would it be easy to accomplish. Putting
away religion is not like taking off your clothes. Religion
is part of man's rational self. Its destruction would be
a violation of what is natural to sane men. Mr. Verrers
has a difficult task before him.

" Is he prepared to try conclusions with the essential
sanity of the human race ?

" He follows on with his ' sin obsession '—quite
logically, if his premises were correct. If what he states
about God and man were true, ' sin ' would be silly ; and
I, for one, would rid myself of the obsession and cheerfully go to the dogs—or the apes !

" Sin may be an inconvenient notion to those who are
dispensing with God. It is a fact, nevertheless, following
from the fact of God, from man's responsibility to the
Author of morality. It is far more comfortable, I know,
to be assured that sin is a mere relic of monkey-nature,
and that men, who once believed they were little less than
the angels, should now rise to the dignity of being little
more than the apes.

" Mr. Verrers contends that priests have fostered the
' sin ' idea in the human race. If so, they must be fools ;
for they bind themselves equally with others under pain
of sin.

" No. Sin is not a ' phantom ' of the human imagination exploited by priestcraft. The fact of right and wrong
is a deep, universal conviction of the human reason. No
degree of culture or civilization can ever shake that conviction. Phantoms pass. ' Sin ' does not.

" I notice that Mr. Verrers inveighs against the people
of England for ' clinging blindly ' to the Christian code
of morality—to a ' man-made morality.' The Christian
code could never have been made by man. It is loftier
than man's loftiest conception of what is right or wrong.

" He regards even the natural moral law as a fiction

induced by fear. Does he understand in the smallest degree what the moral law is? He assumes it to be in conflict with the law of Nature.

"It *is* the law of Nature. It is the law of Nature in man; the natural law of his being. As natural as the laws on which Mr. Verrers bases his own science. He vaunts 'the right of Nature's way' as something 'nobler and higher'; the moral law *is* Nature's way for man. He bids us 'follow Nature.' That is almost amusing. For a few minutes later he upholds *un*natural vices!

"He claims that there can be 'no fixed standard of morality in an evolutionary system.' Why not? Are there no fixed laws of Nature? Of mathematics? No fixed data of science? Why this arbitrary pronouncement in the case of the moral law?

"A man cannot be free, he declares, who adheres to it.

"Why not apply the principle all round? Why not be free from the law of gravity and jump off precipices? Why not be free from two and two making four and say they make five? Why not free himself from the data of his own science and invent biological axioms to his fancy? Why not be free from everything that is fixed?

"If moral freedom, why not intellectual freedom?

"There is no more folly in my suggestions than in his. As well run amuck intellectually as morally; for that is all his moral freedom means—men to give rein to their lusts. If the world is to be turned into a cesspool, why not into a mad-house as well?

"He flings about that blessed word 'freedom' with all the glorious inconsequence of the modern irrationalist; an excellent word for catching the popular ear—'A plea for freedom'!

"May I suggest that freedom comes from obedience to law, not from the disregard of it. He may term it freedom to break from a standard of morality, which happens to have been fixed by the Almighty, and which also happens not to fit into his scheme; but both history and experience of life furnish a damning indictment when he does. Licence is ever termed freedom by its patrons until, in its fetters, they find themselves—slaves.

" I hope I have not wearied you ; but I want you to estimate clearly the basis on which his whole scheme for freedom rests. I want you to realize that every argument he uses, whether against God and religion, or man and morality, is honeycombed with fallacies. I say it without hesitation and I say it deliberately. Mr. Verrers, expert biologist though he may be, exhibits, like many other specialists, the grossest ignorance when he meddles in matters outside his own sphere."

The monk picked up his notes again.

" To come to closer quarters.

" To the proposals which comprise his scheme.

" Are these proposals prompted by a sincere belief in their efficacy, or by a desire to injure the religion he detests ? I wonder.

" What are they ?

" First, he wants Christian marriage to be abolished— ' one of the most heinous inventions ever foisted on mankind ' ; its indissoluble bond ties men and women to ' what is often an irksome and odious union.' ' Legalized unions terminable at will ' would be substituted as more beneficial to the happiness of humanity ; love, if free, would be invested with a grandeur of which it is robbed under ' the iniquitous bondage of Christian marriage.' The present system of ' miserable pretences ' ' clogs the law-courts with unsavoury divorce cases.' The marriage-bond ' occasions adulteries and infidelities,' ' tragedies and cruelties.'

" Very good.

" And where must the blame be laid for all this ? Upon the Catholic Church, upon the ' loathsome injunctions ' attached by her to the marriage union two thousand years ago, and still enforced.

" One is almost edified by the spectacle of Mr. Julian

Verrers lamenting unsavoury divorce cases, and adulteries
and the tragedies of married life. One is also struck by
a sense of incongruity. The cases he bewails are, at any
rate, cases of shattered ideals. The remedy he proposes
leaves no ideals at all. The marriage-bond carries with
it ideals of fidelity, self-sacrifice, unselfishness, of a love
which is lasting. Temporary unions stand for passing
passions, and no more. ' Love must be freely given and
freely received ; it cannot be limited to fixed channels,'
he declares—in plain English, promiscuous lusting.

" This is not love.

" Love endures. It is rooted in something far deeper
than mere bodily desire—in mutual esteem, in spiritual
affection, in home life, in the child. Mr. Julian Verrers
is not talking of love. He is talking of licentious con-
cubinage. He would have men and women like the
animals he tells them they are. No, lower. There is
more fidelity in animal life than there would be in his
temporary agreements. He would have them lower than
the animals."

It must have been a slight movement of hers that
caused Basil to glance at Beauty. There was a white,
strained look in her face. He hesitated. " Anything the
matter ? " he whispered. Her " No, no, I'm all right "
did not quite reassure him. He turned, however, to the
platform again.

" He is very anxious to animalize men and women.

" The impression I received last Monday was one of
over-anxiety on his part. We should expect a man of
science to approach these matters calmly and impartially,
not in a hectic manner. His impatience, the contempt
manifested towards all who might not see eye to eye with
him, the reiterated assumption that those who did were
the advanced and intellectual, the superior treatment
meted out to Christian sentiment, that sneering challenge
to Catholics—it all pointed to animus rather than calm
reason.

"It is that very animus, I believe, which accounts for his over-anxiety to animalize men. Demoralization, he well knows, is the surest method of depleting religion and injuring Christianity. I mention it that you may see what underlies not only this, but all his proposals.

"Such argument as he uses is specious—singularly so.

"So the marriage-bond is responsible for the breaking of it! As, I suppose, the law is responsible for crime! Medical science for disease!

"How many were convinced by this *post hoc, propter hoc* pleading? Is it because of the marriage-bond, or in spite of and in violation of it, that the evils he enumerates come about? The Christian marriage-bond is actually one of the most powerful factors for human happiness, intended by the God Who decreed it, not for the misery, but the welfare of the world. It has produced, not the disasters he attributes, but happiness untold. Blame the traitors to its sacred trust for the disasters! Don't blame the marriage-bond! To do so is gross twisting.

"The bond demands self-sacrifice, I know. Are men the worse for that? No, ten thousand times the better!

"Loosen the bond and you loosen a flood of selfishness with it. Destroy it and you destroy the social fabric— the family. Disintegrate the natural order of society into the unnatural disorder of temporary unions, and you have a chaos of individuals with no natural centre.

"The children born of Mr. Verrers' 'selective breeding' scheme would, as he implies, be State property. Deprive children of the natural care of parents and you deprive them of a natural necessity. Hand them over to the unnatural care of the State and you cheat them of a natural right, of a mother's love, of a father's love, of the magic of that place called—Home.

"'Follow Nature'! Is this following Nature?

"Be sure of this.

"The kind of happiness, associated by vast millions with that word—Home, would vanish for ever under his scheme. That sanctuary of human love, encircled for two thousand years by a rampart of inviolable vows, is the creation of the Christian marriage-bond.

" Let go that bond, and you let go human love.

" ' Loathsome injunctions ' Mr. Verrers calls our marriage laws. We prefer them to his ' freedom,' to the slavery of lust ! "

The monk stopped and looked around.

" I wonder if it would interest you, I wonder if you know what civilization owes to the marriage-bond ? I will show you."

With lightning rapidity he proceeded to sketch its workings in the history of twenty centuries, in the social life of Europe. " Some of you, perhaps, may not have viewed the marriage-bond in this light, as the keystone of that structure called European civilization. Remove that keystone and the structure will collapse," he ended with.

Then :

" I should have preferred to ignore the proposal which comes next in Mr. Verrers' scheme, as unsuitable to deal with at a public meeting. I only treat of it at all in order to counteract, as far as possible, any poisonous effects.

" I allude to—Birth-control.

" In referring to it Mr. Verrers used the expression : ' medical means of preventing conception.' I want you to note that word ' medical.' We might gather from it some medical ruling, some weighty medical authority behind contraconceptive methods. There is nothing of the kind. Medical opinion is most strongly divided. Even experts are in conflict over the harmfulness or harmlessness of birth-control, as also of particular contraconceptive practices.

" I am a qualified medical man myself, still following medical research closely. ' Medical means of preventing conception ' implies some accepted means guaranteed by the medical profession. There is no such thing. There are, though, plenty of self-appointed propagandists gulling the popular mind with dogmatic quackery.

" However, birth-control, or the use of some artificial means of preventing conception, is primarily a moral question.

" It is intimately bound up with the morality of sex relations, and therefore with marriage. Marriage was instituted by the Creator for the purpose of procreation. The marriage right is intended to be used for that purpose. To use some unnatural means of preventing conception is to frustrate that purpose and defeat a natural end. It is therefore morally evil to do so. The laws of the Catholic Church on the matter are not arbitrary, but in accordance with the laws of Nature. The breakage of these laws has already led to a grave extension of immorality among both married and unmarried here in England.

" ' Follow Nature ' ! Is birth-control following Nature?

" It is precisely in this defeating of Nature that the physical danger also of contraconception lies. There is a body of reliable medical opinion now advancing grounds for connecting contraconception, at least indirectly, with disease. I am well aware that the supporters of birth-control could cite other medical views in their own favour ; but I believe that these views are short-sighted. To establish *direct* evil results from our present limited knowledge may be difficult ; but is that any warrant for refusing to see the danger which must inevitably accompany faulty and unnatural functioning of sex ? Every medical man's experience tells him that Nature revenges acts contrary to her ends. Does inexperience in this case, from lack of research, justify recommending the frustration of the primary end of the sex function, the procreation of children ?

" I am not giving a word for word answer to all that Mr. Verrers puts forward on this matter. There is no occasion to do so. For those who stand by morality everything that he says falls by the immorality of the practice he urges. Here, too, the freedom he demands is merely the freedom to lust.

" He asks us for a rational argument against birth-control : I have given one. He challenges us priests for condemning it when we violate Nature ourselves by our celibacy. Can he see no difference between self-control and birth-control ?

" He wants the race thinned out ; the world is over-populated, professions overstocked. Had England no economic troubles with half its present population ? It has yet to be proved that numbers solve this particular problem.

" He blames ' indiscriminate breeding, bringing into the world a multitude of diseased and insane ' ; birth-control will solve this. But so would the segregation of those unfit to propagate, and it would be morally lawful.

" He foresees ' an upcry from Rome.' There will be no upcry from Rome against moral methods leading to a healthier population.

" At the end of his glorification of free-love and birth-control Mr. Verrers, to allay fear, assures us that their reign would not be a reign of licence ; natural virtues implanted in the human species would hold men in check. I reply that the unnatural vices for which he pleads would destroy these natural virtues. Remove the moral code and you remove the moral virtues. Does the witness of history mean nothing to him—that men degenerate into a welter of licence once the barriers are removed ?

" ' The third wide road to freedom.'

" So he terms the last of his proposals. It is a slight variant from the others. It is a scheme for suicide and murder."

The monk stopped, with his eyes on the stalls.

" Why do you start ? That is the plain English for his ' humane system of euthanasia.' It is a scheme for ridding humanity of its ' waste-products,' its ' load of diseased, incurably sick, aged, crippled, and insane ' : their presence is an ' evil ' in the world, to be removed.

He might have extended the scheme. From certain remarks of his I gather that Catholics are the worst evil of all. Why not begin with us ?

" Having previously urged us to go forward on the road of progress, he here asks us to go back. Primitive tribes, he declares, practise these things ; why not copy their example ? Living closest to Nature, they follow her precept—the survival of the fittest. Almost in the same breath he proclaims his scheme ' a merciful system in place of a merciless one.' I may be dull, but I thought he wanted jungle life !

" I am afraid I cannot admire his attempts to whitewash suicide and murder. Neither can I admire his methods. Is it a very admirable proceeding to state that we ' chain life's victims to a living hell ' because we preserve human life at all costs ?

" We do. It is true.

" It is morally illicit to take human life even to escape its pains and burdens. Human life happens to belong to its Creator, not to us. We cannot take what belongs to Him. It is an infringement of His sovereign rights over life and death. We are God's property, not our own. Euthanasia is a crime on natural grounds alone. If voluntary, it is suicide ; if compulsory, it is murder. As suicide it is diametrically opposed to the strongest instinct of human nature, self-preservation ; it frustrates Nature's purpose in ourselves. As murder it frustrates Nature's purpose in others.

" ' Follow Nature ! ' Is euthanasia following Nature ?

" A ' virtuous course ' is it ? Or a coward's policy ?

" ' What more merciful sight than great euthanasic homes standing in every city and town ? ' For those outside these slaughter-houses, yes. Would those compelled to enter appreciate it in this light ? How many *would* enter unless compelled ? How many sufferers *do* take their lives ? They have endless facilities for doing so ; and yet they cling to life. Would Mr. Verrers and his fellow-altruists lead the way into these euthanasic homes if stricken down themselves ?

" May I be quite candid ?

" This euthanasic plan, this ' renunciation of Christian folly,' is nothing less than a stupendous piece of selfishness calculated to rid humanity of a hampering burden upon its pleasure and comfort.

" To the challenge that human wreckage is a ' detriment to the race,' I reply :—Quite possibly, from the materialistic standpoint, which puts an A 1 race as the highest aim of humanity. In the Christian view life's wreckage is a responsibility of honour ; a cross whose shouldering carries with it what a mere physically perfect race would lose—a wealth of self-sacrifice and pity for the broken worth more than a whole world of health.

" There are higher values than those of materialism. There are spiritual values. There is all the splendid tenderness of the human heart that makes humanity so immensely lovable. Take away what calls it forth and you leave men cold, unlovable and cruel.

" Rome will strive to block the euthanasic way to ' freedom,' Mr. Verrers says.

" We shall.

" We know a better way. We are proud to accept the onus of life's wreckage. We are proud of our sacred trust, proud to preserve life, not in ' useless existence,' but as part of an eternal scheme. There is a scheme in which all pain is touched with the divine, by the hands of One Who has endured, Himself ; a scheme in which pain is not worthless, but of eternal value for victim and succourer alike. It is the scheme of the Cross of God."

The monk waited a moment. There was intense silence throughout the Hall.

" I have said enough now to answer, adequately, I think, the main points of Mr. Verrers' two speeches. I have tried to show you what his proposals are worth, and what his scheme for freedom means.

" He claims to speak in the name of science and human progress. I claim to speak in the name of religion and morality.

" Since we are mutually opposed, and our cases mutually destructive, we cannot both be right. If one of us is speaking the truth, then the other is not. He declares that the dogmas of Christianity are in open conflict with the ' findings of biology.' I declare that they are not ; that there can be no conflict between the truths of religion and the truths of science, since God is the author of both.

" Where, then, is the departure from truth ?

" I have endeavoured to show you that to-night ; it is in his presentation of the ' findings of biology.' The hypotheses on which he builds his scheme are not the findings of biology. They are not the truths of science. They are merely the guesswork of materialistic scientists, and false guesswork at that. To furbish up these hypo-heses in the form of a quack drug for the popular palate, a common practice to-day, is not to speak in the name of science, but in the name of materialism. True science repudiates *in toto* what Mr. Verrers lays down as its findings. ' Let the voice of science be heard ! ' he cries. By all means.

" But the voice of Mr. Julian Verrers is not the voice of science.

" I notice that he has the strong support of a certain section of the Press. Most of the writers summoned for his cause, after briefly exposing their ignorance with a display of scientific knowledge, concentrate exclusively on the ' glorious vista ' opened out by this ' Pioneer of human freedom.' Invariably they assure their readers that he is voicing science.

" How many of them are even interested in the scientific aspects of the case ? Even care whether science is behind it or not ? But they do care intensely about what the scheme offers—an excuse, highly palatable to the public for whom they cater, for condoning practices which it advocates, practices already widely prevalent.

" If, instead of his scheme for freedom Mr. Verrers had propounded, in the name of science, a scheme for moral restraint, would he have had their support ?

" Would half England have been aroused, if he had ?

" The first question I think I could answer. The second I find more difficult. England has been aroused, certainly. Why, I am not quite sure. Probably because he has presented a choice. England has been drifting morally for some time, an inevitable consequence of indifference to Christian belief. Suddenly an outspoken challenge reveals whither the drift is leading—to a choice between Christian and pagan morality.

" The excitement is a kind of moral crisis. Mr. Verrers has made the issues clear. For that, at any rate, we may be grateful.

" The upshot, however, is not so clear. Will his challenge have the effect he anticipates ? He assumes that his scheme will have the support of all intellectually minded people, that the restrictions of Christianity are ' intolerable to the modern mind.'

" Is his assurance so well founded ?

" Why did only a section of his audience last Monday acclaim his proposals ? Why has the more responsible Press refrained from approval ? From lack of intellect ? Have his own followers the monopoly of that commodity ? Are their opinions the sole standard of intelligence ?

" I have sufficient faith in the Britisher to believe that he will not be hoodwinked by superior treatment of this kind.

" Neither do I believe that the ' voice of science ' will decide for him between Christianity and paganism. I believe that he is still capable of thinking for himself, in spite of his proclivity for being thought for ; I believe that he is capable of distinguishing between the established facts of science and the assumptions of materialism.

" It is the voice of conscience which will decide, though. And I mean by conscience—reason acting rightly, and not under the influence of base desires ; reason, that is, voicing God's law. There is in every human being the capacity for right reasoning.

" I have appealed to that to-night."

The monk looked at his watch lying on the table.

" I said we might be grateful to Mr. Verrers for making the issues clear. I, personally, am grateful to him for something else—for drawing attention so violently to the Catholic Church. Unintentionally he may have emphasized that, though she is the enemy of all he upholds, yet she is the friend of all who prize decency and chastity, of all who value married love and home and charity to human life. His vehement antipathy to her laws has successfully demonstrated that without them Christian morality would go.

" It is not my purpose to make use of this meeting for propaganda ; but I should like to remark that obedience to those laws does not spell slavery for us Catholics as he insists. On the contrary it spells freedom, freedom from the slavery of the flesh. Obedience to them is obedience to the divine authority behind them. Obedience to divine authority is not slavery ; it is a primary rational act, the due of a rational being to his Creator. If men find obedience to laws essential to success in other departments of life, they will find it even more essential in moral matters where eternal issues are at stake."

The monk picked up his watch and replaced it, slowly, within the folds of his habit.

" Before ending, I should like to make one or two observations on Mr. Verrers' final declamation last Monday.

" It was virtually an invitation to the world at large to set about the destruction of Christianity ; his scheme could not fructify into a universal system of conduct so long as Christianity maintained its sway. And he made it perfectly plain that the destruction of Christianity meant the destruction of the Catholic Church—its ' stronghold.'

" Exactly how her destruction was to be accomplished he did not say ; but I gathered that it would be by moral force, by a method of depletion, by a steady, continual enforcement of his principles by law, until Catholics were compelled to come into line, and so abjure their faith and morality. Or does he look for her destruction by physical force ? I don't know.

" But in either case he is optimistic—very optimistic.

" Does history teach him nothing ?

" The world has for two thousand years endeavoured to force the Catholic Church into line. In every age, from every conceivable source, pressure, whether moral or physical, has been brought to bear : ' All these things will I give thee, if thou wilt but fall down and worship.' That was the offer of a mighty empire, pagan Rome— the pleasures and lusts of the world. She refused. She sees her children flung to beasts and burnt alive. Still she refuses. They die smiling, upheld by some strange power, the name of a Galilean Peasant on their lips. She dies, and yet she lives. The lusts and obscenities of paganism shrink from the divine beauty shining in her eyes. The Roman empire becomes the empire of Christ.

" ' Thou hast conquered, Galilean ! '

" All down the ages she has forced from the world's lips that same reluctant cry. One by one the conquerors of Christendom arise. One by one they fall. And over their strewn corpses she passes on her way.

" I remind you of this, because Mr. Verrers' last words may still be ringing in your ears ; his ideas would triumph universally ' when, and only when, Christianity has been destroyed.'

" He is optimistic—very optimistic.

" He sees the Catholic Church as the stronghold of what he hates.

" Very well.

" Does it mean nothing to him that every earthly kingdom has crashed beneath what she has withstood ? That she survives what no mere human kingdom could survive ? Does he, do those who think with him, hope to succeed where all the rest have failed ?

" May I say this to him, and them ?

" You assume that Christianity is man-made, and can be unmade by man. I assure you it is God-made and depends on Him alone. You say Christians are fools. You scorn us ; but you leave us unashamed. You hope to intimidate ; you will find us unafraid. You shake your fists at Heaven, expecting Christendom to fall. Believe me or not, her future lies in other hands than yours.

" *Were the world's powers to muster, were all its lusts unchained, were hell itself let loose, yet it would not avail. Once more we should die smiling, a Peasant's name upon our lips.*

" *But the Church of God, unconquered, would continue on her way.*" . . . . . .

*   *   *   *   *   *

They stood jammed together on the steps of the main entrance, Beauty and Basil with the Major, watching the immense crowd that had refused to disperse.

The efforts of the police had proved futile ; that sea of heads, stretching away opposite and down Upper Regent Street, would not move until it had a glimpse of the monk leaving the Hall. Traffic had been diverted for the time being. A message had been conveyed to the green-room that it would be advisable for the speaker to leave from the front, and not from the platform door in the narrow side-street, where there would be danger from crushing. His car had, only with considerable difficulty, reached the front entrance itself. It stood there now with a cordon of police keeping a gangway from the vestibule.

" Hell ! " said the Major, wedged tight against Basil. " Get at my cigarettes—left breast-pocket." Basil achieved the task, put one in the Major's mouth and another in his own, and lit them. " If I survive," averred the Major, " it will be with the biggest thirst in creation."

Beauty laughed. She had been very quiet after it was over. The vivid impression of the close of the meeting was still upon her—the monk standing there with his head bent down, as the pent-up emotion of that mighty audience broke its bounds like the bursting of a dam ; the surge towards the platform in which, but for Basil's protecting arm, she might have been swept from her feet ; her own wonder at what she had seen shining in the eyes of men and women all about her—their Faith that had been vindicated before the world. Then Basil's exclamation, as the organ pealed out and the hymn of that Faith thundered forth in triumph : " My God, I wish I was a Catholic ! I say, wouldn't Eric love this ! "

The non-Catholic section in the Hall, though doubtful at first, had unquestionably shown their approval at the finish. There were large numbers of them amongst this Catholic multitude outside now ; they had heard the broadcast of the speech too, and received it even with cheers in places : so she understood from remarks around.

Suddenly, overhead, a loud-speaker trumpeted forth : " The Reverend Father Thornton is leaving the Queen's Hall now. You are requested by the police to observe order and to keep the centre of the road clear."

As the sound ceased, there was a stir in the vestibule behind where the three of them stood. Basil, the tallest, craned his head and saw the swing-doors inside open and a tall figure emerge, accompanied by others.

" Here he is ! "

A passage was made, and Brother Anselm came slowly

through, people clutching for his hand as he passed. He seemed to be taking it all very simply, almost unconcernedly, as if this part did not matter. As he drew near, Beauty experienced a wave of embarrassment, the memory of last Sunday in her mind, also of her note to him that afternoon. He saw her and smiled. A moment later he had managed to reach them. The swarm fell back.

" Well, Miss Dethier ? "

She found her hand in a big rough one, and the grey eyes looking into her own. That was all. But she was suddenly tremulous. . . . He turned to the other two. " Good old Doc," the Major was saying, " you've damned and bl——d——" " Major, I'll wring your neck," the monk cut him short, *sotto voce*. And Basil, his eyes sparkling : " I say, it *was* great ! You don't mind, do you ? " Brother Anselm laughed and put his hand on the boy's shoulder. Basil, enormously proud and confused, in full hearing of the swarmers : " You're letting me drive you back to Hendringham, aren't you—to-morrow ? " " That's very good of you. Call about eleven, will you ? " " Right." " Yes, awfully good of you," put in the Major. " We'll all be there." " You're coming down for the week-end, Major. You promised "— from Basil. They looked at Beauty. " What about our Beauty ? " asked the Major. She looked shyly at the monk : " Am I really forgiven ? I've apologized, you know "—to the others. " Tell Basil to ask you," said Brother Anselm. He began to move away.

The swarm closed in again—autograph books thrust out from all directions. He waved them aside : " No, no ; I'm not the Prince of Wales."

They saw two policemen meet him at the steps. At the same moment he was observed by the crowd opposite. There were shouts. More shouts. A murmur. The murmur grew. Cheering. It rose to a tempest, taken up on all sides. It swept down Upper Regent Street, returning a wild tornado as the monk came into full view, the cordon of police struggling to keep him from the throng. Inch by inch they worked him through the seething press of faces.

Just as the car was gained, something happened.

A man's sneering face, distorted in the white light from above, thrust itself into the monk's. Basil caught a high-pitched jeer : " You ain't done with Julian Verrers, don't you think it ! Take yer b—— religion 'ome with you ! And *that* ! " . . . " That " was a spit, full in the monk's face. There was an ugly rush, stemmed just in time by the police. " Yer dirty divil ! 'Ere, lemme git at 'im ! " " No, you don't ! " came in stentorian tones from the monk, who had quietly wiped his face : " Leave him alone ! " A policeman took the man by the collar and thrust him squirming through the crowd.

" Who the devil was it ? " exclaimed Basil, his voice shaking with rage. " One of that Bolshevist lot," volunteered a man near by. " Verrers goes down with those curs." The incident had taken less than a minute, and had passed unnoticed except in the vicinity.

As the car with the monk moved off, the storm rose again. At a snail's pace it crept to the middle of the road, people giving way slowly and thrusting in hands through the open windows as it passed. Obediently to the request of the loud-speaker the centre of Upper Regent Street had been kept clear.

They saw the car passing down the human avenue, acclaimed from the lungs of thousands.

And then, gradually, the sound moved away.

CHAPTER XI

TWO great desires were born in Basil's soul on the night of that Queen's Hall meeting. The one was occasioned by the meeting itself, the other by Beauty's presence with him.

The first formulated itself in a sincere, if premature and emotional, wish to be a Catholic. He knew nothing about the Catholic religion beyond what Eric had sometimes told him, and Brother Anselm had said on the moors the previous Monday afternoon. He had gone to the Queen's Hall meeting out of interest, his absorbing interest in Brother Anselm. The monk, after his first reserve, had become for him the being of his hero worship.

He had also gone because of Beauty and for the chance of being with her. That Brother Anselm's speech would mean anything to himself had never occurred to him. As he sat listening, however, there rose before his mental vision something of immense import—something which, afterwards, he began dimly to perceive made Brother Anselm what he was, and made Eric what he was. As the monk drove home the stupendous facts before which the schemes of Julian Verrers seemed to dwindle into petty impudence, his whole mentality stirred in response. There was no bias or prejudice against the Catholic Faith to check this response. There was nothing in the way. There was presented to his mind for the first time something great and deep, magnificent and unconquerable; something which had called forth the homage and devotion of those thousands within and without the Queen's Hall.

It was something, too, which claimed his personal attention and brought him face to face with himself. In the short space of an hour he had experienced a kind of spiritual metamorphosis.

Until the time of Eric's tragedy he had given no thought to anything beyond the superficialities of youth. The two brothers had done all the usual things together in the usual way—danced, hunted, competed in games, ragged, fooled along with shows and drinks, and occasional lusts of which their natural cleanness made them feel rather ashamed.

Then the thing had happened. Eric had been broken for life.

For weeks after the cripple's return to Hendringham, Basil had wandered about, gloomy and miserable—but puzzled. He had expected an Eric broken in spirit as well as body. But Eric's spirit was not broken. Eric seemed perfectly happy about it all; at times radiantly happy. Slowly Basil began to connect this phenomenon with the religion his brother had " taken up." He began shyly to question him, in spite of Lord Esterton's injunction to the contrary. He discovered that his surmise was right. Then-came the amazing change in his parents' attitude, from hostility towards Eric's Faith to respect for it—ending in the appearance of Brother Anselm at Hendringham.

Those months from last autumn had acted on Basil. Things had been given up, done without a thought before ; things he simply could not do, with Eric lying there like that.

Brother Anselm's advent had arrested him, in one sense, even more. It had focussed his attention on what was beginning to feel like a gap inside. The monk possessed what Eric possessed. They both possessed what he did not. In a respect he felt out of it with them. They had something in common from which he was excluded.

At the Queen's Hall he began to understand ; also that the Catholic religion was a very big thing, not a sort of interest which certain people happened to possess. He saw it as a supreme thing in human life. It was this that wrought the spiritual metamorphosis; the perception of what it was he was without. His spontaneous exclamation afterwards, " My God, I wish I was a Catholic ! " was completely sincere. It formulated a genuine longing.

The other desire, though in no sense in conflict with the first, was a very human one. As yet, he did not express it even to himself.

He took Beauty to the Queen's Hall at Brother Anselm's suggestion, jumping at the chance of playing Don Quixote. Julian Verrers was a danger to her. How dangerous he understood now, after hearing the nature of the man's moral views. Brother Anselm had assigned to him the rôle of safeguarding Beauty; at any rate, so he had drawn, and was delighted. The monk's assurance that she was of sterling character underneath, though spoilt, had gladdened him; for her display on Sunday morning had momentarily soiled her charms. The knowledge that she had made it up with Brother Anselm gladdened him still more; it revealed her secret respect for the monk in spite of, perhaps because of, his firm handling of her.

What her relations were with Julian Verrers, or how far she had gone with him, Basil did not know. One thing he was determined upon, however; to keep her in touch with Brother Anselm in the hope of his influence countering that of Verrers. He did not set very much store upon his own influence; for Basil had no estimate at all of himself or his attractions.

*   *   *   *   *   *

It was nearly eleven o'clock when he landed Beauty at Curzon Street after the tumult of the Queen's Hall meeting.

He helped her out of the car and then went up with her in the lift. At the door of the flat she took out a latch-key and fitted it. The door opened and she went in, switching on a light.

" Er—what about Saturday ? " asked Basil, remaining outside.

" Come in, and we'll talk about it."

Basil hesitated.

" It's a bit late. I ought to be trotting."

" Five minutes won't hurt," said Beauty. " You deserve a drink, too."

Basil still hesitated. He would have given his eyes to go in.

" I think I won't. Thanks very much, all the same."

" Why, what's the difficulty ? "

Basil was getting red.

" Well, it's a bit late, isn't it ? "

She understood then. He looked down, self-consciously. She was outside again, standing before him.

" Basil, I like you for that."

At the sound of " Basil " on her lips, something within him blazed up. It was the first time she had used his Christian name. He had not dared . . .

" I say, Beauty, may I call you ' Beauty ' ? "

" Yes, of course you may," she replied.

" May I, really ? That's ripping of you."

His pulses began to race. He saw her entrancing loveliness ; the white arms unwinding a silken wrap and disclosing the perfectly modelled throat. . . .

" You simply must come down on Saturday—wil you ? "

" After my exhibition ? "

" Yes, of course. That's all finished—Beauty."

" Why do you want me to come, so soon again ? "

Basil stuck.

" What an awful question to ask a fellow ! "

They took stock of each other.

" I suppose it *was* rather shabby. Yes, I'd love to come. We must lick the monk at tennis this time."

" Tough job," said Basil, overjoyed. " We'll try."

He ventured :

" You don't mind Brother Anselm really, do you ? "

She replied without hesitation :

" No, not now. I thought he was a bully. If he is he's a nice bully."

" Masterful ? "

" I suppose so. Yes, very."

Basil ventured further :

" Did you like him to-night ? "

" The way he took that crowd ? Yes, it was rather fine."

" What did you think of that spitting business ? "

" He didn't seem to mind it."

" No," said Basil, " I don't believe he did. I don't believe he'd mind twenty people spitting in his face— like that."

" Like what ? "

" Well—for his religion."

" Oh." Non-committally.

Basil ventured further still :

" How did you like the—er—speech itself ? "

She played with the silken wrap.

" It was interesting."

" Did you like what he said ? "

She fidgeted.

" In places. He talks very well," she added quickly. " I like his voice."

" Yes, but——"

" I say, Basil, do you mind if we ring off that number ? "

He had been unwise.

" Sorry."

He had intended to lead up to Julian Verrers. He dare not now. He looked at his watch.

" Well then, Saturday. You'll come down with the Major ? "

" Yes. I'll phone him in the morning."

There was a pause.

" Well, good night—Beauty."

" Good night, Basil. Thanks tremendously for taking me."

" My hat, Beauty, I'd——" He stopped just in time, and began walking hurriedly down the stairs.

At the landing he turned and looked up. She was still standing there, watching him. He waved, and her hand went up in reply. He continued down the stairs, treading lightly—listening. At the ground-floor he stopped.

Down the lift-shaft came the sound of a door closing to

CHAPTER XII

§ 1

AFTER reading the papers for over an hour, Eric decided that he had done enough. He had studied the criticisms mainly, contained in the leaders.

The speech itself he had listened-in to last night. So also had his mother and father. Of the scene outside the Queen's Hall afterwards he had known nothing until the papers, a dozen in all, had arrived this morning, giving graphic descriptions of the crowd and its amazing enthusiasm. Its numbers seemed almost incredible, the estimates varying from eighty to a hundred thousand.

On the whole, so it appeared to Eric, Brother Anselm had an even Press.

The speech itself was undoubtedly the event of yesterday. *The Times* and other of the weightier journals agreed that the monk had put a good moral case against Mr. Julian Verrers. He had done some hard hitting, but it was clean and straight. With certain statements about the Catholic Church they could not agree, but they were only such as were to be expected from one of its priests. The less responsible papers headlined catchy passages and omitted the more serious arguments in deference to the popular palate, sensationalizing minor points out of all perspective. Only a few were definitely hostile, levelling charges of " mediævalism " or " narrow-mindedness " at the monk. One genius, in a leader, suggested that he was an " emissary of Rome, commissioned to capture the public imagination in favour of Romanism in the guise of a moral reformer."

It was not until the organs of Rationalism and some of

the more pagan weeklies came out during the following week that serious opposition began, and the speech was declaimed as a " public insult to that brilliant scientist and servant of humanity, Julian Verrers."

The sheets lay now in a pile at Eric's side, rustling fitfully in the breeze which came cool from the surface of the river.

It was his favourite place, this path near the water, sheltered by giant beeches. He had been here since ten o'clock, and it was now half-past eleven. Half an hour ago Spence had come down from the house with a telegram to Lady Esterton from Basil, containing the information that he was bringing down Brother Anselm in time for lunch.

Eric was on tenterhooks for their arrival, filled with excitement over what must have been a veritable triumph for the cause the monk had been asked to espouse. He also wanted to know what effect the meeting had produced upon Basil. He had been hoping great things of it in that direction. He had watched Basil rapidly attracted to Brother Anselm during the past week, reacting to him almost exactly as he himself had done a year ago. He was wondering how far it would lead. He had nothing to go upon so far except the fact that his brother had been questioning him lately, and in all likelihood would be doing the same of the monk.

In the old days Basil had always followed his lead, for better or worse. As boys, whatever he did Basil must do too. As men it had been the same.

When the tragedy had come, and with it the complete change in himself, his brother had gone through a period of bewildering mental pain, cut off at a stroke from the hectic life they had lived together. They could no longer do things together. There had come a mystery into his life too that Basil could not understand, before whose presence he was shy and ill at ease.

They were more at home now, however ; and could rag each other again. The invisible barrier was breaking down under Basil's probing process ; slowly he had conned a sense of the supernatural. He was veering in Eric's direction. Things, the " old things," were being given up. Basil would no longer go up to town with " that hunting crowd " to make a night of it. The looser members of that set, welcome enough in the " old days," were not encouraged at Hendringham now and rarely came, especially since the change in Lord Esterton.

Basil was responding to his leader once more—uncertainly and sniffing unfamiliar air as he came, but following.

Whether he would follow all the way was Eric's problem. Basil meant an enormous lot to him ; but he meant an enormous lot to Basil too, and he was human enough to appreciate that the human factor would count. There was Brother Anselm too. There was Beauty now as well —another factor. For Eric was questioning whether he might have been mistaken, and Beauty prove more than just a " topping girl " like the others.

If so . . . ?

Things had moved more quickly than he imagined.

They arrived at one o'clock, Basil at concert pitch, Brother Anselm unconcerned with the fact that England was discussing him.

" Put up the flag ! " shouted Basil, as he sprang from the car and ran up the steps to Eric. " I say, Eric, it was terrific ! It was absolutely *it* ! It——"

" It-tit-tit," from Brother Anselm, following more leisurely.

" Well, Eric ? "

All through lunch Basil flowed on, describing every detail of last night, from the crowd to the man who spat.

" No, Mater, not *at* him—right bang in his face ! " he was saying.

" Splashed the crowd. Thousands drenched," from Brother Anselm.

Or :

" Dad, it took twenty police to get him to his car."

" And twenty more to get him in," from the monk.

And so on.

Afterwards, when Eric was alone with Brother Anselm down by the river, he proceeded to work :

" Does Verrers know yet it was you ? They call you ' Father Thornton ' in all the papers."

" He does without a doubt," replied the monk.

" Does he ? Does he, really ? "

" I saw him this morning."

" *Saw* him ? "

" Basil was held up in a block at Piccadilly Circus. There was a car close up against ours, and Julian Verrers was in it."

" Good gracious ! "

" He stared, and then looked away. And he stared not because he was surprised to see me, but to make sure it *was* me. He had followed us."

" No ? "

" There was a Daimler going into the Park at Hyde Park Corner. It was the same Daimler, because it was the same chauffeur. He obviously told his chauffeur to turn and follow. He had seen me."

" This is horribly exciting," Eric ejected. " But does he know it was you last night ? "

" There was a morning paper in his hand. It was the one which headlined me as ' The monk from Issano,' and contained a large, very clear photo of myself. He could hardly have failed to recognize 'Father Thornton.' He probably knew last night ; you may be quite certain he was listening-in. He would recognize my voice. Even if he did not, seeing me in London this morning would be enough for an astute man like Verrers. Oh yes, he knows now."

Eric watched the river flowing before them.

" Does he look the same ? "

" Very much. I had a minute in which to study him before we moved on, his side face. His self-possession is marvellous. He knew, of course, I was looking, but he never betrayed it. He was a mask. I had the impression, though, that he wanted me to see him. It was meant as a kind of gesture, I fancy."

" Oh. Defiance ? "

" Probably."

Eric considered.

" What will he do next ? "

" I've no notion." The monk mused. " I doubt if he'll risk another speech. He would find it difficult to get the same hearing as before. There might be opposition ; the public will be awake now. Some of the papers are already hinting it."

" So I noticed."

" Verrers can sail with the wind, but not against it. He is brilliant and compelling while he's having his way ; he cannot brook opposition, though. Even the mild antipathy at his own meeting last Monday irritated him. He lost weight badly at the end—and, incidentally, made it easier for me last night. No, I doubt whether he could carry through if things turned against him. Under serious opposition he would lose control ; that malice of his wou d run him amuck."

" Like at Issano—that afternoon ? "

" Yes."

" Pretty awful, that afternoon," said Eric.

" It was not pleasant," replied the monk.

Eric contemplated the blue patches in the foliage overhead.

" Supposing he doesn't get his way with Beauty Dethier ? " he asked.

" Then it might be dangerous for Beauty Dethier."

The monk stretched, lay back in his deck-chair and contemplated the blue patches too.

Eric turned his head :

" In what way ? "

" I can't say. But Verrers stops at nothing to secure his ends."

Eric thought.

" Supposing Basil attracts her—from him ? "

" It might be dangerous for them both."

" They'd have to be warned ? "

" They would."

For a time Eric did not speak.

The monk immersed himself in the drowsy hum of insects. The green and gold overhead was shimmering hypnotically in the summer afternoon.

After a long interval :

" Has Basil said anything about himself ? About last night ? "

There was no reply. Eric looked sideways.

Brother Anselm was asleep.

The Major came down with Beauty the next day, Saturday, in a drizzling rain all the way from London.

Tea was in the drawing-room awaiting them. They came straight in to find the others gathered there, Brother Anselm and Basil just back from an unsuccessful afternoon's fishing in the river. They had landed nothing, to the Major's joy, who, after tea, handed the monk his fishing-basket with a stuffed fish from a glass case in the hall. Lord Esterton followed with Eric into the billiard-room to find the Major laid out on a settee, with Brother Anselm sitting on him and Basil spanking with the stuffed fish.

" I'll make a speech about this at the Queen's Hall," was the Major's declamation after being released.

The four of them got to work at billiards.

Beauty came in.

She went and sat over by Eric in the corner. Her attitude to him was different somehow from on her first visit. She was more at her ease with him. Eric was quick to notice it. There was some subtle change in her too. She was gentler. As they talked she followed Basil's movements at the table. She called him " Basil " when they spoke. Basil had called her " Beauty " straight off as she entered the drawing-room. They had a new, slightly self-conscious way of looking at each other.

But there was something else about her which Eric noted—a kind of preoccupation, as if something were lurking in the background of her mind. It was when she was silent. She would recollect herself and begin talking rather fast. Once, when he turned to her, he caught an unmistakable look of fear in her eyes.

The Major, fooling at the billiard-table, dispelled for a time the problem. He was partnered with Brother Anselm against Lord Esterton and Basil, and was ragging the latter unmercifully, humming *Beauty's Eyes* whenever it came to Basil's turn. It ended in a scuffle in which Basil, red in the face, and Beauty, roused from her quiet, launched a united attack with cushions upon the tormentor. The Major secured and wielded the now dilapidated stuffed fish in self-defence.

When they had sobered down and the game was over, Basil drew Beauty away from the others. Eric saw them slip out of the room together.

The Major went off with Lord Esterton, and Eric and Brother Anselm were left alone. The monk continued practising strokes at the table.

" Isn't there something curious about Beauty Dethier ? " asked Eric at last.

The monk laid down his cue.

" Tell me your impression."

" Sort of goes quiet—something on her mind," said Eric.

" Fear ? "

" Yes."

Brother Anselm rested himself against the billiard-table.

" The Major tells me that she mentioned Verrers and herself on the way down. Nothing much ; but it may entail a good deal. He needn't worry, she informed him ; she was not going any further with Verrers."

" Oh ? " said Eric. " Really ? That's splendid."

" I imagine a climax has come in their relations," the monk observed.

" Yes ? " Eric added : " But—the fear ? "

" The climax has probably been unfavourable to Verrers. I'm simply guessing ; but it's possible he may be showing his teeth in consequence, and she's becoming afraid."

Eric frowned perplexedly.

" Couldn't you get her to talk to you ? "

" I wish I could. She's shy of me—in case I should broach religion. But I'll try."

Eric seemed more satisfied.

" How does Basil strike you ? " he changed abruptly.

" Basil," replied Brother Anselm, " will sail straight ahead now."

" What, with Beauty ? "

The monk laughed.

" I was not alluding to that. No, religiously."

Eric's eyes lit.

" How do you know ? "

" He tried three times on the way down yesterday to tell me something. Can you guess ? "

Eric could not speak for a moment.

" I think so."

" I didn't let him. He's far too excited over Thursday night yet."

The other was thrilling to it.

" Oh, monk, this is grand ! Is he serious ? "

" He's serious enough. It's better to wait until he's calmed down, though. Were you expecting this, Eric ? "

" I've been hoping. But . . ."

There was a moisture in the eyes that met Brother Anselm's.

" Monk, how glorious ! "

§ 2

Sunday morning brought a blaze of sun once more, drawing the scents of Nature after yesterday's rain.

Brother Anselm, who was saying the nine-thirty Mass at Windern, left with Eric at nine o'clock. As the car turned into the road at the bottom of the drive, they saw Basil and Beauty making their way, by the short cut over the fields, in the same direction. Whatever her motive may have been, Beauty was kneeling there at Basil's side as Mass began.

When it was over and the monk had made his thanksgiving, he came out to find the usual little gathering round Eric's ambulance. As Basil wheeled his brother to the car outside, Beauty loitered behind a little. The monk dropped behind too. She came up to him.

" May I have a talk with you some time ? " she said quickly.

" Yes, any time you like," Brother Anselm replied. " After lunch ? "

" Very well. Thank you."

At the gates outside the church a small crowd was gathered. The word had gone round who the monk was,

Brother Anselm was waiting on the terrace at two-thirty.

Beauty came out from the hall, looked about and saw him. She came forward.

" Could we find a place where we shall be undisturbed?'

" Certainly," said the monk.   He reconnoitred. " Under the elms ? "

" That would do," replied Beauty.

They walked over the lawns, the monk carrying a couple of deck-chairs from the terrace. He set them up in the shade, and they sat down.

" Now, tell me all about it."

" May I smoke ? "

" Do."

She lit a cigarette in silence, and flung away the match. Her fingers were trembling slightly.

" Brother Anselm, how much do you know about Julian Verrers and myself ? "

" About Julian Verrers a good deal. About yourself a little. But about Julian Verrers *and* yourself I only know what I've heard from the Major, and perhaps Basil."

" Oh ? . . . You know a good deal about Julian Verrers ? "

" I do."

" What ? About him—personally ? "

" My acquaintance with Julian Verrers goes back some years."

It held Beauty up.

" But you never—— I thought you were just a public opponent of his—views."

" I am. But my knowledge of him extends a good deal further than his—views. However, that doesn't matter now. It is Julian Verrers and yourself that you want to talk about, isn't it ? "

" Chiefly."

" Right. Well now, tell me what has happened. You're afraid of him, aren't you ? "

Beauty started.

" How do you know ? "

" Never mind. Begin."

She regarded him irresolutely.

" May I tell you everything ? "

" Do. It will make it easier for me."

The monk settled down into his deck-chair. She drew a long breath, and made a start.

She had met Julian Verrers first at Mrs. Sands-Woodford's and had been attracted by his personality. Their acquaintance had ripened into friendship. At Lady Derringham's it had advanced far enough for him to make a certain proposal to her, connected with his " work."

" He wanted me to join him in his ' cause,' against religion. It really meant becoming a member of some organization to which he belongs, I think ; although I didn't realize that at the time."

The monk moved in his chair, closely attentive.

She had refused to consider the suggestion, however ; partly because the idea " did not appeal " to her, partly because—" Well, a woman is a woman, you know. He seemed more interested in my possibilities than myself." Her refusal had annoyed him at the time. When they met again, however, his chagrin had vanished, outwardly, at any rate. At dinner one night at the Carlton there was a perceptible change in him ; he had struck an extremely personal note. " I may as well be quite honest. I deliberately encouraged him. It was what I wanted—this." Last Wednesday she had invited him to tea at her flat, and a crisis had occurred in their relations. " I meant it quite innocently, but——"

Her voice faltered.

" But he took it differently," the monk remarked. " You wanted him at your feet ; he wanted something more, you found."

There was a sternness in his tone which steadied her. She was reaching a tremulous stage.

" Isn't that rather brutal ? "

" Perhaps. But it's true. Miss Dethier, you needn't tell me more of this than you like."

She dug about in the turf with her heel.

" I think I'd rather you knew exactly what happened."

She told him in detail. The monk listened, nodding at times. Her voice was quavering towards the end. He let her finish, and then asked drily : " What impression did he give you while he was making this—offer ? That he wanted you for yourself ; or for whatever use you could be to him in his ' cause ' ? "

" For myself. The relations he suggested would place me in his hands, of course ; but it was not his motive for wanting me."

" His urgency was for *you* ? You're sure of that ? "

" Quite sure."

There was a graver shade in the monk's face.

" When he left, you were to give him an answer in a week's time, you say ? "

" Yes."

" And how do things stand now ? "

Beauty crushed out the end of her cigarette against the arm of her chair and dropped it. In the deep blue of her eyes the monk could discern that same look of fear.

" That is what I'm coming to. I know it won't sound nice to you, but I virtually decided the same night to accept his offer. I was still fascinated by him, as I had always been, and I—I knew that, in the eyes of the world, I should be Julian Verrers' wife. If something hadn't happened——"

She paused uncertainly.

" Something happened. Brother Anselm, do you believe in psychical experiences ? "

" Sometimes," murmured the monk. " Yes ? "

" It's not very easy to describe."

He listened to a faltering account of what had occurred in her bedroom, the attempt to sever with the past by destroying her Prayer Book and beads. " I don't think I really intended to go further ; but I was in doubt about the crucifix—what to do with it. It was on my mantel-piece, and I went up close. I should probably have taken it off and put it away—if the thing hadn't happened." She explained how, all in a moment, a hostility to the crucifix had come upon her. It was as if another personality were in the room driving her on to destroy it with the rest ; she had even looked round, half expecting to see a presence. She had become frenzied and clutched at the crucifix to break it in two. " I should have done so, if——"

" Go on," said the monk.

" If the psychical experience had not intervened."

" What was the experience ? "

" You—your eyes seemed to be looking at me ; just as I was going to do it. It was near where the crucifix was standing. I can't remember any more, except that I was terrified, and stumbled away from it. I think I nearly fainted. I didn't dare go near it again."

Brother Anselm remained silent. She waited. After a while he remarked :

" So that is why you sent the note ? "

Beauty nodded.

" Can you explain ? " she asked.

" There might be two or three explanations. Probably it was the mere projection of an image from your own brain. You were strung up and in the abnormal state when delusions do occur. Let's leave the explanation alone, though, shall we ? The experience in some way caused you to reconsider your decision, is that it ? "

She had expected a different answer from this matter-of-fact one.

" It pulled me up," she replied, and then went on to tell him of her curious find the following morning, the inscribed symbol indicating some society to which Julian Verrers belonged. She described it in detail ; and how it was then she understood what would be expected of her if she accepted his offer. It had filled her with dread of him. There had been moments of uncanny fear before, in his presence ; but she had put it down to her own nerves. It had become a terror now, which only left her when she had definitely decided to refuse his offer. Without waiting for the week to expire she had written to him on Friday morning, saying that under no conditions could she do what he wanted. He had answered by return. She had received his reply on Saturday morning.

" That is what he says." And she handed a square white envelope to the monk.

" You wish me to read it ? "

" Please."

He took out a folded sheet, opened it and read :

" DEAR MISS DETHIER,—I have just received your strange letter. I do not know how far I am expected to take it seriously. Certainly I shall not do so. Since you have not observed the week agreed upon, may I be allowed to follow your example ? I shall call at Curzon Street on Tuesday afternoon about four-thirty.

" May I remind you that it was your previous encouragement that led me to speak as I did on Wednesday. If you were merely counting upon me for a slave at your feet and no more, I am afraid you misjudged—JULIAN VERRERS.

" P.S.—I have reason to suspect that Father Thornton's speech last night has some connection with your sudden change. If this is correct, I am surprised that you should be so easily scared by ecclesiastical thunderings.—J. V."

Brother Anselm folded up the letter, replaced it and handed it back to Beauty.

" You decided to refuse him before you came to the Queen's Hall, didn't you ? "

" Yes. On Thursday morning."

The monk stood up, and began to walk to and fro with his hands behind his back.

" He intends to force you to his will." It was muttered to himself, but she caught it. He stood still and watched the fleecy clouds passing over the line of the beeches down by the river.

" Brother Anselm, I'm afraid—horribly afraid," broke out from the girl behind him.

He turned round. There was a beseeching look, inspired by genuine fear, in the blue eyes now.

" What are you afraid of ? "

" Of him. He's not going to leave it at this."

He studied her closely.

" Miss Dethier, are you prepared to humiliate yourself ? Would you apologize to him for having—led him on ? You see, to an extent you've brought this on yourself. Julian Verrers is not a man to play with."

" I'll apologize—anything. But that won't satisfy him."

" No," said Brother Anselm. " It won't satisfy him ; but it will weaken his assumed right over you. Do you see ? "

She thought.

" Shall I write ? I can't face him on Tuesday. I simply cannot. I may be a coward, but I can't."

" What are you afraid of ? " It was the second time he had asked the question.

" Of himself—his power," she answered. " I don't know how to put it, but there's a kind of lure about him— something sinister. It frightens me ; but it draws me on too against my will. Can you understand ? "

" Perfectly. And you don't want to take any further risks ? "

" No."

" Will you act on my advice, then ? Write to him, apologizing for your share ; but say that your decision is final and that you do not wish to see him on Tuesday. Write by to-night's post. Will you do that?"

"Yes." There was relief in her face. The cloud returned, though.

"But supposing he *does* come on Tuesday? . . . I'll have to be out. Do you think he *will* come?"

"Er—yes, I think he will."

There was an assurance of it in his tone.

"Well, then, I'll say I shall be out."

"No. Say nothing either way. If he means to come in spite of your wishes, he will merely choose another day. No, leave it as I suggested."

The fear was upon her again.

"But I can't—I daren't let him find me alone—after that letter."

"He will not find you alone."

"What do you mean?"

"He will find the Major and myself having tea with you," replied Brother Anselm.

CHAPTER XIII

IT was not until Monday that Brother Anselm at length gave Basil an opportunity of unburdening himself.

In the morning there was tennis—a return of the sets they had played the week before, the same girl, Molly Turner, having come over to partner with Brother Anselm. This time Basil was on his mettle, and he and Beauty nearly succeeded in pulling it off against their opponents, losing by a game only in the last two sets.

The excitement of it took some of the anxiety out of Beauty's eyes, the monk observed. So did Basil, to his relief. Brother Anselm had told him and Eric as much as was necessary concerning the cause of it.

To the Major he had given a full account, with Beauty's permission, of how things stood. He wanted him prepared for eventualities, should Julian Verrers persist and come to the flat. His move had been received with enthusiasm by the Major. " It's to let Verrers understand," the monk had explained, " that he'll have us to reckon with as well as Miss Dethier if he attempts to force her to his will."

" Will he try a second reckoning—after last year ? " the Major had remarked with a gleam in his eye.

" I don't know," the monk had replied. " He did not relent then, remember. I doubt if Verrers ever relents. He will be relentless with Miss Dethier. We may baulk him to-morrow, but——" The monk had stopped. " Verrers is a man who can wait. He waited last year— and then struck back. He'll wait now."

" What'll be his game ? "

" I can no more tell than you."

" He'll strike back ? "

" Somehow, yes. I should say so."

" What, at us ? "

" Miss Dethier, more likely. We know the man, and he'll remember that ; he won't take risks again. No, Miss Dethier. She's afraid of it herself. It's not her nerves, but something in him that frightens her ; she's found that out."

" Damn that son of Satan ! " exclaimed the Major.

The monk had waited and then said meditatively :

" It won't be child's play keeping that man from her. It's not merely Julian Verrers now. It's Julian Verrers mad with passion for a woman he wants."

" God made that girl too darned lovely."

Brother Anselm had smiled in spite of his seriousness, and then added in the same deliberating tone :

" Of course I might——"

" What ? " asked the other.

" Never mind."

The monk had lapsed into silence, thinking.

" If that snake . . ." The Major had ended in expletives.

The party agreed upon a quiet afternoon ; for they were riding up to the moors after tea.

" Coming down to the elms ? " asked Basil, drawing aside Brother Anselm when lunch was finished. They went off to the same place where the monk had listened to Beauty's tale the previous afternoon. He spread himself on the grass. Basil followed suit.

" Now, get it off your chest. Why do you want to be a Catholic ? "

Basil's mouth fell open.

" But—but, how do you know ? "

" That's what you were going to tell me on Friday, isn't it ? "

" Er—yes, I was. . . . Is that why you choked me off ? "

" It was. Never mind that, though. Why do you want to be a Catholic ? "

" Well——" Basil ran his fingers through his hair. " Well, I want to."

" Exactly. But why ? "

" Well, Eric's a Catholic."

" Certainly. But you can't be a Catholic simply because Eric's one."

" Oh no, of course not. I didn't mean that was the real reason."

He suddenly became very earnest. " It's much more. It's what Eric's got. What you've got. Don't you understand, Brother Anselm ? "

" Possibly. When did all this start ? On Thursday night ?"

" Oh no. Long ago. It was things Eric said, when I asked him. Last Christmas, quite."

" Tell me the whole story," said the monk.

Basil raised himself into a sitting posture, with his arms drawn round his knees.

He was not an adept at self-analysis, and he found it by no means easy to elucidate the process by which his present stage had been reached. But he managed to unfold his mental workings sufficiently. His desire was due, not to being swept off his feet on Thursday, but to a genuine persuasion which had been growing steadily, if subconsciously, for some time. It was the change in his moral outlook which, for Brother Anselm, confirmed Basil's sincerity.

The monk saw in those renunciations of " the sort of things a fellow does," the clearing of a boy's soul from the first false values of life. An emptiness had followed, and a blind groping about after new values ; a slow appreciation of his brother's inward happiness, a realization of some supernatural secret possessed by him and unpossessed by himself. The monk perceived now, too, the *raison d'être* of Basil's jump from those amazingly elementary questions last week to his present conviction—for conviction it undoubtedly was ; the more he sounded him the more sure he became. His own unvarnished answers to those questions had discovered to the boy's mind the source of Eric's secret and with it an insight into what, without knowing it, he sought—something definite and tangible to grasp.

Thursday night was a climax only. That compelling vision of the Catholic Church, the calm assurance of what she was and could be to him, her magnificence and grandeur had called forth the homage of his whole soul.

It took Basil the best part of half an hour to explain all this. Except for occasional questions, Brother Anselm had listened in silence.

" Do you understand now ? " Basil asked at the end, as the monk lay back on the grass.

" Yes, I understand ; quite," replied the recumbent figure.

" What's the next thing to do ? "

" The next thing to do is to wait, Basil. If at the end of a month, say, you are of the same mind, then we might see about your coming under instruction."

" Instruction ? "

" Yes. You would have to be taught the Catholic Faith."

" Oh. How long would that take ? "

" It depends on yourself a good deal. From three to six months, perhaps."

" Oh . . ."

" Do you ever say any prayers, Basil ? "

Basil looked shy.

" I tried last night. I asked Eric. He told me what to do. Gave me a book."

" Good man," said Brother Anselm. " Now look here. . . ."

The monk set to work on the virgin soil of Basil's soul.

*   •   •   •   •   •

It was quite a cavalcade that set off from Hendringham for the moors after tea that evening.

The grooms led the horses round to the front, snorting and scattering the gravel to be off. Basil helped Beauty to mount a mare of her own choice and then swung astride on his own. They started away down the drive together. Brother Anselm and the Major followed, the monk on the same big chestnut as last week.

Outside the lodge gates the soft crunch of gravel changed to the hard clatter of the main road. Then Windern, with people gaping from their doors at the ring of hoofs resounding down the street. Beyond it the road began to climb. They eased off into a jog-trot for the two miles up to the wilds of heather and gorse above.

"Look damn well, those two," remarked the Major, half-way, of the couple in front. He pulled up and took something out of his side-pocket—a tiny camera, and levelled it at the pair ahead. "Keep quiet!" to his horse.

There was a click.

"What's that for?" asked the monk, who had pulled up too.

"Show it J. V. to-morrow. Hand it him with the bread and butter."

Brother Anselm leaned over and made a grab at the camera as the Major was putting it back, but missed. The Major chortled, and then gurgled as he found the handle of the monk's riding-crop between his collar and his neck. "Keep it for evidence, then," he gasped. The monk released him.

At the top of the ascent they cantered after and caught up the others.

"How's that?" cried Basil with a jerk of his head at

the view stretched below. It was like a giant coloured map. All four drew rein. " Like it ? " he asked Beauty. She nodded without speaking, her eyes on the panorama of brown and golden fields. " See Hendringham ? " He pointed. They made it out beyond a belt of woodlands to the east, the white front with the river running beneath. To the south lay Windern, its smoke curling bluely and lazily upwards in the heat.

Brother Anselm saw Basil following Beauty's gaze as it travelled over the vista and returned to Hendringham. He caught himself wondering whether Beauty knew, what he himself had only learnt yesterday, that Hendringham would now come to Basil ; Eric had renounced the inheritance of it in favour of his younger brother on the plea of his own incapacity.

" Let's have a rip ! " The Major broke the spell.

They wheeled their horses round, and off the road. There was an expectant champing and snorting. The springy moorland turf was to their liking ; they padded delicately to its feel, ears pricked up to the coming gallop. A little coquetting along sideways, some trotting steps, a canter, glossy necks straightening out—and they were off.

Then the splendid thrill of cool air whistling by, the steady thud of hoofs, and squelch of saddle-leather.

They kept in line until the pace began to tell and the faster pair carrying Beauty and Basil pulled ahead.

" 'Ware sheep ! " shouted back Basil. " Keep left ! "

Brother Anselm found some difficulty in swerving his big chestnut off the straight to the lead of the two in front. The Major's horse on his right responded more willingly. They had a glimpse of startled sheep scattering at their approach, and one stupid animal doing a skelter on its own across where Beauty and Basil were coming. They heard Basil yell at it. The sheep continued on its blundering track, bewildered by the nearing rush.

What happened the two behind could not quite see ; but apparently the animal stopped suddenly in front of Beauty's mare, to be sent staggering, caught by its front hoofs.

" Whew ! " Brother Anselm heard the Major's whistle—the violent swerve of the mare had nearly unseated Beauty. They saw Basil close in, lean over and get a grip on her riding-habit. She righted herself in the saddle. The sheep was on its legs again as Brother Anselm and the Major passed.

But something was wrong in front.

The mare was refusing to slacken to Beauty's efforts. Basil, wisely, was not interfering, but leaving it to her rider and keeping neck to neck. For a distance this continued. Then Beauty was sawing with the bit.

" That mare's bolting," called the Major.

For some reason Basil was pulling in his horse. Beauty was carried ahead alone. Then Basil was spurring and thrashing with his crop, endeavouring to catch up on the other side, her left.

The monk, all in a moment, understood.

Basil knew the moors. A ridge of rocky ground ahead marked one of the precipitous dips dotted about on these uplands. The mare was making blindly towards it. To the left there was a slope down. The only chance was to head her off to the right of the ridge.

They could do nothing but follow hard on that flying pair.

" Oh, hell ! " caught the monk's ear—a rasping sound from the Major ; for Basil did not appear to be regaining his lost ground. He was digging furiously at his horse's flanks. They only knew he had caught up by a forward crouch of his figure, and his crop raining blows on the mare's head.

The ridge was coming close.

He must have been to the fore of the mare now ; for he was pushing as near as possible and striking at her nostrils with his fist. The steady pressure and pounding were having effect; she was veering from that dead straight line. He was making some sign to Beauty. She was leaning back with her weight on the right rein.

They seemed to be at the ridge itself. A hissing sound came through the Major's teeth. . . . The monk felt the horrible tension of it even at that pace. Then——

Basil had drawn away and, next moment, driven the full weight of his horse on to the mare's neck. It shook her stride badly, but she did not go down. Instead, the impact swung her to the right, just clear of the last jutting rock concealing the drop below. Basil's horse, locked against her on the inside, missed it by a hair's-breadth.

" Ah ! "—a shout of triumph from the Major.

On they went, Basil steadily punishing the mare and forcing her more and more to the right, until she was heading for a steep ascent that could be seen a quarter of a mile away. As they neared it and the ground began to rise, her pace visibly decreased. Basil was ready for the swing that she tried to make to the left. There was a violent tussle, in which he secured the reins under the bit, keeping his horse against her as he did so.

She was mastered.

Digging at her with his spur, he kept her on up the hill. It was a matter of moments now. He was able to turn his head to Beauty and say something.

The mare faltered as the ascent steepened. Then she slowed down and, quite abruptly, halted, her front legs planted firmly apart. Basil flung himself from his horse without letting go her reins from his right hand. On the ground he changed them quickly to his left and caught Beauty swaying from the saddle, just in time.

Brother Anselm and the Major cantered up. They dismounted and ran to where Basil was holding the girl away from the mare, now viciously kicking. She had not fainted, but seemed dazed and unable to stand. The monk picked her up bodily and carried her away, clear of danger.

The Major helped Basil with the mare. They succeeded in tethering her, quivering and sweating, to a boulder some yards off, and then returned.

Beauty was sitting on a tump of grass, looking white and shaken, Brother Anselm standing by. She smiled wanly as they approached.

"Got a flask on you, Major?" asked the monk. The Major produced one. Beauty drank a little at Brother Anselm's command. Some colour stole back into her cheeks.

"Sorry to be such a fool," she said, glancing up timidly at Basil. He was silent and shy now that it was over.

"Feeling better?" he asked awkwardly.

"A bit stupid, that's all."

The Major handed Basil a cigarette, lit it, and another for himself. They waited until Beauty had recovered sufficiently to stand up and walk about. She seemed all right.

Basil suggested riding back to Hendringham and fetching his car for her; but she refused: "I'd sooner ride back, if you don't mind. It's only nerves."

"You'll ride my gee, then. You're not going to get on that mare again," said Basil firmly. "I'll change the saddles. . . . Nerves? Good heavens, Beauty, you've got the nerve. . . . Darned few women would have stuck on."

"Now, you sit still for a bit, Miss Dethier," interrupted Brother Anselm. "If you want to ride back."

"Doctor's orders," said the Major.

"Oh yes, I'd forgotten you were a doctor." Beauty laughed. She was fairly well herself again, but obediently sat down.

Brother Anselm and the Major strolled away in the direction of the mare. Basil remained standing, pulling at his cigarette rather rapidly.

"Won't you sit down?" said Beauty.

He flung away the cigarette and seated himself beside

her in silence. She was fingering the grass, her head down. When she looked up and turned to him there were tears in her eyes.

"Thank you, Basil—very, very much." The words came tremulously. "It was a pretty near thing, wasn't it?"

Basil did not answer.

He was not thinking of those rocks, or himself. He was thinking that it was Beauty he had. . . . He was conscious only of blue eyes and a golden head, and a hand that rested impulsively on his knee—all the loveliness of her so perilously close. . . .

CHAPTER XIV

WOULD he come ?

To outward appearances Brother Anselm and the Major were unconcerned. They might have been there just to have tea with Beauty in her library. The girl herself, too, was remarkably calm now that the moment had come.

The Major was diverting her by examining with great interest a snapshot which he had taken from his pocket. " Incriminating evidence," he called it. " Can't show it you, no." It was not until the monk had deftly seized it from him and transferred it to his own pocket that the Major quieted down and asked :

" What time did he say ? "

" Half-past four," replied Beauty.

" Um." The Major looked at his watch. It was a quarter-past. He started drumming on the table. " What do we do ? Sit like this till he turns up ? "

" Don't you think we're rather too conspicuously waiting for him ? " suggested Brother Anselm.

" What, start tea ? " said Beauty.

" I think so."

She pressed a button.

The three of them had said good-bye to Hendringham that morning. Basil had been very quiet over his farewell to Beauty, as if holding himself in with an effort. They had reached town by midday, Brother Anselm and the Major arranging to be at the flat in Curzon Street by four o'clock.

Yesterday's experience had left Beauty unharmed. The shock of it had done her good in one way, by forcibly diverting her mind from Julian Verrers for the time. Last night, at Brother Anselm's "orders," she had retired early. She had stayed up long enough, though, to catch fragments of a conversation on the terrace outside the drawing-room, while she and Lady Esterton were having coffee after dinner.

" . . . Good old Youngster "—Eric.

" Damned smart ! Damned smart ! "—the Major.

" It was pretty close, then ? "—Lord Esterton.

" Yes, very close "—Brother Anselm's deep tone. " If Basil had lost his nerve . . ." Beauty had missed the end of the sentence, and only picked up odd phrases following, sufficient to tell her that the monk was giving his account : " . . . took the only chance . . . extreme risk. . . ." A whistle from Lord Esterton. " . . . few men would . . . amazingly quick thinking——"

" Hullo, everybody ! " Basil's voice had come from a window, interrupting. " Are we going to have billiards ? "

The clock on the mantelpiece struck the half-hour.

Beauty put down her tea-cup. Brother Anselm and the Major stopped talking.

Would he come ?

The monk's calm demeanour was immensely reassuring to Beauty ; she could never have faced the ordeal alone. The Major was twinkling with expectation.

" Ah ! "

She started at a sharp ring of the electric bell. Brother Anselm moved his chair to the centre of the room, nearer Beauty and exactly opposite the door, and reclined his big person in it, his legs crossed. They heard the maid cross the hall and the front door open. Then a man's voice and the door closing.

" Are we to look surprised ? " whispered the Major hurriedly.

" No, like hard-boiled eggs," answered Brother Anselm, to relieve the tension. Beauty had gone white. . . .

" Mr. Verrers," announced Marie.

There were steps into the room.

Nobody moved.

" Mr. Verrers," said Marie again, louder.

" Thank you, Marie," said Beauty without raising her eyes.

The door closed.

Silence.

When she looked, he was standing poised very erect with his back to the door, staring at the monk. At her movement he turned towards her uncomprehendingly.

" I think you know—Father Thornton and Major Brandreth ? " she heard her own voice saying. He ignored the remark completely. Brother Anselm and the Major remained motionless. . . .

" I don't quite understand," he said at last.

' What don't you understand ? " she replied. Her confidence was returning. He hesitated, uncertainty and suspicion in the deep set of his eyes.

" I expected to find you alone."

" No doubt. You got my second letter ? "

" I did."

" Well then ? "

He indicated with a gesture the presence of the other two : " I'd prefer to discuss it with you alone."

" There is nothing to discuss, Mr. Verrers."

" On the contrary, there is very much to discuss. But, as it's a purely private matter between us, I shall choose another occasion."

He laid his fingers on the door-handle.

" Please understand, Mr. Verrers, that what I said in my letter was final."

He frowned impatiently.

" I came here to——"

" You came here in express disregard of my wishes."

" Miss Dethier, I've already reminded you that this matter is private."

There was a touch of irritation now.

She sensed, more than saw, Brother Anselm stirring.

" On the contrary," came quietly from the monk, " the matter is known to Major Brandreth and myself."

Verrers half faced round in the direction of the voice.

" So this has been arranged ? " It was addressed to Beauty.

" Yes, it has been arranged," the monk answered for her.

" I spoke to Miss Dethier." Verrers brushed aside the interruption.

" If you have anything further to say, perhaps you will say it to me—or, if you prefer, to Major Brandreth." The monk uncrossed his legs.

The words revealed the situation to Verrers. A flush swept his face and receded, leaving him white with suppressed anger. With an effort he controlled himself.

" Since when has Father Thornton constituted himself your spiritual adviser, Miss Dethier ? "

" I have not constituted myself Miss Dethier's spiritual adviser," Brother Anselm replied, unperturbed. " Neither has Miss Dethier ever approached me in that capacity. If you are insinuating that her decision to refuse a certain offer of yours was directed by myself, you are mistaken. Miss Dethier and I only met recently. Her decision was made before "—he turned to Beauty, interrogating her permission. She nodded—" before she consulted me, as a friend."

" Thank you for your priestly interference." For the first time he addressed the monk directly.

" *Friendly* interference, please. Or shall we say— protection ? "

Verrers assumed surprise. " Protection ? "

" Your letter to Miss Dethier certainly showed me that she was in need of protection. That is why Major Brandreth and I are here."

" That letter was private."

" That letter was a threat, to force Miss Dethier to your will. As such she had a right to show it to me. It was a threat to a defenceless woman. Do you deny it ? "

" Kindly don't assume the right to question me, Father Thornton."

Brother Anselm stood up, facing the man squarely. He put his hands behind his back.

" Have you anything further to say ? " He waited. " No ? Then, Verrers, the door is just behind you."

There was a dangerous glint in the black eyes.

" Am I to understand that——"

" That I am requesting you to leave ? Yes. You came uninvited, and you came for a particularly dishonourable end."

" That is a matter of opinion."

" For you, perhaps. Before you go, I might mention that if you attempt to enter this flat again, or in any way interfere with Miss Dethier, I shall not scruple to act immediately."

Verrers smiled sarcastically.

" Melodramatic—but interesting, Father Thornton. Legal measures ? "

" No. Your methods are not punishable by law. No, Verrers—public measures. Shall I suggest them ? "

He waited.

" At present you are known only in your public life. Privately you are unknown. The capacity, shall we say, in which you act is unknown. It could be made known. Do I make myself clear ? "

The nonchalance was dropping from him.

" Do not forget," added the monk, " that all the evidence required is upon your person at this moment."

Verrers' right hand moved unguardedly.

" Precisely. In that little gold case on your watch-chain. I notice you are very much aware of its contents—as also are three other people in this room."

Verrers moved back a step, still maintaining a kind of wariness. Then, without warning, he swung round upon Beauty :

" So——"

" No, Verrers, to me, please ! " The monk motioned Beauty back. " So what ? "

The other stood there in defiant silence.

" If you wish to know, I obtained the knowledge quite legitimately, and by accident. And I shall not hesitate to use it if it becomes necessary. That will depend upon yourself. May I once more call your attention to the door ? "

A strange glitter was suddenly in Verrers' eyes, a wild—— " Now then, control yourself ! " came sharply from the monk.

The man wavered.

Then without a word, he opened the door and walked out. The monk closed it after him. Beauty went across the room quickly and pressed a button.

Marie's footsteps were heard, and, next, the front door shutting. . . .

The affair had taken fifteen minutes.

Fifteen intense minutes.

Beauty had sunk into the depths of her arm-chair, and was regarding the monk bewilderedly.

" Brother Anselm, what was it ? Why did he go—like that ? "

The monk stirred himself.

" He had no alternative."

She was mystified. The Major leaned forward and tapped him on the knee.

" Doc, was it bluff ? "

" No. Why should it be ? "

" What put the wind up, then ? "

" The fact that I knew something, and he guessed it."

" But what ? "

Brother Anselm regarded the tea-cups thoughtfully.

" I told you what that little thing means—the disc with the Latin words that he wears ? "

" Some organization, yes," replied the Major.

" You interpreted that much, Miss Dethier," said the monk. " Have either of you any inkling of what that organization is ? "

They had not.

" Did it occur to you that Verrers left in that way, not because I invited him to leave, but to safeguard himself— to conceal from us his own sheer fear ? "

" Oh ? " from the Major.

" Now listen. You'd better know this." He settled himself. " The organization to which he belongs is not a rationalist association of the ordinary kind. It is a society whose existence is secret to its members, officially at any rate, with headquarters in France, Paris actually. I happened to learn a good deal about it some years ago from an apostate Catholic whom I reconciled to the Church. He had become a member, and left owing to the dread of what he found. I made no attempt to drag anything from him. This is what he told me of his own accord :

" The society has no name, but a symbol only. Every member must be an apostate Catholic. He must also take two oaths of initiation. Under the first he swears to work by every means in his power ' against the Faith and the Church.' I'll tell you about the second in a moment.

" He described fairly fully its activities. He showed

me his own symbol of membership, similar to Verrers' one which you found, Miss Dethier—a gold disc, inscribed with *Contra Fidem et Ecclesiam*. Next, he asked me to take charge of it; he had a superstitious terror of the thing. I refused, naturally, and advised him to destroy it. On questioning him, I learnt this "—the monk leaned forward:

"Under the second oath the initiate binds himself to wear the society's symbol always, upon his person. Verrers does so, you notice, in that curious little gold case. This is for the purpose of recognition by other members, so I learned. On no account, however, must the disc itself be seen except by members themselves. This injunction is rigidly guarded. Death is, according to the oath, at any rate, the penalty for its breakage—as in Freemasonry for the divulging of its secrets. The severity of the measure is necessary, I imagine, to ensure secrecy for the schemes of the society; the words on the disc would constitute incriminating evidence, too. Apparently even an accidental breakage of this second oath is liable in the same way. Miss Dethier, I wonder if Verrers acknowledged what you returned to him?"

"No, not a word."

"And he will not. Do you see why?"

"It would be written evidence against himself? His admission that I had seen it?"

"Exactly. Have you got it now, Major?"

"I've got it, Doc. Go on," said the Major.

"Remember," continued the monk, "I only threatened to expose him to the public—as an agent, of course, of a diabolic organization. He wouldn't appreciate the exposure, it's true; it would turn public opinion against him. It was the other thing that silenced him just now, though—danger from another quarter. There are members of the society working here in England who would draw their own conclusions if the facts about him came out. A disclosure, by them, of his carelessness to the society's headquarters would render him liable to the extreme penalty. He was quick enough to see that ; and quick enough to keep silent when he did see it. A fool would have betrayed his fear. He was wise enough— to go."

The tale had absorbed them. It left the Major muttering his own amazement to himself.

Beauty was still subdued. She asked :

" What will he do, do you think ? "

The monk replied in a deliberating tone :

" I think he will keep—the contract, if only to save himself."

" You do, really ? "

" I do."

There was a look of immense relief about her. She was slowly realizing the effectiveness of the monk's move. The haunting fear of days was lifting.

Brother Anselm ruminated.

" Miss Dethier, this is rather gratuitous advice perhaps. He won't interfere with you now, in the way he intended, I firmly believe ; but, for all that, you can't afford risks. I suppose it will be impossible to avoid him altogether ? "

She considered.

" At dinners and things ? "

" No, I suppose you can't. But, as far as it's humanly possible, keep clear. Julian Verrers does not forget, and he does not change."

" You're afraid of what ? " she asked.

" I'm not afraid as long as you give him a wide berth. I'm only afraid of that passion you've roused. With a man like Verrers it won't easily die down. It's underneath that he's dangerous ; you can't trust his cool exterior."

" Beauty," supplemented the Major, " can you see him

with all his bl——d dignity gone, blazing with fury and striking blindly with his fist—at the Doc, shall we say ? "

She looked startled.

" Quite honestly, I can't."

" Well, it happened once. You've got to keep that snake out of striking range, that's what the Doc means. You were going to look after yourself with him a fortnight ago—make a lap-dog of him. He's a reptile, see ? "

" We're not saying this to frighten you," remarked Brother Anselm. " It's to put you on your guard against a man who is relentless and unscrupulous—and can become violent on occasions, that's all."

It had a subduing effect.

" You're hinting delicately, aren't you, that I've been a fool, and you can't quite trust me not to repeat it ? "

" You've got it, kid," said the Major.

" You're a brute, Major. Will you trust me this time ? " It was to them both, and came very humbly.

" We shall," said Brother Anselm.

He rose, observing :

" We never finished tea."

" I'm going to finish mine," said the Major. He went over and helped himself from a decanter of whisky on a side table.

" Shall I ring for some more ? " asked Beauty.

" Not for me," replied the monk. " I must go."

Beauty left him with the Major for a minute. When he came out into the hall, she was there waiting for him.

" Brother Anselm, you're a dear. I'm very, very grateful. Thank you enormously for what you've done."

The monk took his hat from the stand and smoothed it with his hand.

" I've done very little. It's somebody else you should thank."

She did not comprehend.

" Have you no idea ? Somebody at Hendringham. Somebody you've rather ignored."

" Oh ? Who ? "

" Eric," said Brother Anselm. " I'd trust his prayers before any efforts of my own. He's rather a wonderful person, you know—or rather, you don't know. Have a talk with him next time you're there. You've been fighting shy of him."

She looked away.

" I'm going to say something to you, Miss Dethier. You came to me because you were in danger ; but you don't seem to realize yet how the danger was brought about. You allowed yourself to be influenced by Verrers because your religion was becoming inconvenient ; his ideas were plausible enough to strengthen your excuse for dispensing with it. Isn't that true ? "

" Brother Anselm, I'm sorry, but I'd much sooner not discuss this."

" I daresay. It's of more consequence to yourself, though, than Verrers."

She hung her head.

" I've begun, and I'm going to finish. . . . No, please. I want you to listen. Somebody's got to tell you the truth. You were flattered by a man of his standing taking an intellectual interest in you. If you'd been a good Catholic you'd have shunned him like poison, and there would have been no trouble. It gratified your vanity ; more so, when his interest became personal in another way. You expected the usual kind of adulation— and then he presented his terms and the rest followed. It was your Catholic instinct that refused those terms, but only at the last moment. It might have ended very differently."

He stopped. She was not appreciating it.

" Miss Dethier, you took me into your confidence because you trusted me. Can't you trust me now ? It hurts you to be reminded of your religion, I know ; but I should be a poor sort of friend if I didn't do it—and a poor sort of priest too. Your religion is far more vital to me than any mere danger from Verrers—to yourself, too, if you could see it."

She looked up.

"Can you learn nothing from that crucifix ? I mean, from the fact that you couldn't break it ? That was the turning point of your severance from Verrers."

"No, no. It was the—psychical experience."

"It was your conscience revolting against the horror of what you were going to do. It was your religious instinct that saved you from that act—and from yielding to Verrers, too. And you don't wish to admit it."

"Oh, it was my moral outlook, of course."

"My dear girl, where did you get your moral outlook from ? "

She did not answer the question. Instead she broke out impetuously :

"Oh, Brother Anselm, I know what you want. You want me to come back to my religion—and I can't. It's no good—I can't."

The monk's grey eyes met and held hers, searchingly.

"Yes, you can. That is why I want you to talk to Eric."

He moved towards the door. As she opened it he said :

"You know where I am in town, if you want me ? "

"Yes. . . . Oh, Brother Anselm, do you think me horribly ungrateful ? "

"Have a talk with Eric," he replied. "Good-bye."

And he went.

She returned to the library.

The Major was reading a newspaper on the divan by the window, a glass of whisky at his side. He put down the paper as she entered, and she divined that he had stayed on for a purpose.

"Beauty, I've—— Hullo, still worried ? "

" I'm all right," she replied quickly.

The Major refrained from comment.

" Got something interesting for you, Beauty. Remember that morning in Kensington Gardens ? Said I was mysterious about Julian Verrers, didn't you ? "

" You were."

" Well, the Doc won't let out this ; but I'm going to."

Her curiosity was roused. She came over and sat down on the divan at the other end.

" That row you spoke about ? Is that it ? "

" Oh, the row. Yes, and another thing, too. The row was over Eric. I'll tell you that in a minute."

The Major screwed himself round to face her.

" Anything strike you just now—the way they met ? "

" It was different from what I expected," she replied. " I was prepared for—pretty well anything from Mr. Verrers. He was—what shall I call it ? He was tame. He didn't even allude to Thursday night."

" That's his way. He wouldn't. Anything else strike you ? "

She considered.

" He acted as if Brother Anselm were a total stranger. Why did he ? "

The Major smiled.

" It suited him. Didn't want things raked up, especially in your presence. Might be awkward. Said I'd got something interesting, Beauty. Listen."

She did.

Her attention became rapt as the Major unfolded his story—all in his own jerky way.

It was a remarkable story. In spite of the mental reaction following the intensity of the last hour, it gripped her faculties and left her amazed. From the lips of anyone but the matter-of-fact Major, it might have sounded incredible. From him it was a simple narration of the truth.

She knew already that Julian Verrers had served with

the Gunners during the War. It was entirely new to her to learn, as she did now, that not only he, but " the Doc " as well had served under the Major in his own battery ; that " Captain Verrers " and " Captain Thornton, M.O." had met at the Front.

The gist of the story itself was this :

A mutual aversion had kept the two apart, " the Doc " detesting the moral harm of Captain Verrers' presence in the battery. A memorable night, however, had brought them together in an unexpected relationship. The battery had been half wiped out in retreat. Owing to an over-sight, Captain Verrers had been left behind wounded and unconscious, his leg broken, among the dead. The dis-covery that he was missing had been made by " the Doc " after they had retired a mile or so from the scene of the disaster. Unknown, he had made his way back, in the shell-lit blackness of the night, to their previous gun-line : " He must have gone through the devil's own hell. He was hit on the way, and his horse killed. Only had a box of matches for his search among those corpses— and shell-bursts. But he got him. And got him back. One of our infantry officers picked them up with his limber-cart on the road, the Doc done in from loss of blood, and Verrers in delirium. They got Verrers to the dressing-station still unconscious. He never found out who had done it. The Doc came back to the battery four weeks later. I'd done some guessing and made him tell me ; but he swore me into silence not to let Verrers know. Verrers got right, but was put on home service for the rest of the War."

Now came the curious outcome.

" Ever heard of Issano, Beauty ? It's a small town on the slopes of the Alps—Italian side. I was stopping there last year about this time. Found Verrers in the same hotel. Hadn't seen him since the Front. I heard from him about Eric Esterton being smashed up. Eric and two others had picked up with Verrers out there and done

one of the mountains with him. Rope had broken—you know that part, though. They'd got Eric down to a monastery place above Issano. He was being looked after by one of the monks. Well, we went up one afternoon. Found Eric in a garden place in an ambulance. Verrers allowed me about a quarter of an hour with him, and then sent me off to look at the monastery. Got the shock of my life there. Who do you think came along ? "

" Brother Anselm," said Beauty promptly.

" It was."

" Basil said his monastery was on the Alps somewhere," Beauty explained.

" Oh ? Yes, it was the Doc, large as life. I'd lost sight of him since the War. Never even heard he'd become a monk. Staggered me, I can tell you, running into him like that. Now, here's the rum part. It was the Doc who was looking after Eric, and Verrers hadn't recognized him. They'd steered clear of each other in the battery, you see. It was years afterwards, too. The Doc had spotted him at once, the night they brought Eric to the monastery. Hadn't given it away, though. I learnt all this as we talked, the Doc and I. Verrers was still with Eric in the garden, but the Doc had no notion until I mentioned it. Never forget his face. ' We'll join them,' he said. My God ! it was a hell of a row. Verrers had got rid of me to get hold of Eric and blast the Doc's influence out of him—religion and all that. He'd been at it before. Beauty, I'll never forget it—the Doc standing there and blazing at him ; lashed him like a dog. Never seen the Doc like that before. Verrers tried the superior stuff, but it didn't work with those eyes fixing him. Went mad suddenly and struck out with his fist. The Doc had him in a vice next moment—arm up like a piston-rod, jerked him straight and held him there ; let him feel his strength for a bit. It finished Verrers. He went after that. And he was still in the dark, mind, about the Doc, who he was."

The Major picked up his whisky.

" That was the row." He sipped and put down the glass. Beauty waited, absorbed.

" It wasn't pleasant with him at the hotel after that, I can tell you. We were barely on speaking terms at times. Eric's two friends were still there, too. Didn't much matter, though. He was out in his car most of the time, and I was up at the monastery a lot. Always liked the Doc, but I'd have licked his boots now—the way he was looking after Eric and pulling him through that time. Anyway—Verrers didn't go."

The Major cleared his throat.

" Now here's the last thing. It was the day before we were leaving. The Doc gave us a sort of Italian beano at a village up in the mountains—a place where you go for the view. He brought Eric up in a car. The rest of us, Eric's friends and myself, joined them there. Well, we were having drinks on a terrace place outside a *caffè*. Suddenly a car draws up at the gates, and out steps— Verrers ! Darned awkward. Verrers saunters on to the terrace and looks at the view, then sees us. Held him up for a moment. He took the shock well, though—came and sat down with us ; laid himself out to be nice. Couldn't quite make it out myself. Began to wonder whether he was going to climb down and apologize to the Doc. Anyhow, he got us all listening to him ; you know that way of his. Didn't get suspicious, myself, until I saw he was isolating the Doc from the talk. Didn't guess what he was up to even then—until it came."

The Major took another sip.

" It was darned cleverly done. He steered that talk to the War. Knew we'd all been out there, but took it for granted that the Doc had been at the monastery all through. Never mentioned names, but made it quite clear what he thought about Englishmen who kept out of the War, and what *we* ought to think—all, mind you, in an impersonal kind of way. The Doc sat there looking away into the distance, saying nothing—and then suddenly suggested to Verrers to talk *to* him instead of *at* him. Verrers went headlong into the trap and began hinting some unpleasant things, straight at him. The Doc never answered—not a word. Just went on looking away over the mountains. It didn't suit J. V. Wasn't going according to programme. He wanted to rouse him. All of us silent, too ; we'd taken our cue from the Doc. You could see the glitter coming in those black eyes—that's the danger signal with J. V. He tried things about monks hiding away from the War in their monasteries—cheap stuff, but he was losing control. Doc still mum. Then it came. He saw red suddenly and called the Doc a ' cowardly shirker.' That finished me."

The Major rubbed his hands together. His eyes had a gleam in them.

" I needn't tell you how it was done, Beauty ; but a few minutes later Verrers was sitting there speechless. He'd learnt how a ' cowardly shirker ' of an M.O. in my battery had got him back that night at the Front—and who the M.O. was. The Doc tried to save his face for him a bit by going into the *caffè* to pay the bill, while he was being told. It dazed him—couldn't even speak. The Doc was grand, when he came back—hated him knowing and was sorry for him, but wouldn't he think a bit better of religion ; it was his religion that had made him do it."

The Major paused, trying to recall the impression.

" Beauty, it was darned queer, what followed. Remember what the Doc said just now—Verrers doesn't change ? "

She nodded, too intent to speak.

" Not a psychologist myself, or I might explain it better. The Doc said afterwards J. V. couldn't have acted differently, being what he is ; he'd a satanic obsession against religion. Well, he sat there like a stone, eyes like slits—the Doc pleading. Made me feel lumpy, that great rough chap being gentle when he could have eaten him up. It wasn't any good. J. V. stood up suddenly and laughed. Frightened me, that laugh ; sort of laugh a damned soul would give—mocking. Not, mind you, at the Doc ; at himself—the idea of changing. Then he went across the terrace to his car without a word. We didn't see him again. He'd gone off when we got back to the hotel."

The Major drained his glass, stood up and began to walk about. Beauty remained still. The dramatic force of the tale had left her tongue-tied. It was some time before she said :

" Thank you, Major. I'm glad you've told me that."

The Major smiled.

" See now why they were strangers this afternoon ? It was the first time they'd met since last year. J. V. wasn't risking any allusions. Trusted the Doc to do the stranger, if he did."

Beauty stroked the nape of her neck.

" How very weird ! "

" Thought he was tame, didn't you ? " said the Major. " He was. Sarcastic and all that over the Doc stepping in. All the same, he was being darned careful. You can't go far with a man who's saved your life."

A thought struck her.

" Good heavens—if the public knew ! "

" The public will never know. The Doc'll see to that. He'd not take advantage of him in that way. Don't you breathe a word of this, Beauty. Promise ? "

" I won't, Major. I promise faithfully."

She suddenly wrinkled her forehead.

" Major, what is Brother Anselm really afraid of ? What can he do now ? " She was thinking of herself again.

" J. V. ? "

" Yes."

" He won't do anything as long as he remembers what

the Doc threatened.   There might be trouble if he forgot."

" How ? "

The Major examined her.

" You didn't get what the Doc had at the back of his mind ? He's a medical man, remember. Thinks J. V. can go insane at times. He'd forget then."

Beauty looked astonished.

" But he *is* sane, surely ? "

" As long as things go right and he's getting what he wants, he's as sane as you or me, Beauty. You've not seen him as we have, though. He *was* insane at the end of that row over Eric. He *was* insane when he got that shock about the Doc. Good heavens, he couldn't even show gratitude to the chap who'd saved his life ! He was on the verge just now. Didn't you see his eyes ? Why do you think the Doc snapped out like that ? "

There was a pause.

" But there's no serious danger ? "

" Look here, Beauty, why do you think I've been telling you about—last year ? Wanted you to know about the Doc, of course—but about J. V., too. He *is* dangerous." The Major tugged at his moustache. " The Doc couldn't say it, but I'm going to. . . . Er—you're getting a bit keen on Basil, aren't you ? No harm in that. Basil's a damned fine boy. But, for the love of God, don't go dangling him near Verrers. Got it now ? . . Sorry, my girl."

For the colour had come swiftly to her cheeks.

*   *   *   *   *   *

She noticed it shortly after the Major had gone—the photograph of himself which Julian Verrers had given her only a fortnight ago. The sight of it brought the facts slowly disentangling themselves from the welter of her thoughts.

Her severance with him was complete.

The nightmare of the last few days had lifted, that over-powering dread. She had been released. Julian Verrers, as a threatening presence, was no longer there. He remained a vague danger of the future, no more.

She had been delivered from the consequences of her own folly, at least. . . . Brother Anselm and the Major had done it kindly ; but they had driven home that folly so as to leave no delusions in her mind. She had sought out Julian Verrers for the gratification of her own vanity. The monk had hurt her with that. But it was true.

She knew him now for what he was—a dangerous fanatic blinded by his obsessions to the ordinary code of honour, insensate to all but the ends of an unscrupulous organiza-tion for which he worked. The man himself was con-cealed under an uncannily fascinating exterior, moving in society with the ease afforded by a host of idol-worshippers, known by them only as a prominent biologist with original views on moral questions.

Julian Verrers !   Insane perhaps at times.

She rose and went across to the mantelpiece.

She picked up the silver frame and extracted the photograph. Next she tore it firmly into four quarters and dropped them into the paper-basket beneath her escritoire. No, that wouldn't do ; the maid—— She recovered them and tore them into fragments, wrapped the fragments in a sheet of notepaper, crumpled the package and buried it beneath the litter in the basket.

Then she considered the empty frame.

A thought occurred. " Why not ? " She disappeared from the room. When she came back, it was with another photograph in her hand. And shortly, from the mantel-piece, Basil was looking at her.

●   ●   ●   ●   ●   ●

She returned in the early hours of next morning, dead tired ; partly from the straining events of the last two days, and partly from three hours at a night club.

She returned with a mild sense of shame also, excusing herself, however, on the ground that she had been taken with a party ; the particular night club had been more than doubtful. One dance, at least, had been unblushingly indecent.

Before going to her bedroom she went into the library and turned on the light, and then stood before the new occupant of the silver frame. He had slipped the photograph into her hand the last night as she was going up to bed, shyly.

It was an unusually good likeness—expressive of all the glorious youth that was Basil's. Yes, it was Basil exactly ; the clear, laughing eyes, the slightly parted lips that, yesterday morning, had so nearly said what she had read in his look ; the curly hair upon which her hand had lain as she swayed from her horse at the end of that terrible ride.

Basil.

It was Basil she had dismissed for Julian Verrers at Lady Derringham's. It was Basil who had snatched her from nearly certain death without a thought of the peril to himself.

She leant against the table, her head lowered.

There came a sense, once more, of the monk's grey eyes upon her. This time she felt rather than saw them. They were probing into her soul, bringing self-revelation. . . .

"Beauty, you're detestable !" broke from her lips, aloud.

She buried her face in her hands, as if to hide the truth from her sight. For the truth had come, piercing her with its shame. Until yesterday she had been playing with Basil, as with others, to satisfy her lust for admiration—for his homage at her shrine.

"Beauty, I hate you !"

Until yesterday . . .
She uncovered her face.
Until yesterday . . .
She took the photograph in her hands.

" Basil, I'm sorry. I'm terribly sorry."
And, very reverently, she kissed it.

PART II

CHAPTER XV

§ I

HENDRINGHAM rose gaunt and stark out of a wilderness of white.

The first snowfall of the winter had come, delaying its arrival until the new year, but atoning for the negligence with a foot of emptied sky on earth. From the terrace to the tennis-court down by the river the grounds lay shrouded in cold peace. Beyond the river, glistening stillness stretched away and mingled with the leaden pall of heaven.

Basil, from the window of Eric's room, wondered, not at the beauty of the scene, but how he would get up to town that afternoon.

* * * * * *

Certain things had happened since the day, seven months ago, on which the door of the flat in Curzon Street had closed on Julian Verrers.

In July Brother Anselm had received directions from his superior at Issano to remain in England as long as might be needed for his purpose. The monk had kept close watch on Julian Verrers' public movements. The latter had continued, but confined his activities to small gatherings and drawing-room meetings. No large hall had been commandeered either in London or the provinces.

For weeks after their respective speeches controversy had raged in the Press. The rationalistic, as also the more modernist section, had demanded another public hearing for Julian Verrers, a further defence of his own proposals against the "brow-beating methods of a mediæval-minded monk," as described by one journal. The demand had evoked a surprising storm of hostility from another quarter, the more moderate and conservative papers pointing to the fact that Julian Verrers had already been given two public hearings to the monk's one, and that the monk had been answering an attack rather than provoking one. Most of these papers had made haste to assure their readers that they held no brief for the Catholic religion, and that it was the moral issues of the controversy with which they were concerned ; those moral issues had been ventilated in the full light of day ; the monk had done no more than illuminate what Julian Verrers had veiled ; their rationalistic contemporaries did not deny the interpretation given by him to his opponent's schemes, but objected to the severe treatment meted out. Had it been more severe than the other's treatment of Christianity ?

The effort to reinstate Julian Verrers had been relinquished. Many of the monk's defendants went so far as to express in plainest terms their disgust at the welcome given in the first instance to the "Plea for Freedom," now that its licentious significance had transpired. Brother Anselm had read it all with a certain humour, recalling that some of these very papers had originally assisted in the "welcome."

He read into it something more as well, which gladdened his soul—that deep down in the heart of England was implanted a strong, if vague, sense of morality which had responded generously to his appeal.

The conviction was strengthened week by week, as he journeyed about fulfilling his preaching engagements, the invitations which had followed from the Queen's Hall speech. Wherever he went the same serious hearing was accorded by men and women of every class, of any religion or none. The churches in which he preached, and to which they flocked, frequently proved inadequate. In some places he had adopted the expedient, after emptying the church of its first congregation, of refilling it with a second and repeating his address. His plain, unvarnished discourses on " Moral Questions of the Day," dealing in an extended form with the points raised at the Queen's Hall and others as well, had been published in the Press, series by series.

In this way he had continued to reach a wide public. The effect had been slow but steady. The star of Julian Verrers had begun to wane. By Christmas the monk felt he could rest for a while from his almost unbroken labour of six months.

Of Julian Verrers' mind he was in ignorance. They had never actually encountered each other since that June afternoon at Beauty's flat. Once in November, though, the monk had passed him in Oxford Street, unseen himself.

Of this alone he was certain. However much Julian Verrers might hate what he was doing, destroying his propaganda, yet the man trusted him to keep silent in the matter of their private knowledge. Verrers had kept strictly to their contract himself. Never, by letter or in person, had he attempted to approach Beauty Dethier.

Things had happened elsewhere, during those seven months.

Basil had been received into the Catholic Church at Christmas by Brother Anselm, after a lengthy course of instruction from the parish priest of Windern. Lord and Lady Esterton had raised no objections. They had even seemed to approve. It appeared natural to them that Basil, who had always followed Eric's lead, should wish to be what Eric was.

Basil had written to Beauty telling her of the fact. She had replied hoping he would be happy, but making no comments.

It had disappointed him terribly.

He had hoped that this news, at any rate, would call forth some avowal on her part as to her own state of mind. It had not. He had quite expected that she would return to her religion with her release from Julian Verrers, the main circumstances of which Brother Anselm had related to himself and Eric shortly afterwards. She had not returned. She had been unapproachable on the matter.

It had been the only barrier between them ; but a barrier which had grown more and more formidable in his mind. It had become a kind of barricade against which he had been brought up short. By the time of his reception into the Church he had come to a decision, won at the cost of a hard and bitter struggle. The decision was that he could never ask Beauty for what his whole being yearned until she had come back to what he himself had found—the Faith. In spite of all that she held for him, in spite of all that he had learned to love in her, he could not blind himself to the fact that she was an apostate from that Faith. His self-imposed determination to wait, his very duty, as he saw it, occasioning enormous self-restraint, had fanned, rather than damped, the fire for her within him. In a moment of very human self-pity he had confided in Eric. His brother had firmly approved the line he had taken, and quoted for his consolation, fairly appropriately : " I could not love thee, dear, so much, loved I not honour more."

At first Beauty and he had been corresponding regularly in between her visits to Hendringham. Basil had signed his letters—" your affectionate friend " ; she had signed hers—" your ever grateful Beauty," in reference to his feat on her behalf in the summer. When they met it was in the spirit of comradeship on the surface, both hiding what was underneath and both successfully revealing it—whenever their eyes met, or hands touched. Basil had known how very different she was from " the others " for him from the time of that day on the moors.

He had not been sure, though, of what she felt towards himself until some weeks after the dismissal of Julian Verrers. There had been a gap in their meetings for a time, Basil having been fully occupied at Hendringham with work on the estate. And then one day in the early autumn he had found an excuse for running up to town, and also for calling on her and taking her out to tea.

She had made no attempt to conceal her joy.

With her " Basil, how splendid this is ! " as they sat down in the corner of a tea-shop in Bond Street, she had given him a glimpse of what his absence had meant to her. Her usual light way of looking about, conscious of the notice she attracted, had abandoned her. Instead, she had been absorbed in him, a new, gentle light in her eyes. They had played with tea, thrillingly conscious of each other, tingling with excitement over a wonderful, unspoken secret—talking quickly and eagerly over nothing in particular to hide it.

At the door of her flat, when he left her, the secret had all but been spoken. At Hendringham, when she came down again, there had been a moment when . . . and Basil had suddenly suggested billiards. He had guarded himself against another "moment" next time, she noticed. As the weeks and then the months went by and Basil still held himself from it, she had become puzzled. She saw the pent-up longing that was in him ; she herself was only waiting—hungry for his arms to close about her.

The moment had never come.

Instead, a slight formality had begun to mark their relations. The secret was still there, but it had been locked up.

And it was now January.

* * * * * *

He and Beauty were to meet that night at a dance ; hence Basil's perplexity about getting up to town. The heavy snow put out of question a forty-mile run by car. He decided to drive to Windern station and catch the afternoon up-train.

The dance was to be a big affair, at the Savoy ; mainly people from various hunts. Beauty had written, begging him to come as her " man," enclosing an invitation from a Mrs. Sands-Woodford, of whom he had heard but had never met. The invitation card was headed : " Savoy Hunt Ball." He had accepted.

As he was saying good-bye to Eric after lunch, his brother remarked : " Savoy, isn't it ? " And he suddenly remembered that the last time he had danced there Eric had been with him. He replied : " That's it. Cheerio ! " and went out of the room rather quickly.

In London the snow was not so deep. He drove from the terminus to their London house in Knightsbridge, where a room was always kept in readiness. From there he telephoned for a private car to call later. He had arranged to pick up Beauty at Curzon Street and take her on to the Savoy.

§ 2

" And is this your Basil ? " whispered Mrs. Sands-Woodford wickedly to Beauty, holding her hand with one of her own and Basil's with the other, as she received them. The file of guests following behind, waiting their turn, allowed of no more from Beauty than a " Maggie, it's the Honourable Basil Esterton. You've no respect for your guests," flung back over her shoulder as they passed into the dance hall.

It was a brilliant scene, ablaze with light and movement, the predominant black-and-white of evening dress throwing up the gold or silver favoured by a few women, or a huntsman's red. Scintillating to hidden searchlights were the two famous bands, one at the far end in the full rhythm of a fox-trot, the other at rest near by.

As the fox-trot ended, men who knew Beauty began to make for her. She had already fixed with Basil for most of the programme. Only a few could be favoured. Basil watched the competition and felt immensely proud. He then went about booking his own remainder.

The band resumed. He caught Beauty's eye and manœuvred to her through the crush. Next minute that sea of moving beings had claimed them.

" You're quiet ; but you're dancing perfectly," murmured Beauty after a while.

" I am," replied Basil. " Don't spoil it by talking."

Later :

" How do I look to-night ? "

" Your dress is all right."

" Brute ! "

Or :

" I expect we look extraordinarily well together," from Beauty.

" That girl was referring to me," from Basil.

They had dropped naturally and easily into their old banter. In the car driving from her flat the touch of formality had been preserved. Here the *joie de vivre* was having a dispelling influence. It was as if they had, by mutual agreement, reverted to their attitude of some months ago. As they stopped at the finish, they looked at each other and smiled.

They danced five running, caught by the intoxicating music, their young blood quickening to its weird symphonies, mad or melodious in turn.

" Let's have one more," said Beauty, " and then give it a rest."

" Right ! " said Basil.

When it was over they lingered a moment in the crowd

" Now where ? " suggested Beauty.

They went outside. It was crammed everywhere. " Abandon hope, all ye who enter here," quoted Beauty, inspecting. " Let's try the lounge," said Basil. The lounge was better. Beauty searched. " Hullo, where have those two come from ? Come on, quick ! " A couple had emerged from behind some palms and screens at the other end. They made for the place and discovered an alcove, partly concealed from view by glass doors. There were a couple of wicker-chairs inside. They went in.

" Bagged ! " said Beauty, taking a chair. Basil dropped into the other by her side.

" They've done this rather well," he said, eyeing the festoons and chinese lanterns decorating the lounge outside. " Hardly knew the place."

" When were you here last ? " she asked.

" Ages ago. Before—— Some fancy dress show Eric and I did Mutt and Jeff."

" Oh ? Really ? . . . Poor old Eric."

Basil examined his pumps.

" ' *Poor* old Eric ? ' Why ? "

She looked surprised.

" Well, it *is* rather ghastly for him, isn't it ? "

" Eric doesn't think so," replied Basil. " He's a darned sight happier than all this crowd put together." He jerked his head in the direction of the ball-room.

Beauty made no comment on the remark. Instead, very deliberately :

" Hendringham's up to the neck in snow, I suppose ? "

Basil experienced a sense of annoyance ; she always sheered off like this when their talk showed any sign of veering in a certain direction. He wouldn't answer it. . . .

" I asked you a question, Basil."

Formality was returning from its hiding-place.

" I heard it."

Rude, of course ; but Basil was suddenly determining

not to give in to her, this time. He summoned to his aid
a resolution that had been forming in his mind during the
past week. His courage screwed up.

"Look here, Beauty—I——" He floundered.

She turned towards him.

"Beauty, you *always* dry up like that. I'm sick of it."

He met her stare.

"Dry up ? How ? "

Whenever you think I'm going to bring in religion.
You know you do."

She hesitated.

"Oh, Basil, let's keep off this. I'd much sooner, if
you don't mind."

"No, we won't keep off it," he retorted hotly. ". We're
always keeping off it." He was breathing hard. "Look
here, things can't go on like this for ever. I've been
waiting months——" He stopped.

She rested her elbows on her knees, quickly, with her
face between her hands to hide the rush of colour.

"I know you've been waiting," she said at last. "So
have I, Basil." She had misunderstood him.

He added hastily :

"I've been waiting for you to come back to your
religion."

She saw her mistake. The confusion of it betrayed
itself in her eyes. Basil played nervously with a palm-
leaf, rubbing it with his forefinger up and down. . . .

"So that was it ? And why have you been waiting
for that ? "

"Because the Catholic religion means an immense lot
to me now ; you must know it does. I thought you were
going to come back. You won't even let me talk about it."

"And supposing I don't come back ? " It came
defiantly.

"Then——" He halted. "I can't go on pretending
it's all right between us when it's not."

She said nothing.

" What is it ? Why *don't* you come back ? " he asked
more gently. " Don't you believe, or what ? "

" If you want to know—no, I don't think I do believe."

It was the first time she had vouchsafed even that much
to him.

" Why don't you ? I mean, why do you think you
don't ? You don't seem very certain."

A frown wrinkled her forehead. She was becoming
impatient. He was resolute, however.

" Tell me straight. Was it Julian Verrers ? "

" No," she replied promptly. " It was before that.
Now, I think we'll drop it."

There was a finality in her tone. He watched her face
and realized that, with the remark, she had closed up
like an oyster. It was to be left at this, then.

Very well. . . .

He fought down the storm of longing that suddenly
surged up ; it would cost him all his will power to do it.
She looked entrancingly beautiful, alluringly so to-night
in the dress of sheen she had chosen. Her white arms, her
flushed face, were maddeningly near ; the blue sapphires
of her eyes catching the glimmer from the lights above.

He looked away. Her hard expression was gone. She
was watching him now, in her turn, the woman in her
rising up to meet what he could not hide, what he was
striving to crush.

" Oh, Basil, Basil, can't we go back—to last autumn ? "
She whispered it softly, appealingly.

He was trembling. She moved closer.

" Basil ! "

He wrenched himself from her nearness with a fierce :
" No, damn it all, I'm not going to ! It's got to stop—
the whole thing. I—I can't stand it any longer."

And then in the anguish of the moment the unspoken
thing slipped out.

" I can't go on with it. I love you, Beauty, so terribly
Can't you see ? "

As if to hide her from his sight his hand pressed over his eyes. He waited, all the aching misery of the renunciation he had foreseen flooding his soul—aware that she was very still. From the ball-room the strains of some voluptuous melody reached their alcove.

He felt her hand upon his own taking it down, tenderly. He did not move.

" Basil."

He would not look.

" Beauty, for the love of God, don't make me weak."

She released his hand.

When he had mastered himself he raised his head. She was leaning forward to him, and her eyes were glistening with tears.

" And *I* love you, terribly. You know that, don't you ? " The words fell from her lips tremulously.

" Yes."

He did not trust himself to more than the monosyllable.

" We've the thing that matters, surely ? " She did not see even now.

" We love each other, yes," he answered. " But we can't go on just loving. Nothing can come of it."

Understanding came. It frightened her.

" But——"

" No, Beauty ; I mean this. I'm not going back. It's utterly different now that I'm a Catholic."

" What do you want me to do ? "

He almost smiled.

" You know quite well."

She smoothed the arm of her wicker-chair.

" Do you want me to be a Catholic just to please you ? If I came back it would be for your sake, and the whole thing would be a sham. I shouldn't dare go to the Sacraments like that. I couldn't."

A swift ray of insight came to Basil.

" Then you do believe ' "

She avoided his gaze.

" You couldn't possibly speak of the Sacraments in that way if you didn't."

She fumbled for an answer, but could not find one.

" You said you didn't *think* you believed ; that was your way of putting it. You don't *want* to believe. Come back for my sake ? God forbid ! You couldn't come back unless you wanted to. You don't want to."

" Very well then, I don't. I'll be honest with you now, Basil. I *did* put it that way, to spare your feelings. I suppose, deep down, I do believe ; though I thought I didn't, once. I hate hurting you, but it's true—I don't want to come back to my religion."

" Tell me why."

" Will you still love me, if I do ? " she asked.

" I can't help loving you," he replied brokenly.

She thought.

" You may not understand me ; you may think me mad, but at times I almost hate religion. It binds you to things—believing things, doing things. I hate being bound. I can't even stand my home. That's why I live alone, so that I can be free. I've got to think for myself, Basil. I must decide for myself. I hate being decided for ; the Catholic religion decides things for you. I must have my freedom ; it means everything to me. Besides——" She halted.

" Go on," said Basil.

" How can I give up the sort of life I live ? I'm too mixed up in it all—people and things. If you're a good Catholic you've got to keep clear of ' the world, the flesh and the devil.' I don't, and I don't pretend to. I'm in with a crowd who are simply pagans in their outlook— and morals too. I read books that good Catholics would put on the fire. Oh yes, you may as well know it all—I go with them to shows that are absolutely indecent. They're exciting, though. Some of their night clubs are pretty thick, too—but I go. I don't care for them ; but I like the experience. I like to experience everything

It's my life. I'd have to scrap everything, don't you understand ? "

She was watching for the effect of it upon him.

" Well, Basil, there's the honest truth about myself. I didn't tell Brother Anselm that much."

" How much did you tell him ? " he asked.

" Nothing, except that I couldn't come back."

" When was that ? "

" Last summer."

He thought.

" What did he say ? "

" Oh, he wanted me to talk to Eric. I made no promises."

" For God's sake, I wish you would, Beauty. *Will* you ? "

" What's the good ? What would be the good of it ? "

Basil passed his hand wearily over his forehead, feeling futile and helpless.

" I suppose it's decent of you to have told me," he said at length. " I see what it is now, at any rate. It's all bilge, of course—I'm sorry, but it *is*—sheer bilge. Freedom ? Good heavens ! Do you think that's freedom ? It's all damned nonsense. You can't do what you like. Eric used to do what he liked. I used to do what I liked. We thought we were having a hell of a time, seeing life and all the rest of it. That kind of thing's not life. It's not freedom—it's selfishness. It's making a god of pleasure. It's being a slave to pleasure. . . . Experience ! That's the sort of hectic stuff you read in a novel. You're blinding yourself with that. You know your religion's true ; and you hate it being true, because it gets in the way. You could scrap everything to-morrow, only you're afraid of your own precious happiness."

She hadn't expected this.

" You're cruel ! "

" I don't care if I am. It's true."

He added ruthlessly :

" And it's all I'm going to say."

It was he who was being final now. She had expected some kind of sympathy on his part in recompense for her confession. She was receiving none.

" What are we going to do then ? "

. " Nothing," he replied. " As far as I am concerned it's finished."

" Basil, for pity's sake be sane."

" I am being sane."

There was a long silence before he said, in an expression-less voice : " You were coming down for the week-end, weren't you ? Do you mind if we let that stand, or my people will begin wondering ? We'll have to get through it, somehow."

" I'll come, if you think it's best," she answered.

" After that——"

He left the sentence unfinished. But the two words conveyed enough. A sudden, sickening desolation possessed her.

" Basil ! . . . But I love you."

Her voice broke as she said it. She laid her hand upon his shoulder.

" You love yourself more," he replied bitterly.

And at that moment it happened.

Basil became aware of her touch upon his shoulder suddenly changing to a grip. He looked up to see her attention riveted apparently by something outside the alcove where they were sitting, a frightened expression in her eyes. He followed their direction.

Two men had paused opposite the open glass door of their retreat, a few yards away. One of them was staring. He seemed to hesitate, and then took a step forward. His head came into the radius of light above the glass door.

For a moment Basil assumed the action to be merely bad manners on the part of someone who was taking advantage of the lounge being a public place.

" Ah ! . . ." from the girl at his side.

The man had moved nearer quickly and was at the entrance, craning his head forward to envisage them more clearly.

Without saying a word he took in first the girl, slowly, deliberately, smiling cynically as he did so—and then the man who was with her, as if to make sure. He nodded to himself, confirming something. Then, without warning, the man's black eyes were gleaming into Basil's, his face distorted insanely.

" What's up ? " came from the background.

In a flash, at the sound of the other man's voice, the insane look went. He drew back, turned round and left them.

The whole incident had taken a few seconds.

Basil was too amazed to speak, his mind grappling with some vague familiarity about the man. He remembered the girl at his side, and found her leaning back, very white.

" Who on earth was it ? "

She answered, as if in a trance :

" Julian Verrers."

CHAPTER XVI

§ 1

BROTHER ANSELM re-read both letters, and then put them down on the desk before him. He leaned his elbows upon it.

After a while he began to pick off the torn edges of the envelopes undecidedly. Next he replaced the letters and rose from his chair. He walked out of the room, down the corridor outside to a door marked " Rev. Prior," and tapped.

" Come in," from inside.

He entered. The Prior was dealing with his morning's correspondence. He did not look up, but said : " Yes ? "

" May I have permission to be away for the week-end, Father Prior ? " asked Brother Anselm.

" Where ? "

" Hendringham."

" You've no engagement ? Preaching ? "

" Not this Sunday."

" Certainly, then," said the Prior.

He turned to go.

" Will you say a prayer for my intention, Father Prior ? "

" I will."

" Thank you."

Brother Anselm retired and went back to his room.

He began to pack, slowly and absorbedly, his mind all the time on the contents of those two letters—one of them from Beauty, the other from Basil.

It was Beauty's letter that raised the immediate problem ; for from it he learned that the thing which he had feared had happened—Julian Verrers had found Beauty and Basil together, and under circumstances which had betrayed to him their relations. There was no hysteria in her description of the incident, though there was fear in every line. She conveyed, as accurately as possible, her own impression : " He was registering Basil carefully for some purpose, I am quite certain of it—as certain as I am that a moment later the malicious jealousy in his face was that of a momentarily insane man. I remembered afterwards what you and the Major told me about him, that he can become violent at times. I believe he would have done something violent, if the other man had not called. I feel that he *will* do it, if he can. It's Basil I'm afraid for, more than myself."

Basil's letter, written from Hendringham, was a pathetic outpouring of what had happened between Beauty and himself, the breaking off of their relations. He was utterly miserable about it, but convinced that he had done the right thing. The Verrers incident he treated more or less lightly, or pretended to. He besought Brother Anselm to come down to Hendringham on Friday, if he possibly could, and " cheer me up " ; also his presence would ease the situation between Beauty and himself. He could " cheer up " Beauty too ; the Verrers business had " got on her nerves."

It was Friday to-day. They had both written the day before, Thursday.

Altogether there seemed to be good reasons for going down to Hendringham—the main one being the uneasiness in his own mind that Julian Verrers might " do something." It was not only Beauty's account, but also Basil's " P.S." that had disquieted him : " Forgot to say that I was rung up at Knightsbridge this morning, just before I was leaving for Victoria. Somebody wanted to know whether I was in town for the week-end. Said I was returning to Hendringham. I was going to ask who it was, but they cut off. Felt a bit puzzled afterwards, that's all."

Why should Basil have mentioned the trivial incident ? The monk could only surmise, just as he could only surmise about the incident itself.

He had decided that his place was with Basil and Beauty for a day or two. He had hoped for a few days' quiet in which to complete a series of articles on which he was engaged. It was not to be.

He had finished his packing, and was studying a time-table for an afternoon train to Hendringham when a lay-brother entered and announced someone to see him.

Brother Anselm went down to the waiting-room and, to his surprise, found the Major there.

He was in a state of suppressed excitement.

The monk took him up to his room, planked him in a chair, and gave him a cigarette.

" Doc, something's up," he began.

" Verrers ? " suggested the monk.

" You know then ! . . . How much ? "

Brother Anselm told him, and gave him Beauty's letter to read. The Major scanned it.

" Now listen, Doc," he said. " I heard from Beauty yesterday, much the same as she tells you. I'd have come straight along, only hadn't time. I phoned, but you were out. Decided to act immediately. Didn't like the look of things, knowing Verrers. He could play hell in that state. Don't laugh, Doc—but I had J. V. watched, at once."

" Really ? "

" There's a taxi-rank opposite his place. Chose my man and promised him a fat tip. Did his job all right. He followed him to Victoria this morning, inside too. J. V. booked for Horsham. My man phoned that from the station. Know where Horsham is ? "

" Sussex ? . . . Why——"

" Yes, Horsham's three miles from Hendringham."

He waited for the effect of this.

" What do you think, Doc ? "

Brother Anselm looked grave. It was either very significant or purely accidental.

" Had he any luggage ? "

" A suit-case," replied the Major.

" Um."

The monk walked to and fro with his hands tucked into the sleeves of his habit. He stood still and looked into the fire.

" I'm catching the two-thirty for Hendringham, Major. Could you manage to come down with me ? Get through to Lady Esterton from here."

" You think—— ? "

" I think we'd better be together."

Lady Esterton, answering the trunk-call, was delighted. Basil, also, put in a welcome from the other end. The Major did not enlighten them as to what lay behind the sudden visit. They had decided not to alarm the family unnecessarily.

§ 2

Basil and Beauty managed to conceal the situation between them fairly well that night at Hendringham. During dinner Lord and Lady Esterton noticed nothing.

Beauty had arrived about six o'clock, after Brother Anselm and the Major. She and Basil were to be told nothing about the presence of Julian Verrers, probably three miles away, they had decided. It would be value-less to inform them at the present juncture, especially as it was within the bounds of possibility that the man had gone to Horsham merely to fulfil some engagement.

The monk had had a talk with Basil after tea, before Beauty's arrival.

He had found him very sore at heart, but resolute. As he listened to the whole story of how the crux between the two had arisen, he began to appreciate Basil in a new light. The boy had a sterling strength of character, almost beyond his years. At the cost of immense self-sacrifice he had immolated himself on the altar of an unwavering principle. There was no self-righteousness over it, just the great pain at his heart. "Basil, you've done the big thing," he said at the end. "Perhaps it will bring your Beauty to do the big thing too." That and Brother Anselm's rough hug of sympathy had brought the tears to Basil's eyes, but acted like balm upon his soul. It had meant an enormous lot to him that he could pour it all out into the monk's big heart, and still more that the big heart could understand, and share his pain.

To Beauty, in a corner of the hall, Brother Anselm had only said in a matter-of-fact way : " Thanks for your letter. Don't say anything to Lady Esterton about Julian Verrers, or Lord Esterton either. It's no good alarming them. You'll have to trust the Major and myself to do our best." She was looking pale and nervy, and he had not wanted to disturb her further. He had added : " By the way, you haven't talked to Eric yet, have you ? " She had lowered her eyes uncomfortably.

After dinner he and the Major went to Eric's room, when Spence had settled the cripple in bed. They had agreed to let him know about the presence of Julian Verrers at Horsham. Eric had a calm way of viewing things and nothing ever perturbed him. Also he might be able to help.

Of the occurrence itself at the Savoy, they discovered, Basil had already told him, also about Beauty and himself. The latter matter, by tacit understanding of its delicacy, they did not discuss in the Major's presence, as he was not a Catholic. On the way down in the train Brother

Anselm had informed him of the main facts. The Major's comment had been : " Darned queer thing your religion ; but I take it the boy knows what he's about. What a hell of a mess ! "

Eric listened quietly to the relation of Verrers' move.

" There are only three hotels at Horsham at which he could stay," he suggested. " Why shouldn't Spence go over in the morning and make enquiries ? Spence is no fool, and absolutely safe ; the other servants would know nothing. If Verrers is still there he'll find it out, or I don't know Spence."

Brother Anselm and the Major agreed. Eric pressed a button in the wall. Spence appeared and stood before them, impassive.

" To-morrow morning, Spence, you're a private detective," began Eric.

" Yessir."

" There are three hotels at Horsham, as you probably know, owing to your drinking habits (Spence was a teetotaler). You are to find out whether a Mr. Julian Verrers is staying at either of them. You have your own methods in these matters ; they are thoroughly discreditable, but may be useful on this occasion. Don't loiter with barmaids (Spence disliked all women), but come back and tell me results as soon as possible."

" Yessir. Excuse me, sir, but is it Mr. Julian Verrers the atheist ? "

" It is Mr. Julian Verrers the atheist."

" Excuse me, sir, but could you describe his appearance ? "

Eric motioned to Brother Anselm.

" He's tall," said the monk. " Very erect and wirylooking. Peculiarly black eyes and very straight features ; hair black, too, slightly grey over the ears. He would be described as strikingly handsome."

" Thank you, sir," said Spence. He bowed and retired.

They waited for a few moments.

"Have you a map of the locality anywhere, Eric?" asked Brother Anselm.

"There's an estate map of Basil's on that table over there, I think. Do you mind looking, Major?"

There was. The monk spread it out on his knees and studied it.

"There's the main road from Horsham through Windern passing the bottom of your drive," he said slowly, tracing it with his finger. "And the short cut from Windern to here through the fields. That comes out into the main road opposite the lodge. Those are the only ways of reaching here from Horsham, Eric?"

"No other possible way, unless you make a circuit of about twenty miles. The river's in the light. There's only one bridge in this part, and that's the one in the grounds."

"In that case," said Brother Anselm, "anyone approaching this house from Horsham would, under ordinary circumstances, have to use the drive and cross your bridge?"

"He would," replied Eric.

Brother Anselm retired at half-past ten.

In his bedroom upstairs, before undressing, he opened the window wide, leaned on the sill and for a few minutes ignored the cold bite of the air.

The snow that had fallen earlier in the week still lay thick over the grounds. They lay peaceful and silent under the hush of a star-lit heaven, their whiteness showing up objects in dark outline. The monk could see the sweep of the drive indicated faintly until it disappeared into the black of the pine-wood about a hundred yards from the front of the house, to the left. He could just detect the swirling sound of the river passing under the bridge. The bridge itself was hidden in the trees.

He was about to pull the casement to, when . . .

His body was suddenly rigid. . . .

He stepped back and closed the window—noisily. Then drew the curtains to, waited, went to the corner of the room and switched off the light.

In the darkness he crept back to the window, drew back the curtains very slowly, and began to open the casement again, also very slowly and without any sound, first peering behind him to ascertain that there was no mirror at his back.

Then he watched.

So for a minute . . .

He caught his breath. Next moment he was leaning forward, every muscle tense, his eyes straining in the direction of the pines. . . .

In the morning, as the car which had taken him to Windern for his Mass reached the gates of the drive on its return journey, Brother Anselm told the chauffeur to stop.

" I'm going to walk up the drive," he said.

" Get your feet wet, sir," remonstrated the chauffeur.

" My dear man," replied the monk, " I spend half my life in the snow. Ever been in the Alps ? "

" No, sir."

Brother Anselm jumped out. The car proceeded on its way up the drive.

He got to work.

First he noted the position of the lodge—thirty yards back from the drive itself and bushes in between. Any man could open the gates quietly and pass it unobserved, especially at night. He walked slowly up, studying the surface of the snow, particularly at the sides where it was free from car tracks. About fifty yards on he came to a halt, bent down and found the fresh impression of footmarks. They were long and narrow, and pointing up the drive. He went on, and met the same footmarks, this time pointing down the drive. He returned, passed through the gates again out into the main road, and stood for a while stroking his chin. Then he crossed the road to the stile opposite from where the footpath across the fields to Windern began. He climbed over it, and found what he was looking for. He went along for a short distance, examining, and smiling to himself. There were two clear tracks of those long, narrow footprints, one leading towards Hendringham, one away towards Windern.

He returned. Now he walked quickly up the drive, observing here and there on the way. He crossed the bridge and reached the point at which the wood on either side ended and the snow-covered lawns opened out. Here he turned off from the drive and followed the footmarks as they passed to the left, two distinct tracks again each way and close to the edge of the tree-belt. At the point where the line of the wood veered down to the river with the gardens, he paused. The footmarks ended here. They ended with two deep impressions side by side, and pointing towards the face of the house.

After breakfast Brother Anselm went in to Eric.

" I don't think Spence will need to go further than Windern. Probably Julian Verrers is there now, and not at Horsham. He was watching the house last night."

Then he told Eric certain things, had a consultation with the Major, and telephoned to Scotland Yard. They had a man free next morning, Sunday; not before. He would be at Windern as early as possible.

About twelve o'clock Spence returned to say that " Mr. Julian Verrers " was stopping at the Queen's Arms Windern, under an assumed name.

§ 3

Basil was doing his best to keep up an outward appearance of his usual relations with Beauty, keenly alive to the mockery of the position. As far as possible he avoided being alone with her ; he would risk no weakening on his part.

To-day was Saturday. On Monday she would go ; and, though he strove not to contemplate what that going meant, the anguish of it was gnawing with cruel persistency at his heart. On Monday she would go out of his life.

After lunch he suggested to Brother Anselm and the Major a tramp round the estate as the best thing to do, with the snow still on the ground. They welcomed it, without admitting to one another that it would be a relief to the tension on their nerves. For they were both waiting now, and they were waiting in the dark.

The monk had a momentary qualm about leaving the house, but decided to risk it rather than rouse Basil's suspicions. Verrers would be unlikely to visit the place by daylight. They would be back by four.

The three of them went off.

Lord Esterton retired for the afternoon to his study. Lady Esterton went up to her room to rest.

In the billiard-room Beauty found herself left alone with Eric.

Eric went on reading the book from which he had glanced up as the door closed on his mother. Beauty, rather unnecessarily, picked up a log and threw it on the blazing fire by which she was sitting. Eric's ambulance was on the other side of the fireplace and at an angle to it, his profile towards her.

After a while she picked up a paper, and began reading.

Then she put it down, clasped her fingers under her chin and gazed into the flames. Eric put down his book, wriggled on to his side in his rather painful way and said :

" Why not tell me all about it ? "

She unclasped her fingers and looked up at him, slowly. The inevitable had come. Brother Anselm's " Have a talk with Eric " dinned in her ears.

" Would it be any good ? " she replied. " Basil's told you, I suppose ? "

" Everything," answered Eric. " The Youngster's my brother, you see."

" I could only tell you what you know already."

" Never mind. Tell it me yourself."

Very well, she would.

She began with what she had said to Basil at the Savoy, her eyes upon the fire, finding immediately that it was a far more difficult matter telling Eric. Her apology for herself came haltingly. She gave exactly the same reasons for not coming back to her religion that she had so often given to herself and, a few days ago, to Basil ; but, as she advanced, she was conscious of a certain unconvincing ring about them. The sincerity with which she had answered Basil did not come to her aid. Rather, a sense of insincerity grew as the very same phrases passed her lips.

She began to falter, under an indefinable feeling of conducting her own defence. And yet—Eric was saying nothing. He was merely listening.

At the end he asked :

" Would you like me to make any comments ? "

She could have said " No." But she did not. He was compelling her, though perfectly politely : " May I ask you this ? "

She nodded helplessly.

" Would you kneel before the Blessed Sacrament, and say what you've just said to me ? "

No answer.

" You wouldn't dare."

No answer.

" Forgive me, Beauty. But you see, don't you ? "

The directness of it hurt her to the quick. He said immediately :

" Now, let's just think it out."

He settled himself.

" You want freedom, as you call it. Well, now, didn't Julian Verrers offer you the very kind of freedom that you're after ? Why didn't you——"

" Oh no," she interrupted hastily. " I think his ideas are hateful."

" But you said freedom to do as you like, to believe what you like. Freedom to act as you like. Isn't that his idea exactly ? I read through every word of his Queen's Hall speeches."

" He goes too far," she said.

" He draws his principles to their logical conclusion, that's all. Why don't you ? Your principles are the same."

" But my—moral sense revolts from it."

He shifted his position.

" Supposing you lost your moral sense, as Catholics do, mind you, who stay away long enough from their religion ; what would prevent you from agreeing fully with his ideas then ? "

She saw his point. It perplexed her for a reply.

" Let's put it another way. Supposing Basil threw over his religion and did what *he* liked—went to the dogs morally, women and all the rest of it—would you love him as you do ? "

" No. You know I shouldn't."

" I do. But Basil would only be acting on your principles."

She was in a corner.

" Look here, Beauty," he said, " doesn't it come to

this really ? If you were consistent an l had the courage to face your own notions, you'd very soon scrap them ? "

She said nothing.

" I'm going to hurt you again. In your heart of hearts you don't believe in them. You've devised them, however subconsciously, to hide your selfishness from yourself."

She winced. He was striking her, striking hard. She tried to summon her anger and stop him, but could not.

And he struck on.

" You are out for yourself. You are out for pleasure, all the pleasure you can get. You say you love life ; you like to ' experience.' Boiled down, that means you love what appeals to yourself. If you were immorally inclined, you would be an immoral woman ; you'd fling your moral sense to the winds with all the rest, and, as likely as not, you'd be with Julian Verrers by this time."

" Oh, how—— ! " The protest died on her lips.

" You trade on your attractions to secure what you want—adulation, excitement, amusement, whatever you can get. It's yourself all the time. And you don't want to see it. You cloak it all under—' passion for freedom,' ' experience,' ' life.' There's nothing original in it. It's merely the modern method of excusing self-seeking."

And still he struck on.

" You say Basil's unable to ' appreciate your ' view.' Thank God, he is ! My dear Beauty, instead of pitying yourself, appreciate *his* view. Do you think he's going to ' appreciate ' your selfishness, however much he loves you ? Are you blind to what it's cost Basil to stick to his principles ? Would you really respect him if he weakened, when he knows that self-love is at the bottom of your apostasy ? You believe all the time. You're afraid to come back for fear of sacrificing your own happiness— what you consider your own happiness."

He struck even deeper.

" At the back of your own mind, even now, there's an idea that Basil may climb down—yield for love of you.

Basil will *not*. After Monday he'll bring everything to an end, unless——"

She was suddenly in tears. He waited while she fumbled for her handkerchief. They were tears of self-pity, he knew—perhaps of humiliation, too. He wanted more than that.

When she was calmer :

" Look here, Beauty, you may think I've been cruel. I haven't wanted to be. It's only because I want things to come right between you and Basil—and there's only one possible way. You *do* love Basil, don't you ? "

She nodded.

" Isn't he worth a little self-sacrifice ? "

" He's all the world to me," she cried.

Eric waited. . . .

She stood up and began to walk about restlessly. After a while she leaned with her hands upon the billiard table, looking out through the window, unseeingly, at the waste of snow outside.

There came an impatient sigh.

Eric moved on to his back, and lay there with his eyes on the window, too. . . .

" No, you're not cruel."

It was more to herself than him.

" Oh, Eric, is that really—myself ? "

He did not answer.

" Does Basil . . ."

He kept still.

There was another long interval

It was broken at last by :

" Eric, I'll try. I *will* try."

She went slowly across to the foot of his ambulance and looked into his face.

" I'm very weak, Eric. Will—will you pray for me ? "

" You know I will. It's the only little bit I can do."

The tears welled up again. This time she ignored them.

There was peace after the storm, a quietness about her, as she sat down again by the fire.

She remained pensive.

" I want to know something," came at last. " I hope you won't mind."

" What is it ? "

" Do you know what I said to Basil about you ? "

" No."

" That it must be pretty ghastly for you—like that."

He laughed.

" Do you really think so ? "

" I used to."

Eric pondered, and then wriggled again on to his side, facing her.

" It *was* ghastly for a bit."

" Tell me about it, Eric. Will you ? "

" Oh, well—I say, Beauty, don't mind me. Wants a bit of powder, doesn't it ? The others might——"

She laughed quite happily, and set to work on her face. " Eric, you're worse than Basil." When she had finished : " Go on. It's about yourself I want."

" Yes," he said slowly, " it was hell, at first."

He thought.

" Brother Anselm had told me I'd be always like this. He looked after me at the monastery, you know. I was finished, I thought. You know Julian Verrers was there at the time, at Issano, don't you ? "

She nodded.

" He came to see me up at the monastery. I was in the mood for him, and listened. It was all against God. He left me with nothing to live for. There was nothing to hang on to. I went mad with despair and—I tried to put an end to it all. Brother Anselm saved me just in time."

" Eric ! "

" It took a good while, but he sort of built me up, gradually. It was himself partly. Beauty, he was grand. You know his rough way, and then that tremendous tenderness underneath ; he helped me grope out of that awful darkness. I found there was more waiting for me than I'd lost. Verrers guessed what was happening and tried again. Brother Anselm was ready that time. Has he ever told you what happened ? The row ? "

" No. The Major did, though," she replied. " He made me promise not to breathe a word about it."

" Oh ? . . . You know, then. And what came out later ? What Brother Anselm did at the Front ? "

" Yes."

She whispered :

" Eric, it was magnificent."

There was a moment's reflection.

" Was that why you became a Catholic ? "

" No," said Eric promptly. " It staggered me, of course, but I'd decided before that. Brother Anselm got me as far as God, and then he left me alone. I used to watch Mass in the monastery church, and Benediction. There's a great crucifix there, hanging above the choir. Just that—and the Blessed Sacrament. There was a ray of light on the crucifix one evening from the sunset. I think it was after that evening I wanted more—something definite. I asked Brother Anselm, and he told me. It was God's Kingdom—I was still outside that. I knew nothing of it all until he explained—grace, the Sacraments, the Faith. The rest was fairly easy ; easier than for most people. There was nothing in the way. Everything had been taken from me, you see. There was only my will."

" It was easy to believe ? " she asked. Her eyes were intent upon him.

" Yes, honestly, it was. Quite. God did that part."

" God ? "

" Why, yes. Who else would ? "

A log fell from the fire. She picked it up with the tongs and replaced it. As the flames blazed up she shielded her face.

" Yes, I suppose . . ."

She lapsed into introspection. It was as if some slumbering memory had stirred. Eric watched her.

" You gave up your will ? "

He nodded.

" Tell me. When you accepted the whole thing, did you—feel free still ? "

" I knew what freedom was for the first time."

" Truly ? "

" Truly. What you called freedom just now is not freedom at all. It's slavery—slavery to false values of life."

She made no attempt to contradict.

" Beauty, has *your* freedom satisfied you ? Honestly, does the life you live satisfy you ? "

She pressed her fingers over her eyes, and drew them away slowly.

" Honestly ? "

" If you want the humiliating truth—no."

A quick light was in his face.

" You've been finding that out ? There *is* nothing in your life to satisfy. Look here, Beauty. You've got a soul. You've got an immortal soul. You're made for God, not for trumperies. Your soul's craving for God. You can't be free until you submit to Him—and that means accepting what He says—His truth. The whole world can't give you *that* freedom ; and it's the only kind worth having. Truth does set you free. That's not a thing to say. It's a fact."

" But how ? How ? "

" Because if you accept it, you accept God. You possess God. You can go out then. Nothing matters. You're free. Oh, Beauty, I wish I could put it better ; but don't you see ? All *your* things end in blind alleys— and you're caught. There are no blind alleys in God. He's endless. He always satisfies. And there's always more."

She was listening, closely intent at his eagerness.

" Eric, how do you know all this ? You've experienced it ? "

" It's one of the elementary truths of the spiritual life," he answered.

With that he left it. His tremendous conviction had arrested all the faculties of her soul.

The wearied look of an hour before had gone.

She was gazing far away through the window at where the disc of the moon was rising, large and yellow in the haze, above the white expanse. The evening star hung twinkling, crystalled in the deepening blue.

Eric became aware that the room was nearly dark, except for the flicker of the firelight on the walls.

She stood up.

" You've been very, very good to me. And I *am* going to try."

She moved towards the head of the ambulance. Her eyes rested on his emaciated figure lying there.

" Yes. You've nothing left ; and yet you've more than me."

The pathos of his shattered body, the unearthly beauty of his face struck her with peculiar force.

" May—may I kiss you, Eric ? "

She stooped down and put her lips to his forehead. Then raised herself.

" You won't tell Basil anything, yet ? "

" Right," said Eric.

She looked at her wrist-watch, and started.

" They ought to be back. It's after four."

He sensed a change in her, an alertness, and guessed instinctively what it was. Her absorption had driven it from her mind ; it was returning now.

" What are you thinking about, Beauty ? "

" Oh, I'm stupid ; but I can't shake it off. You know what happened at the Savoy ? About Julian Verrers ? They've told you ? "

" Yes."

" I've been afraid ever since ; even here. It's a kind of presentiment, and I can't help it."

" Are you afraid for yourself ? "

" No, I don't think so."

" For Basil ? "

She paused.

" In a way. But——"

" Who then ? "

" I simply don't know. It's just there."

She was standing with her foot on the fire-rail. After a while, since he said no more, she turned towards the ambulance.

He was lying very still.

It might have been the firelight playing on his face, but she thought he was smiling—a strange, far-away kind of smile.

" Eric ? . . ."

He did not hear.

He seemed to have forgotten her presence. A flame leapt up and lit the pallid features. What it was she saw about him she never understood ; but an impression was borne upon her of a curious radiancy.

She was not afraid ; just mystified.

She moved away, but turned again and looked, her fingers on her lips. Then, very quietly, she went out and closed the door.

CHAPTER XVII

§ 1

DINNER that Saturday night was as usual at half-past seven.

The gong boomed punctually, and half a minute later Brother Anselm descended the stairs from his room dressed, except that he was wearing thin boots instead of pumps. In the drawing-room, while they were waiting for Lady Esterton, he drew the Major into a corner and whispered something.

At dinner he seemed preoccupied. The Major, too, was quiet. Usually he kept them all amused; to-night, for some reason, he was not in the mood. Conversation, at first about their walk through the estate that afternoon, grew fitful. Soon Lady Esterton had to make it; an effort not often required of her. Beauty, though looking less strained than during the day, seemed absorbed, too. It left Basil, opposite, making occasional observations to his mother. By the time of sweets Lady Esterton was wondering what was wrong. A depression seemed to hang over the meal.

Once or twice she caught Brother Anselm looking at his wrist-watch, and Lord Esterton addressing remarks to him that he did not hear. There was an atmosphere of impatience about the monk that was quite unusual. She, wisely, rose after dessert without any lingering, and, taking Beauty with her, left the men to their port.

" Will you excuse the Major and myself, Lord Esterton ? " said Brother Anselm soon after the door had closed.

Lord Esterton looked up, surprised.

" Certainly, certainly. Nothing wrong, I hope ? "

" May I leave out reasons ? " replied the monk, moving towards the door. Basil sprang up to open it, confused.

" Certainly," repeated Lord Esterton. The Major followed Brother Anselm.

Outside :

" Now," said the monk, " get on your boots quickly. I'll be on the drive. Join me without them seeing you, if possible."

The Major found him three minutes later with his overcoat on, standing in the snow near some shrubs, at the point where the drive swerved down towards the pine-woods. The moon was brilliant, at the full, throwing up objects in dark relief from the white surface of the grounds. It was bitterly cold.

The monk came forward to meet him.

" We're too conspicuous," he said. " Come into the shadow—here, by the house."

There he whispered :

" Stay here and watch. If he comes it will be before they shut up, probably. He's in one of his insane moods and we'll have to be prepared for violence. I couldn't tell you in the drawing-room, but Spence was at Windern again this evening. They're having difficulties with him at the hotel. There may be nothing for you to do. I'm going to keep him from the house altogether, if possible. I'm going down the drive now to watch at the bottom by the gates. If by any chance I miss him, remember he can't approach the house without crossing the lawns. You're bound to see him in this light. Whatever happens I shall be back within an hour. If he does come, it will be before then, unless I'm completely wrong. Is that clear ? "

" Got it, Doc," said the Major.

Brother Anselm turned and began walking quickly down

the drive. He found the half-frozen snow crunching to his tread. The sound might give warning, he realized, and kept to the side, where it was softer. He entered the black shadows of the pines. It was difficult to discern objects here at any distance ; the bright patches of light, striking through the trees on to the road, were confusing. Over the bridge the woods were thicker, until a gap came, exposing him to the full flood of the moon. To avoid risks he made a circuit to the right amongst the trees, keeping an eye on the road all the while, and returning to it further down. Five minutes later he was at the gates. The lighted windows of the lodge, thirty yards away behind the shrubs, glowed friendlily. He found the gates open ; they were locked at eleven, he had ascertained. He went through.

The main road, running straight to right and left, was empty. He searched for a shadowed place for his observation post. The only available one was across the road under a big tree, close to the stile from where the short cut over the fields led to Windern. He crossed and stood close to the trunk. From here he could see down the road in both directions and also along the fields.

He had not waited long when a thought occurred.

He climbed over the stile and walked a few yards along the pathway. In the moonlight the two tracks of footprints he had found in the morning were still clearly visible. There was no . . .

An exclamation broke from his lips.

He plunged his hand in the pocket of his overcoat, drew out an electric torch, switched it on and bent down. There, in the frost-hardened snow, ran a *third* track of the same long, narrow soles, not so deeply impressed, but quite distinct. They were pointing in the direction of the stile. He followed them, climbed over the stile, making a hasty examination on the other side, and crossed the road. At the gates the circle of light from his torch moved here and there, remained stationary at one point, then passed through and a few yards up the drive wandering about uncertainly. Finally, it came to rest at where the snow lay thick again. The monk was on one knee now, making quite sure. His eyes travelled questioningly in the direction of the house. . . .

Somewhere Julian Verrers had passed him !

He remembered the moonlit gap and his circuit round it through the trees. Standing up, he thrust the torch back into his pocket. For a moment he was still.

Then, unbuttoning his overcoat and wrenching it off, he flung it into the shrubs and set off at a steady run up the drive. . . .

    •   •   •   •   •   •

After the Major had watched Brother Anselm disappear into the pine-woods, he paced to and fro under the wall of the house, observing all the time the line of the trees.

His vigil had not been kept for more than fifteen minutes, before a thing, unbargained for, occurred. A patch of yellow light suddenly added itself to the white glisten on the terrace, still unswept of its snow.

" Damn ! Oh, damn ! Who the hell——? "

He knew exactly what had happened. Somebody had pulled apart the curtains of the drawing-room window. He thought rapidly. Those curtains had to be drawn again somehow. The others would be in the drawing-room by now. One of them, in fact, had done it. The room would be exposed to full view from outside.

" Oh, damn it all ! "

If he went in he would have to give some excuse for the strange behaviour of Brother Anselm and himself (they were probably discussing that already), and also an explanation for wanting the curtains closed. It would be almost impossible to avoid rousing suspicion, even alarm. Still, those curtains must be drawn.

He would give that yellow patch two minutes to disappear.

He did. It was still there.

There was nothing else for it. He took a look all round. No sign of anything. He went hastily to the front doors and let himself in. Crossing the length of the hall he paused outside the drawing-room, feeling rather foolish. He opened the door, went in, and stood there blinking before the brilliance of the electric chandelier.

Lord Esterton was standing at the window, inspecting the night. Behind him lay Eric, his ambulance drawn across the space where the curtains, wide apart, should have hung. Engrossed in the moonlit scene without, neither of them noticed the Major's entrance. Beauty and Basil did. They were in the lounge chairs under the circle of the chandelier's blaze, and in a direct line back from the window, both reading.

" Hullo, Major ! " said Basil, looking up. " Come and give an account of yourself."

The Major smiled uncomfortably.

" Lord Esterton, can I speak with you for a minute ? " he said.

Lord Esterton had turned at Basil's voice. (The Major remembered afterwards that Eric had not.)

" Yes, yes. Come into my room." Mystified, he came away from the window past Beauty and Basil, and was in the act of putting his arm through the Major's. . . .

" Eric ! What's up ? " exclaimed Basil.

They moved round swiftly.

Eric was jerking himself painfully, frantically into a half-sitting position—holding himself there with one hand on the rail of his ambulance, his eyes darting to the window and then back at Basil.

" Eric—— ! "

There came a reverberating, deafening explosion—and the crash of shattering glass ! . . .

For some seconds they remained stunned, staring at the window in which were great cracks radiating from a jagged hole in the centre.

"My God! What's happened?" It was Lord Esterton.

Then Basil sprang up, his body tense and craning forward. . . .

"Get down, man! Get down!" shouted the Major.

§ 2

When, some days later, Brother Anselm was able to piece together more clearly the events of that terrible night, he recognized that, humanly, the central tragedy of it all (if tragedy it could be called) might never have occurred, had he not left the house, or had the Major not gone within. Under the inscrutable decrees of Providence they had both made mistakes, though with the best intentions. For all their precaution a man insane on the point of revenge, but perfectly sane in his cunning and plans, had succeeded—not as he intended, but, nevertheless, at the cost of a bitter sorrow.

In the hands of Providence he had to leave it.

The events themselves were to him, in the happening, a series of vivid impressions following one another with lightning rapidity : a drama driving violently along to a climax, allowing no time for thought, but only the swift mechanical action of his brain throughout.

•   •   •   •   •   •

He reached the bridge, labouring for breath from the long uphill run along the drive. There, to recover his wind, he dropped into a quick walk, peering ahead to the open archway where the trees ended and gave place to the white expanse of lawn.

He emerged from the shadows a minute later, slowed down, and listened.

Everything seemed as usual. The Major was not visible, but it was difficult to discern things in the darkness under the house with the dazzle of snow in between.

He gave a low whistle.

There was no reply. He went on, exposed to the glare of the moon for the hundred yards up to the house. And then, abruptly, he stopped.

" That won't do." The porch until now had obscured it from view—the wide square of the drawing-room window fully lit up from inside.

" That will *not* do." Even from this distance he could see someone standing inside, silhouetted against the brilliance behind, and then moving away. He looked in the direction of the front doors, made up his mind, glanced. . . .

His breath caught.

Another figure was there—stealthily raising itself over the low parapet on to the terrace, observing carefully . . . straightening . . . raising an arm to shoulder level. . . .

The monk was running at full speed as the report came. In a few seconds he had gained the terrace-steps, and was making straight across the space still separating him from where the man was standing, preparing to take aim a second time. He slipped on the glassy surface of the terrace, but recovered himself. The man turned, saw him and hesitated. Next moment he was on him, his right hand gripping, jerking up the revolver, his left getting a hold, the wild eyes of Julian Verrers glaring into his own.

He was a madman, with a madman's strength ; for the revolver was being twisted down again at the window. The monk swung him round by the collar of his coat, gripped and flung him to the ground. Without waiting he was on the prostrate figure, pinning him down, struggling for the revolver. His weight on the man's chest, he began steadily unlocking those fingers of steel. There was a sudden tug which left his own fingers about the muzzle—then a blinding flash. . . .

Without changing his position the monk held up his right hand to the light. It was completely numbed. The upper part of the middle finger, blown to bits, was hanging by the skin, blood welling.

Verrers, with a violent twist, released himself and was on his feet, backing and levelling the weapon once more— not at the monk, but at someone in the background, the muzzle dodging for its target. Then a voice—the Major's, was shouting, " Keep away, Basil ! Keep away, man ! " and the Major himself was rushing in.

The monk was up at the same instant, and together, shielding their heads, they went for him. It was desperate work, but it succeeded ; for Verrers, confused, shot wildly into the darkness behind them, and at the same instant received the monk's left full in his face. He reeled, still gripping the revolver, and staggered back. As they were about to close in he sprang away, slipped on the glassy surface and came down on his elbow. The force of the impact must have released the trigger ; for, as he hit the ground, the revolver spoke once more.

He twisted over. His head fell back, the body jerking hideously. Then he lay still. . . .

They came and bent over him.

" My God ! That's done it," said the Major breathlessly.

With Basil's help they moved him into the light of the window. Brother Anselm made a hasty examination. There was a hole in the side of the head from which blood was oozing. They undid his clothes. The monk felt about the heart ; then pressed open the lids of the eyes. They were glazing already.

"Dead," he remarked quietly, and remained kneeling there, his lips moving.

He looked up to find a group about him—Lord Esterton, Spence, and some of the servants, all of them bewildered.

"Better bring him in, hadn't we?" It was Lord Esterton.

Between them they lifted the body, carried it across the terrace to the front doors and inside. In the hall Beauty was with Lady Esterton, both white-faced and horror-stricken. "In here," said Lord Esterton, and opened the door of his study. Within, they laid the body on a couch.

"Could someone get a sheet?" asked Brother Anselm.

It was Beauty who brought it in. She stood behind them while Brother Anselm was closing the dead man's eyes and then came forward. The monk looked up and saw her.

"You know who it is?"

She nodded, staring at the body. Julian Verrers' mouth was twisted grotesquely into what was almost a grin. She shuddered.

They covered him with the sheet.

Outside in the hall, as they came out, Lady Esterton met them, moving away from the huddled group of servants who were questioning and frightened.

"What has happened?" she asked. "I can't understand."

Brother Anselm and the Major told her, and who the dead man was.

She was still uncomprehending. For they found it difficult to explain why it was Basil he had wanted. Beauty interposed: "May I tell you—when we're alone,

Lady Esterton ? Brother Anselm, your hand's hurt, isn't it ? " She was the first to notice the handkerchief which he had bound round.

"It is, a bit," he replied. "I wonder if you'd —— Come into the billiard-room, will you ? "

Beauty followed him.

In there he said : " I don't want them to see this. Can you stand nasty sights ? "

"I'll stand anything for you. I believe you've saved Basil's life."

"Get some bandaging," he said. "And iodine, if they have it. Oh, and scissors, and a bowl of water."

"Now, cut," he said, after she had returned. "Go on, cut straight through. It's only skin—that."

"Oh——"

"Go on, cut ! . . . Where's Eric all this time ? "

"He was in the drawing-room," she managed to reply, obeying with the scissors.

He went across to the fire, placed at the back of it the blood-soaked handkerchief and what it contained, came back and washed the dripping stump of his middle finger in the bowl of water. The water reddened.

"Iodine ? "

Next she was binding.

"Tighter, please. . . . Tighter. . . ."

When it was over he just said : " Thanks."

They were both very white.

There was to be no reprieve that night.

"Oh, somebody, come quickly ! "

The anguished cry from Lady Esterton startled them.

In the drawing-room they found her, near the window, bending over Eric.

" Brother Anselm, quick ! He's——"

" Let me come, Lady Esterton." He drew her aside. That something was wrong he saw at a glance.

" Eric ! " he said.

Eric did not answer. He was lying with his head partly over the side of the ambulance, moaning. The monk put one hand under his shoulder, and with the other supporting his head raised him carefully. As he did so there was a sound of dripping, and then he saw what he prayed in his heart Lady Esterton had not—a dark pool on the floor.

" Oh, what is it ? "

" I can't tell yet, Lady Esterton. Will you find Spence ? I'm going to get him on to his bed."

As she disappeared :

" Miss Dethier, quick ! Go and put the bandaging and everything in Eric's room."

When she returned : " Now, handkerchiefs, as many as you can. Soak all that up." He pointed. " Put then on the fire. Find Basil or the Major first. They're outside somewhere, I think."

He wheeled the ambulance across the room, out into the hall and down the passage. Lord Esterton's voice at the telephone upstairs was informing the Windern police-station.

In Eric's room he placed the ambulance alongside the bed, and began taking off the coverings. Spence came in, hurried and startled, and next moment the Major and Basil, who was looking frightened.

" Is Eric ill ? " he asked in a queer, strained voice.

" Shut the door," said Brother Anselm. " Now, help me lift him on to the bed. Spence, put your hand there. Major, under his legs."

Eric lay unconscious. The monk set to work, moving his head cautiously. It was the neck he wanted to examine.

" Was he by the window for that first shot ? " he asked, without turning.

" Y-yes. Right in the middle," replied Basil in real fear now. He had seen the blood. " I'd forgotten it."

The monk's head was bent down low.

" Forgotten what ? "

" He pulled himself up, just before it came. I couldn't make out what he was doing quite."

The monk paused, his back straightening.

" Turn on that table-lamp, Major, and hold it close here."

The Major did so.

After a while the monk put his fingers on Eric's wrist.

" Could a car be ready, immediately, Basil ? "

" Y-yes, of course."

Spence received directions and went out.

" Now listen carefully, Basil. I want you to telephone, at once, to the priest at Windern. Tell him you'll be at the presbytery shortly. Ask him to have everything ready for the last Sacraments, including Viaticum. Drive down there and bring him back with you. Does Eric's doctor live anywhere near the presbytery ? "

The monk's short directions were conveying understanding. A terror was gripping at Basil's heart as he replied : " Yes, quite close."

" Will you get on to his number, Major, when Basil's finished, and ask him to be waiting ? Bring him with you too, Basil." The monk's thumb had been pressed on Eric's neck while he was speaking. He reached out his other hand and gripped Basil's arm.

It steadied the boy.

Left together, the Major's eyes met his.

" Yes," said Brother Anselm, starting to bandage. " It's a matter of a few hours. There's a bullet in the neck—the first one it must have been."

The Major paled. For a moment he was silent. Then his face was crimsoning with rage.

" Doc, that damned——"

" No, Major, don't ! He's dead."

There was a moan from the figure on the bed. The monk continued bandaging. As he was completing the task, Eric moved. His eyelids were flickering and opening. He looked about in a wearied, puzzled way before he knew them.

" Would you telephone now, Major ? Tell Lady Esterton I want to be alone with him for a few minutes. I'll let her know."

In less than half an hour Basil was back.

He took the Windern doctor into the drawing-room and then led the priest down the passage to Eric's room. At the end of it, through the open billiard-room door he caught sight of the others waiting. That silent gathering and the unfamiliar hush about the house were poignant. They knew.

Lord Esterton saw Basil and came out, haggard and stricken. He took the priest's hand, but said nothing. Basil tapped on Eric's door.

Brother Anselm appeared, took the priest aside, and whispered. The priest went into Eric's room, closing the door.

" The doctor ? " the monk asked Basil.

He followed to the drawing-room. Basil remained outside, pacing the hall restlessly. After a short while the door opened, and Brother Anselm beckoned him in.

The doctor was standing by the mantelpiece, a short, spare man in glasses.

" Where were you, Basil, when he fired through the window ? " asked the monk.

" Sitting there, under the chandelier."

" What, here ? In this chair ? "

" Yes."

The monk sat down in it.

" What were you doing ? "

" Reading."

" Leaning back ? "

Basil thought.

" Yes, I was."

The monk leaned back, and turned his eyes to the window, as if gauging something.

" Eric pulled himself up suddenly, just before it came ? "

" Yes."

The monk rose.

" Sit here, Basil, just as you were sitting at the time."

Basil did so.

" Now look at the window—at that hole. Was Eric's head in a line with it, from you ? "

Basil considered.

" Yes, it would be. I should say exactly."

The monk looked across at the doctor.

" Did there seem any particular reason for Eric pulling himself up at that moment ? "

" I didn't have time to think about it ; it all happened so quickly. I had an idea he was doing something odd ; I've never seen him pull himself up in that way. I called out, I believe."

The monk pondered.

" The Major was in here, wasn't he ? "

" Yes."

" Could you ask him to come in for a minute ? "

When he appeared, Brother Anselm put a curious question.

" Major, the first thing Eric said just now was about Basil. He asked whether Basil had been hit. That means he knew at the time that Basil was in danger of being hit. Did his behaviour suggest anything ? "

" What, pulling himself up like that ? Doc, that darned rush put things out of my mind. He must have seen him, I suppose. Remember him peering at the window, Basil ? I take it he saw the revolver and was trying to get out of the way."

" He looked round at me, as well," said Basil.

Brother Anselm nodded, and looked at the doctor again.

" Come here, Major," he said. He led him across to the window, and indicated an imaginary line from the hole in the glass to where Basil had been sitting.

" That was the line of his fire, Major. Remember, it was Basil he was aiming at. Eric was not in that line while he was lying down ; his head would be here. He was, though, when he'd pulled himself up."

He was watching their faces and speaking slowly.

" Eric was not trying to get out of the way, Major. He was trying to get *in* the way. And he did."

Basil sprang up with a cry, and stared at the monk. Brother Anselm came away from the window and laid his hands on the boy's shoulders.

" You'd sooner know it ? "

" Tell me ! "

" He wouldn't say so, just now. Eric took that bullet— for you, Basil."

§ 3

There was silence in the night. Silence over Hendring- ham. Silence in the room where Eric lay.

The doctor from Windern had left. There had been little for him to do. His examination of Eric's condition had confirmed Brother Anselm's opinion. It was a matter of hours. The shock itself would have been sufficient in the cripple's enfeebled state, let alone the loss of blood. He had bled severely from the artery in the neck, apparently in a semi-conscious state, forgotten in the confusion of the struggle outside ; not one of them had known that he was hit. To operate had been out of the question.

It was while the priest was still with him that Basil had found his father and mother and, broken-heartedly, revealed the truth of Eric's wound. He had flung himself down into a chair and buried his head in his arms. Not until Brother Anselm had come in and a bandaged hand had stolen round his neck could the boy's torn soul be calmed.

" Oh, Eric, my splendid Eric ! " had escaped the mother's lips, as the meaning of it dawned—a proud light shining through her tears. And to Beauty, in the midst of her amazement, there had come a flash of memory—the strange ending to her talk with Eric in the afternoon ; Eric lying there, in this very room, suddenly silent and unaware of her, the firelight playing on his face lit up by a mysterious, unearthly joy.

*　　*　　*　　*　　*　　*

The clock in the hall struck midnight.

They were there now in his room.

He was fully conscious, lying very still, a ghastly pallor telling its tale. The pain that had flooded in with his return to consciousness and amidst which he had received the last Sacraments had subsided, so the priest from Windern said, as the Host of the Viaticum passed his lips. The hand that had been clutching distressingly at the sheets now hung quietly over the edge of the bed, the clothes of which were drawn down, exposing the heavily bandaged neck.

He was aware of everything, his senses curiously alert to what was going on around—to his father being called from the room just now, to strange voices in the hall. He had asked what it was and Brother Anselm had told him—the police from Windern. He had learned already about Julian Verrers.

As the last stroke of the clock died away he stirred. His eyes looked about the room and rested on Basil, who

was sitting beyond at the foot of the bed. Something in
his brother's attitude seemed to arrest his attention.
Without moving his head, for he could not, he whispered
feebly :

" Youngster."

Basil, his hands pressed over his eyes, did not hear.
Beauty rose and touched him on the shoulder. He
looked up. She pointed to a hand which was stretching
out.

In a moment he was there by the bed on his knees,
Eric's hand in his own.

" What's the matter, old man ? " came in the same
weak whisper.

" Oh, Eric, Eric ! "

" Tell me."

" Oh, Eric, why did you do it ? "

They saw a smile transform the drawn features.

" Why not, Youngster ? "

Basil could not reply. He let go Eric's hand. Next
moment he was jerking with great sobs, then crying out
his very heart.

The brother's hand groped about, and rested on the
Youngster's curls.

      .   o   ●   ●   ●   ●

The clock in the hall struck one.

Brother Anselm went quietly round the bed to Lady
Esterton.

" Try and get some rest upstairs," he said in a low
voice. " One of us will come for you at once, if there's
any change."

She yielded only under pressure from Lord Esterton
who, too, had seen the strain telling on her nerves. As
she passed through the hall to the stairs, the Major and
the priest from Windern were coming out of the study.
Together they had been in to lay out decently the body of

Julian Verrers. The act had stilled, to an extent, the tempest raging in the Major's heart.

Lady Esterton stopped the priest.

" Father, I'm going to lie down for a little. There are some prayers you—have ? "

" Prayers for the dying," he replied.

" When ? "

" I'll come for you, Lady Esterton," said the Major.

With the mother's departure the tension in the room relaxed ; for the strain she was enduring had communicated itself to the other watchers by the bed.

A peculiar peace began to release itself, replacing the earlier agony. It centred in the figure on the bed.

There had been a horrible moment shortly after Basil had broken down—Eric choking suddenly for breath, and Brother Anselm lifting him bodily into a position to ease the struggle. It had not recurred.

There was peace now.

And with it Beauty found herself able to think.

In spite of physical exhaustion her perceptions were becoming acutely alive to certain things.

They related to herself.

Lying there dying, Eric, who that very afternoon had shown herself to her and struck at her self-love, was striking deeper still. For she saw the self-immolation of his act for Basil as the price of her own folly. He was the victim of a mad vengeance which, but for her, would never have been wreaked. Had she not played with the passions of Julian Verrers that bullet would never have been fired. In piercing him it had pierced her own soul, too, with bitter remorse.

Were the others seeing it as she saw it ? Would they attach to herself blame for the tragedy ?

No. Instinctively she knew they would not, even in their hearts. At the most they would see her only as the occasion of Verrers' insane deed. Actually she was no more. Not for one instant could she have foreseen the result of her relations with him. Yet—at that moment she would have given her life never to have crossed his path.

She suddenly remembered he was dead—his body cold and stiffening in the room across the hall. His death would be in the papers, a public sensation. How much would come out ? " Death by accident " ?

She looked at Brother Anselm keeping vigil at the head of the bed. The monk was allowing himself no respite, priest and doctor in him both alert. She marvelled at the strength of the man, at the self-effacement with which he had concealed the real injury to his hand. That he was suffering acute pain she could tell from the veins in his forehead. Only his will and powerful physique were enabling him to endure. Eric's description came to her mind : " His rough way and then that tremendous tenderness underneath." The " rough way " had saved Basil from Julian Verrers, she knew that from the Major ; the " tremendous tenderness " was there now in the grey eyes keeping watch.

Basil ?

He was sitting a few feet from her. His face, an hour back quivering with grief and horror, was calm again. He was ready now for what was coming. His eyes were closed. He was saying his rosary.

A yearning swept through her to kneel at his feet and pour out her remorse, plead with him not to lay this thing to her charge. A wild fantasy surged up—would he cast her from his sight ?—" Eric's blood is on your hands ! "

The morbid exaggeration vanished as quickly as it came. She perceived what lay behind it ; the fear of her own heart lest she should lose his love.

Should she tell him what she had promised Eric ? And more, what she had resolved ? Subconsciously that resolution had been forming while she watched. In some mysterious way Eric, his life ebbing away, had completed the work begun that afternoon.

Should she tell Basil ?

No. Not yet. There could be no intrusion upon—— She trembled to think what the next few weeks would be to him. She would have to wait.

She would have to do it first, too.

It would not be easy. It would have to be a definite breaking with the past. The severing of many ties. Things would have to be given up before she could return to the Sacraments. The relinquishing of them would severely test her.

There must be no bribing Basil with promises. She must wait until she had proved herself.

*   *   *   *   *   *

The clock in the hall struck two.

It was near the half-hour when Brother Anselm spoke quietly across the room to where Lord Esterton and the Major were whispering with the other priest.

" Ask Lady Esterton to come down, will you ? "

They started. The Major went quickly to the door, and the priest over to Brother Anselm. The monk was bending down with his fingers on Eric's wrist. The others drew near. They saw what he had seen—the change coming.

" Yes, Father," he replied to a question from the priest, who at once opened his office-book and knelt down. They did the same.

The door opened softly and Lady Esterton came in, followed by the Major. The sight of them kneeling there bewildered her for an instant. Then its significance brought her with a low cry to the edge of the bed :

" Eric, my son ! . . . my son ! "

He had lapsed into unconsciousness and did not hear.
The mother took his hand to her lips, weakly crying.
Lord Esterton was at her side, his face working piteously.
In the background the Major knelt down, awkwardly.
He hung his head. Spence crept in. The Major made
room.

The Litany for the Dying began, Basil responding
unsteadily with Brother Anselm as the other priest said it.
Then came :

" Go forth, O Christian soul, out of this world, in the
name of God the Father Almighty, who created thee ; in
the name of Jesus Christ, the Son of the living God, who
suffered for thee ; in the name of the Holy Ghost, who
sanctified thee. . . ."

The great dismissal rolled on, accentuated in that
deep silence.

Beauty listened.

" In the name of the holy and glorious Mary, Virgin
Mother of God ; in the name of the angels, archangels . . ."

It was the first time she had heard the rite. The
tremendousness of it gripped her.

" In the name of thrones, and dominations, cherubim
and seraphim . . ."

The clarion call was awakening her soul, unseen hands
tearing at its wrappings.

" In the name of all the Saints of God. . . ."

There followed prayers, pregnant with pleading,
strong, pitiful, sweeping up to an Eternal Throne, opening
flood-gates, calling down from blazing heights a stream of
light upon one who was passing through the shadows.

" By Thy most sacred agony . . ."

There was Someone Who understood. Someone Who
had descended from His Throne. Who had become Man.
Who knew, and had, Himself, endured. Someone Whose
everlasting arms were reaching down . . .

The terrific reality was borne upon her.

As the priest's voice died away, the still figure in their midst moved, almost imperceptibly; moaning, rallying back to a brief consciousness. Brother Anselm leaned over and whispered the Holy Name in his ear. They saw the lips moving, repeating it.

There was a long pause. They watched.

To Beauty's quickened senses there came in that silence some difference in the room. It was a living silence now. A silence filled with a vast, overwhelming Power. The horror of the night was vanishing at the touch of a mighty Hand.

A coal fell from the fire.

She looked at Eric's face. There was the same mysterious radiance as she had seen before, intensified. All trace of suffering had gone. The features were perfectly still. He was back in that peace from which he had momentarily returned.

Outside a gale of wind was springing up, whistling eerily round the house, stressing the hush within.

Still they waited.

A shadow was creeping over.

The clock in the hall struck three.

The breathing altered as the last stroke died away. Brother Anselm bent over. Eric's lips were parted in a kind of wondering smile. . . .

Then his head fell sideways, a little.

CHAPTER XVIII

§ 1

THE policeman was sure of it.

He observed her carefully. He had a good memory
" It's 'er all right."

He had recognized her at once. He remembered the
occasion on which he had observed her before, months
ago, last spring in fact. It was at this very spot—the
Brompton Oratory beat. She had stood on the pavement
there talking with—— " There won't be no Julian
Verrers this time," he thought.

She was walking up the steps to the Oratory's main
entrance. He followed her with his eye. She disappeared
through the doors.

" No, there won't be no Julian Verrers." He resumed
his swing, trying to recall the conversation he had over-
heard that day. There had been something about religion
which had not interested him. They had arranged to
meet somewhere ; that had interested him more. He
had thought about it afterwards, depicting a romance to
the beginnings of which he had, accidentally, been privy.
He had even seen himself opening the paper : " There
yer are—' Engagement of Mr. Julian Verrers to ——.' "
It had not appeared. What had appeared two months
ago was : " Tragic death of Julian Verrers."

He had devoured the sensation to the smallest detail.
A public furore had gathered round the mysterious
affair ; for mysterious it certainly had been. The enquiry
into the case had been conducted in strictest privacy, the
Press being given only meagre information.

A storm of protest from the same had at length elicited

a statement which, though sufficient for its purpose, had, if anything, further whetted public curiosity. It was to the effect that the court of enquiry was completely satisfied with its own verdict that Julian Verrers had met death accidentally. Unimpeachable witnesses, including the Roman Catholic monk, Father Thornton, had given evidence which placed the fact beyond question. The circumstances under which it had happened, however, could not be made known. The public must rest assured that the motives for this concealment were entirely honourable. The officials of the enquiry were in possession of the full facts. Out of deference to the request of Lord Esterton, at whose country seat, Hendringham, the tragedy had occurred, they had decided to issue their verdict and no more. Delicacy and respect for the feelings of certain others, brought into the affair by accident, forbade the publication of what could only cause them pain and embarrassment.

With that the public had to be content.

For weeks, however, sensation-mongering journals had refused to drop the excellent copy afforded. Every conundrum was proposed, every accessible fact ferreted out :

Why had it happened at Hendringham ? What had Julian Verrers been doing there at all, with Father Thornton, his public opponent, a guest at the place ? Why had the death of the Honourable Eric Esterton occurred the same night ? Why had Father Thornton been in a London hospital for the amputation of a finger immediately afterwards ? This last discovery coupled with another—that Julian Verrers had been in possession of a six-chambered army revolver at the Queen's Arms Hotel, Windern, where he was staying at the time, close to Hendringham— had produced a thrill. Had there been . . . ? Vague, carefully worded innuendoes had followed.

The public had finally wearied of the problem, and the world gone on its way.

It was all fresh in the policeman's mind; the last echoes of the event were only now dying away. He wondered what the girl whom he had just seen knew about it. She had been a friend of Julian Verrers.

He observed her, about half an hour afterwards, coming down the Oratory steps, slowly and pensively. He swung carelessly towards the gates. "Gawd, ain't she lovely!" As she came through, a large limousine drew up at the pavement edge exactly opposite.

"My dear Beauty! Is it really you?" An extremely smartly dressed woman jumped out. "Jackson, wait here!" she flung back, and next moment had the girl's two hands in hers. "Dear child! what on earth—— Come inside the gates; we can't talk here. Constable, *do* you mind the car standing just *one* minute?"

"That's all right, mum," said the policeman.

They passed through and a few yards to the right inside the railings and stopped. The policeman waited, and then resumed his beat, to the right along the pavement outside the railings. As he passed where they were standing something appeared to catch his eye in the traffic. He paused with his back to them and listened. . . .

"But, Maggie, I did write."

"Oh, you wrote. But you didn't tell me anything."

"Sorry, Maggie, but I couldn't."

"Why not?" The second voice sounded impatient.

"If you really want to know, I didn't intend to. You saw what the court of enquiry said?"

A laugh, not very pleasant.

"Really, Beauty! Please don't refer me to the papers. I asked you as a friend, privately."

"And as a friend, privately, I've nothing to tell you." There was a quiet finality in the tone.

"You're politely asking me to mind my own business, then?"

The first voice said : " I'm not going to quarrel. Let's talk about something else."

" Aren't you forgetting that Julian Verrers was a personal friend of *mine* ? Considering that you met him at my——"

" I'm forgetting nothing. I'm not at liberty to speak, that's all. Now please, Maggie."

There was a wait.

" Very well, we'll talk about something else. Why have you been avoiding me ? "

The policeman turned round carelessly and became interested in the façade of the Oratory. He resumed his original position : " Colours up grand ! "

" You've changed. What's the matter with you ? "

" I suppose I have. Yes, Maggie, I have."

" Oh ? In love ? What are you blushing about ? "

After a time :

" I've come back to my religion, if it interests you."

The policeman caught a gasp.

" Is this a joke ? "

" Oh no, it's not a joke."

Something in the way it was said must have arrested the elder woman.

" Dead earnest ? " she asked at length.

" Dead earnest."

Another interval.

" You've given me quite a shock."

" I'm sorry."

" So that's why you've been keeping away ? "

" If you put it like that. I've had to give up a good deal ; the sort of things that—— Well, Maggie, you know."

" The sort of things I do ? "

" Er—some of them, yes."

A ripple of merriment.

" Beauty, you're a gem ! Who's been reforming you ? That Father Thornton person ? "

There was no reply.

" My dear, for the love of Heaven, don't look murder at me ! "

" Then, for the love of Heaven, don't say stupid things!"

The policeman pulled at his moustache, and moved away a little.

" You don't understand, Maggie. I'd rather not discuss it, if you don't mind."

" I understand that I'm not a fit person to associate with. So that's why—— Really, so I'm to be a moral leper now. Are you treating all your friends like this ? What a delightful religion ! "

Silence.

" My dear child, who on earth's been getting round you ? People don't do this kind of thing nowadays. It's simply not done."

Still silence.

" Is it a pose, or what ? "

" Any more questions, Maggie ? "

" Really, Beauty ! I'm quite serious."

" So am I. But I'll answer nothing while you're like this. Good-bye, Maggie."

A rather high-pitched laugh.

The policeman smartened up, strode in a business-like way to the left, cast an eye on the limousine, went round through the gates and approached the pair. . . .

" You'll come to your senses. Nerves, my dear. It'll pass."

" Good-bye, Maggie."

" Excuse me, mum, but we've orders—— "

" Oh constable, the car, yes. Well, good-bye, dearest."

The extremely smartly dressed woman flounced away through the gates, gave an order to the chauffeur and then jumped inside the car. It drove off. The girl walked slowly towards the other gates to the right. Outside she quickened her pace and disappeared up the Brompton Road.

The policeman watched her out of sight and then took

up his beat, meditatively. " Didn't 'alf like it, that dressed-up bitch."

The conversation had been highly interesting, but highly tantalizing. " That girl knows about Julian Verrers. Knows more than the 'ole blooming public. And she ain't going to tell. . . . Don't blame 'er either, if she was in with 'im." The problem simmered. " Taken up religion ? . . . Don't look like Julian Verrers." Next, he smiled to himself : " Nosey didn't get 'er change. Serve 'er b—— well right."

Final apostrophe : " Gawd, ain't she lovely ! "

§ 2

Brother Anselm was worried.

On the desk before him lay a pamphlet.

Its title was boldly printed : " Julian Verrers' Scheme for Freedom." Underneath : " Two famous Speeches and some Comments." The make-up was unusually attractive, with an artistic cover design.

He had been examining the contents.

First came the verbatim of the dead man's " Plea for Freedom " and " Christianity, the Enemy of Freedom," delivered at the Queen's Hall last year ; then fifty pages of " Comments."

The latter, he had discovered, were no less than a scientifically veiled appeal to the baser passions of man, emphasizing and expanding the worst side of Julian Verrers' proposals. The intention of it was plain. It had been issued to reach the public before the memory of the man faded. It was also a challenge to all the work he himself had been doing for the last nine months.

He had come in to find it waiting for him with the afternoon's post. A note enclosed was signed : " Some-

one who once met you." It contained a few lines to the
effect that the sender would call next morning to see him,
if he could spare a few minutes ; would he look at the
contents of the pamphlet first. He had done so.

His soul was filled with disgust.

He rose, flung open the windows of his room and
returned to his chair. He picked up the pamphlet again,
and became puzzled. There was no publisher given, or
printer. Neither was there any author's name to the
" Comments." The publication was not for sale then,
in all probability. It was plainly intended for the public,
though.

He re-examined the note enclosed with it. Who was
the sender : " Someone who once met you " ? The
hastily scribbled lines conveyed no more than the un-
satisfying signature.

Their tone suggested friendliness, no more.

That problem would have to wait until to-morrow
morning. The purport of the pamphlet itself required no
explaining, however. It was a malicious attempt to undo
the influence of his own labours during the last year.
Julian Verrers' death, so he had imagined, had released
him from his task. He had succeeded in countering,
more or less effectively, the influence of the man's seductive appeal. His own incessant lecturing and writing had
met with a response far exceeding his anticipations. With
the man's end he had concluded his work was done.
Already he had written to the Abbot of Issano to this
effect. The reply had come that he was to return to his
monastery at the end of March. A week more was left.
And now . . .

As if from the grave this taunt had been flung. A few
pages of printed matter, the " Comments " of a satanic
genius, someone who had followed closely his own appeal
to the moral sense of a nation, and who now held up that

appeal to carefully veiled derision. There was no attempt at reasoned argument. The writer was relying solely on the psychological force of his " Comments," on the suggestion which ran throughout them, and was summed up on the last page :

" In the long run human passion must prevail. No matter what arguments may be produced for Christian morality, no matter what conventions and taboos society may decree, in the end the imperious claims of instinct must have ascendancy. Instinct demands release and will find it, howsoever you may endeavour to chain it down. You cannot appoint to sexual urgency fixed channels. You cannot say to it : ' Thus far and no further.' It recognizes no law, save that of satisfaction. It desires, and its desires must be fulfilled. When satisfied it rests. When rested it resumes its wander-lust.

" Those are the facts, and against them men are power-less. The world will move on, irresistibly impelled, and claim the reign of freedom awaiting human love.

" Julian Verrers is dead. His work will live."

At eleven o'clock next morning a lay-brother announced someone waiting downstairs.

" Man or woman ? " asked Brother Anselm.

" A man."

" I'll see him up here."

He was shown in a minute later, a middle-aged man.

" Sit down," said the monk. He scrutinized his visitor without moving from his chair. His appearance suggested friendliness. The eyes were kindly. There was a peculiar pathos about the face, heavily lined beneath a crown of prematurely snow-white hair.

" Where have I seen you before ? " asked Brother Anselm.

"You reconciled me to the Church, about five years ago," the other replied.

The monk raised his eyebrows, as it came back to his memory. This was the man who had once been a member of the organization to which Julian Verrers had belonged.

"Yes, I remember you now, very well. It was at Issano."

He could recall it all—the man telling him what he had done, and what he had been. The horror of realization had driven him from the organization's headquarters in Paris. He had come to the solitudes of the Alps well-nigh demented with remorse, as with the brand of Cain upon him. Staying at Issano he had one day found his way to the monastery. He remembered the man's awful introduction of himself: "I am a murderer of Christ," the little golden disc he had shown him in proof of what he said, the things he had heard from his lips. He had stayed at the monastery for a month. He had been reconciled, come back to the Sacraments and then left, his soul at peace with God.

"Yes, I do remember you, indeed. Tell me about yourself. What have you been doing since then?"

The man told him. He had been in London, earning his living quietly as a bank clerk, and practising his religion. There had been no attempt on the part of his former associates to trace him, as far as he knew, until by an impetuous act of his own he had betrayed himself.

He had been present at the Queen's Hall on the night of Julian Verrers' second meeting there, and in a moment of uncontrollable fury had shouted at him. Others in the hall had supported him and the proceedings had terminated in disorder.

"So you were the disturber," the monk remarked. "I was listening-in and heard it all. That shout was very informing."

"Of what?" asked the other.

" That Julian Verrers was an apostate Catholic. You called him a Judas."

The man nodded. He went on. His impulsive action had nearly been his undoing. Whether Julian Verrers had recognized his voice as that of a former associate in his work *Contra Fidem et Ecclesiam*, he did not know. What he did know was that Verrers had afterwards discovered his name and address and revealed his whereabouts to the society's headquarters. Only by changing his abode three times had he succeeded in losing himself once more.

At the end of the narration the man said :

" May I ask you something ? "

" Go on," replied the monk.

" What really happened to Verrers ? I only know what was in the papers. I was as puzzled as the rest of the public. You were in the affair, Father, weren't you ? "

" Julian Verrers met his death accidentally," replied the monk shortly.

" It got about that he was making an attempt on your life."

" I know. And I wrote to the papers stating that the notion was utterly false."

" Yes ? "

" Julian Verrers would in no case have attempted my life. I was once able to do something for him which he never forgot."

The man looked surprised.

" I am not going to tell you what it was. But it held him back from ever attacking me personally, even on the platform ; and, most certainly, from attempting my life at Hendringham that night. That gratitude of his, for it was that, was the one spark of honour left in him. And he preserved that spark of honour to the end."

The man stroked the nape of his neck.

" I'm glad you've told me that."

He asked no more ; but he was still curious. He was looking at the monk's right hand resting on his knee.

" No," its owner replied to the unspoken question. " That was accidental, too." He glanced carelessly at the stump of his middle finger. " I'm sorry, but I'm not at liberty to say more. Now——"

He picked up from his desk the pamphlet which he had received the day before. " Why did you send me this ? "

The other's expression changed. He was alert suddenly.

" You've read it, Father ? "

" I have."

" Can you guess why I sent it to you ? "

" I imagine because of what it contains."

" Certainly. Do you know anything about it, though ? "

" I can see it's the work of someone who hates Christianity, and incidentally myself ; also that it is diabolically subtle. And it is certainly one of the most loathsome productions I've ever come across. Beyond that I am in the dark."

The man rested his arm on the monk's desk.

" It was handed to me by a clerk in the bank where I work, who happens to have a dislike of religion. I asked him where he had picked it up. He said it had been sent him ; he didn't know from whom. He had read it with gusto ; it was a welcome publication and he hoped I should enjoy it too. I flung it away ; but picked it up afterwards when he was out. I read it through the same evening, and discovered what I am going to tell you. It was the " Comments " that gave me a clue to its origin. They are written, as I daresay you've noticed, in a peculiarly flowing style. It swings almost into metre at times. There's a touch of the pedantic in the phrasing. There are expressions here and there that only a Frenchman would use. I was struck by the style at once, for the simple reason that it was familiar to me ; as familiar as its author. The man who wrote those " Comments " is a member of the *Contra Fidem et Ecclesiam* organization. He and Julian Verrers worked together for a time in France ; in fact before Verrers came to England."

The man glanced up to note the effect of it upon the monk.

" Go on," said Brother Anselm. " You still follow the movements of these people, then ? "

" It's not difficult—when one has been with them."

The white head lowered.

" One learns things inside ; for instance, that out of fifty men one may be incautious, especially if he is beginning to sicken of the work. The one I am thinking of is decidedly incautious. He talks. It's because he talks that I can tell you still more about that pamphlet."

Brother Anselm leaned forward with his elbows on his knees. " Yes ? "

" I have learned, first, that I was right about the authorship ; secondly, that the author himself was in England soon after Verrers' death. He came over with the purpose of taking Verrers' place and lecturing in public. Although he is a Frenchman he talks perfect English, just as he writes it. He found feeling too high, though, to risk it—that suspicion about Verrers. He also found that you had a public hearing far beyond what he had imagined. He decided to adopt another means of influencing the public. The other means is that pamphlet."

Brother Anselm took it up again and opened it at the inside title-page.

" Apparently it is not for sale, although it is written for the public. Why's that ? " he asked.

" I should say because he wants to make certain of it reaching people widely, and to put it on sale would be a doubtful proposition, as regards results. What I do know is that he has chosen to circularize instead of sell it. It is to be circularized in a big way, too. He will work through agents in various parts of England. The expense will be heavy, but their funds will meet it easily."

" How many have been printed so far ? " asked Brother Anselm.

" I don't know. It is to be three million altogether."

The monk gave a low whistle.

" He expects to send through the post three million copies ultimately, to selected addresses. He has begun already."

Brother Anselm moved restlessly.

" So that is what you've come to tell me ? "

" Yes."

" With the idea that I should do something in the matter ? "

The monk looked keenly at him.

" Are you quite sure of all this ? Remember I've no means of corroborating what you say. I've nothing but your word. I'm not distrusting you, but I must be certain that your information is absolutely accurate."

" My dear Father, it's because I'm quite sure of these facts that I'm here. I shouldn't have come to you other-wise."

" Quite so. But I've to be very cautious before I do anything. I don't 'doubt your word for a moment ; but I do know that inaccurate information can leak out, as well as accurate. You see, unless it's to be the sort of campaign you believe, it would be wiser to ignore it altogether."

The man moved his chair forward.

" You don't doubt my word, then ? "

" I do not."

" Will you believe my word for this ? "

" I will."

" Well, I wanted to confirm the information. I went as far as ascertaining for myself whether this immense number of copies was actually to be printed. It was not very difficult to discover the printing firm. Neither was it very difficult to find someone to show me over it. I examined the machinery with great interest, especially the press through which I saw a likely sheet being poured out. A man was stacking up these sheets at the side. I picked up one casually. It was this pamphlet. I remarked to the man that there couldn't be much of a sale for this sort of stuff. He said he didn't know about the sale, but it was the biggest order they had ever had—three million copies. There seemed to be no secret about it, as far as he was concerned."

The monk rose and began to walk about the room. He put a picture straight on the wall, and kicked a coal into position on the fire. Then he stood still with his back to it, regarding the floor. . . .

"Yes, that settles it. Thank you."

CHAPTER XIX

" AND now . . ."
 Beauty pulled out the sliding leaf of her escritoire
and settled herself. From a pigeon-hole she took a
sheet of notepaper, and from the inkstand a fountain-pen.
She stroked the nib upon her blotting-pad. Then she
rested her cheek upon her hand.

She had waited ten weeks for this moment. From the
day early in January when she had left Hendringham
after Eric's funeral until now, nearly the end of March,
she had neither seen nor heard from Basil. At Eric's
graveside in the little Catholic plot at Windern they had
stood together. At the difficult luncheon afterwards they
had sat side by side. Then their good-bye. The mourners
lingering or hurrying off had allowed of no privacy,
mercifully easing the cruel moment. It had just been,
" Good-bye, Beauty," and " Good-bye, Basil," as the
car taking her to the station moved off. For a moment
the impulse to speak had striven powerfully with her
resolve to say nothing yet. " Basil, wait ! It's going to
come all right ! " had leaped to her lips. She had stifled
it, though. Instead, their eyes had met for one fleeting
instant, the dumb agony of her going, as well as over
Eric, in his ; yet steady resolution too.
 And she had been right, she knew.
 The thing had to be done first. Kneeling at Eric's
death-bed the decision had been made ; never should she
appear in Basil's eyes as if bartering promises to retain
his love. That decision she had kept to.
 And now the thing had been done, that Basil had longed
for, and Brother Anselm, too.

A month ago, one Saturday afternoon, she had knelt amongst the penitents at the Oratory waiting for her turn. When it had come the priest had been surprisingly gentle. She had left the confessional trembling with a new happiness and knelt before the Tabernacle. Next morning she had made her Communion. At the flat, afterwards, she had cried out her joy in faithful Marie's arms. And Marie, devout from childhood, had understood and been immensely happy, too.

Freedom.

Eric had been so utterly right. She had found that out at once. " Dear God, tell Eric," she had prayed last night, after four weeks of experience ; of her soul's opening out to the radiance of Divine love. One by one the chains of earth had snapped, giving release into the supernatural world.

" And may I tell Basil now ? " she had added.

For she had waited to test her motives ; hungry all the while to let him know. " Come back for *my* sake ? God forbid ! " he had exclaimed that night at the Savoy. She had been afraid lest it should be that, merely to hold him. All through the hard weeks following their good-bye she had crushed down the thought of herself and their love. Day by day she had recaptured the vision of Eric's showing, the eternal things he had unveiled to her on that last day of his life. Not until she had been able to kneel and say : " For Thy sake, not Basil's," her lips upon the crucifix she had tried to break, had the assurance of her own sincerity come.

Eric had been so utterly right.

With the initial act of self-surrender her faith had sprung to life, like a fire from smouldering embers, snatching the trumperies of the past from her grasp burning them to ashes in its blaze.

So utterly right.

Her experience had confirmed his own. Like the dawning of the morning on a mountain's golden height, the splendour of the Unseen had burst through the shadows of the seen. Dazzled, humbled, wondering before the immensity of it all, she had crept back—a little child.

Freedom.

Step by step she had found her way to the road along which it lay. She could look back now and see the false turns from which she had been driven. She had sought her liberty in unbelief, Julian Verrers' way, and found, instead, licence stalking naked and unashamed. She had immersed herself in the world; its mad, hectic pleasures had allured her with their tinselly glamour, but never satisfied. She had met Basil and been given his great love; her own had gone forth to his. Like a dividing sword her self-interests had clashed between them. Blindly she had refused the sacrifice of them, until in one short hour Eric had stripped her self-love bare.

His act for Basil, costing his life; that supreme renunciation for the brother he loved had completed it.

From that moment of understanding she had gone forward.

It had not been easy. It had meant a steady, deliberate renunciation of the past; of friends whose ways could no longer be hers, Mrs. Sands-Woodford first. Each in turn had thought her mad. It was impossible to make them understand. Their pagan outlook, their morals, their whole environment sealed their eyes to all that was not of this world.

The renunciation, too, of many pleasures. Of the very doubtful things ticketed under " experience." The ceaseless round of self-enjoyment labelled " life." These things were utterly incompatible with the supernatural life of the Faith.

For ten weeks she had tested herself, the time she had decided upon before letting Basil know. She had wanted to reserve the news for Brother Anselm as a great surprise.

She had written to him once asking after his hand, adding a postscript : " Pray for me." He had replied that there was a little less of him than before, that was all ; and that he remembered her at Mass every day. She had wondered if he had guessed anything.

The ten weeks were up.   And the moment had come.

She began to write :

" BASIL,—Would you like me to tell you something ?

" Do you remember that night at the Savoy ? What you asked of me ? Well, I've done it.

" I've waited before telling you.   I wanted to do it first. And I wanted to do it in the way you spoke of. You said it would have to be done for God, not for you. And it *has* been done for God ; that I can honestly say.

" Oh, Basil, it's all very wonderful. It was Eric who made me see. I *did* talk to him, though I don't think you ever knew. It was just before the thing happened that night. I'm going to tell you everything when we meet. We can meet now, can't we ?

" I want to talk about Eric, too. Oh, my dear, you're aching over him still, I know. But how glorious it was ! I think of it like that, always.

" Basil, if you knew how utterly glad I am that you refused to give in ! I mean, to insist on my coming back first. Our love could never have been——"

The sharp whirr of the telephone-bell interrupted her. She laid down her pen, and went out into the hall to answer the call, glancing at the clock on the way and wondering who could be ringing her up at six in the evening.

" Hullo ? "

" Is Miss Dethier in ? " came from the other end.

" Speaking," she replied. " Yes ? Who is it ? "

There was a pause.

" Basil. I say, Beauty—sorry to be so sudden, but—— "

" Basil ! "

" Yes, it really is. Hope I haven't frightened you. I say, will you be in if I come straight along ? "

" But—— Where are you ? Where are you speaking from ? "

" Knightsbridge. I could be at Curzon Street in twenty minutes."

" But, Basil ! . . . Why, has something happened ? "

Another pause.

" You don't mind my coming along, do you ? "

" No. Oh no, of course not ; only—— "

" Right. I'll come now."

She stood there regarding the mouthpiece in a dazed way, and then slowly hung up the receiver. She went back into the library and sat down, staring vaguely, trembling.

What on earth could it be ? Basil ?

She had scarcely recognized the strained, feverish tones. What was he coming for ? Her eye caught the unfinished letter to him lying on her escritoire. She went and placed it with shaking fingers inside the blotting-case.

What did it mean ? . . .

His ring startled her when it came, though she had been waiting for what seemed an eternity. She glanced at the mirror, trying to keep calm. The door opened and Marie announced him. She came forward slowly. He was standing before her. The door clicked to behind him.

" Basil ! "

They did not shake hands, but stood taking each other in.
He looked strange.

" Take your coat off, won't you ? " She strove to be
natural. " Come and sit down."

He took off his coat without speaking, flung it on a
chair and then came across the room in a quick, fierce
way. She moved back slightly. He remained where he
was, watching her. There was a fever in his eyes.

" Basil, what's the matter ? Why have you come ? "
she managed to say at last.   " Won't you sit down ? "

He ignored the invitation.

" You know why I've come. You must know," broke
quiveringly from his lips. " Beauty, I can't stand it any
longer ! "

She understood quickly, then.

There was no mistaking his look, the hunger in it,
the air almost of guilt. His working features told her
everything.

He had given in. He had given in at the very moment
when . . .

" You're upset, Basil," she heard herself say. " It's no
good talking till you're calm. Now look here, my dear,
sit down ! "

He obeyed in a sort of mechanical way, his eyes still
upon her.

" Cigarette ? Here you are."

She found matches and struck one for him. He put the
cigarette to his lips, and she lit it. Then she chose one
for herself, slowly. She wanted time. She let the match
out and struck another, unhurriedly, thinking rapidly all
the while. She lit her own cigarette, watched it glowing,
and then threw the match on the fire. Her quiet deliberate-
ness steadied him.

She sat down in her leather arm-chair opposite after
pushing it further away, and inhaled, intimating that he
was not to speak until she was ready. It gave her time for

what she wanted—to gain possession of herself for what was coming.

" Now. Tell me quietly."

He began jerkily, but his voice became more controlled as he proceeded. He told it all without once looking directly at her. He told her this.

For the first few weeks after their good-bye he had succeeded in steeling himself to the loss of her. He had absorbed himself in the work of the estate at Hendringham and tried to forget. Eric's death, too, had stunned him into a kind of insensibility to things. As the first shock of it began to wear off, however, a terrible loneliness had crept in ; he had lost the two people in the world whom he loved above all others—Eric and herself. He had struggled on, resolute to keep to his decision at whatever cost to himself.

Last evening a climax had come.

Nearly three months had gone and she had given him no sign of doing what he had hoped for. He had taken down her photograph from its place on his mantelpiece with the intention of destroying it. He had gone as far as taking it from its frame.

Then, all in a moment, it had happened.

His love for her had surged up, overwhelming him with the force of a torrent, sweeping everything before it, except that life without her was more than he could bear. All night long he had lain awake, arguing, reasoning with himself. By the morning he had made up his mind. In the afternoon he had driven up to town. " Beauty, do you see why I've come ? I've tried to do without you, and I can't ! "

Before she could stop him he was on his knee before her, gripping her hands, trying to draw her to him. . . .

" No, Basil ! No ! " She disengaged her hands, half-pushing him away. He stood up, flushed and breathing quickly.

" Why not ? " he cried. " What's to stop us now ? "

She stood up too, facing him, understanding only one thing—that it would require all her strength to resist. One moment of weakness and, at her own hands, his ideals would be shattered to the dust. Instinctively, while he was talking, she had perceived that this was not the real Basil ; it was a Basil who had failed in a moment of despair. If she yielded while he believed that she was still an apostate from the Faith, she would be an accessory to his surrender ; nothing could come of their love, he had declared, until she returned.

" What's to stop us ? Don't you see ? Beauty, can't you see ? I want you to marry me."

" You said you could never marry an apostate," she replied.

" I've altered my mind. I've come round to your view."

" And I've altered my mind and come round to yours." He started. " I don't think a Catholic should marry an apostate. I've changed my opinion."

" Why ? "

" Never mind. I have." She added firmly : " You have not ' come round.' You've just been making a shame-faced apology for acting against your own strongest conviction."

It stung him.

Then a sudden, engrossing fear expelled all else. He came close.

" You don't love me. Is that it ? "

" I love you so dearly that I would rather die than dishonour you," she answered.

It banished the horrible doubt from his eyes ; but brought puzzlement.

" Dishonour me ? "

" Yes. It would be dishonouring if I took advantage of you like this. Would you respect me if I did ? "

He drew back slowly.

Deftly she had made him understand. She was taking

the onus of his honour upon herself, giving him a chance to retrieve his surrender.

He dropped into his chair, staring unheedingly at the window. She remained standing there, acutely sensitive to the anguish of the struggle. The strange reversal of their position struck her. He had been adamant once. It was her turn now. She saw the curly head lowering.

" Basil, be brave ! Be yourself ! " She went and laid her hand upon his shoulder. At her touch he sprang up. " I'm to kill my love for you ! "

The cry was a sword of agony piercing her own heart. With one word she could tell him everything, show him the letter she had just been writing. But his action had sealed her lips, tied her hands. He must not know ; he must never know, until he had once more renounced her —an apostate from the Faith, as he thought her still to be.

" I can't do it ! Beauty, for God's sake——"

" I'm not asking you to kill your love," she intercepted him.

" You are ! What else can I do ? "

She did not reply. There was only one answer : " Wait." She could not give it without hinting at the truth about herself. An inkling of it might bribe him back to his principles ; and there must be no bribing back. He must do it unaided by any ulterior motive.

She must act quickly.

It would be cruel to herself. It would be agony for him. But it had to be done. Suddenly she was weak and shaking. The strain was becoming almost unendurable. She steadied herself, her hand on the edge of the table.

" Basil, do you love me ? "

" My God, you know I do."

" Will you do what I am going to ask ? Will you trust me ? "

He hesitated, frightened.

" Will you, Basil ? "

" I'll try."

It was not enough.

" Will you ? " (" Dear God, please help.")

She steeled herself against the mute appeal in his eyes, knowing well that, for him, the death-warrant of their love was being signed.

" Very well, I will," came in a hoarse whisper. " What do you want ? "

" Do this," she answered quickly. " Leave me now. Then write and tell me that you will never marry an apostate."

He was still . . .

Then he stood up heavily, moved in an unseeing way to where his coat was lying across a chair, and picked it up. The face that he turned to her was haggard, piteous.

She was aware that he was still waiting. She closed her eyes, pressing her hands over them.

He was still waiting. . . .

" Go, Basil, go ! . . . Basil, for pity's sake . . ."

He fumbled for the door.

CHAPTER XX

§ 1

SHE had doubted whether he would understand Whether a monk could understand the pain of a woman's love.

She doubted no longer.

She had told him everything—the talk with Eric, the effect of it and of his death upon her, the return to the Sacraments. He had guessed it immediately, as soon as he saw her standing there in the plain little waiting-room. "*Deo gratias!*"

His gladness first. Then compassion for what had happened to Basil and herself. She had told him that next, hiding nothing. He had listened, without comment, until the end. Then into the grey eyes had come the " tremendous tenderness," reflecting her pain as if it were his own.

" My poor child ! "

After a while she looked up.

" Was I right ? Oh, Brother Anselm, was I right ? "

" Absolutely," he replied. " You were very splendid, Beauty."

It was the first time he had called her " Beauty."

" It was like sending him to his death. Was that splendid ? "

" You martyred yourself to do it," he said.

She studied the floor.

" It's Basil I'm thinking of. I'm frightened about him. It's nearly a week now and he's not written."

" You needn't be afraid for him."

" Why ? Why are you smiling ? "

" Basil's not going to do anything desperate," he remarked.

She became curious.

" Have you heard from him ? "

" I was at Hendringham last night. I went down to say good-bye to them. He——"

" You've seen him, then ! "

" I have. I had a talk with Basil."

" Oh, tell me ! Is he all right ? "

" He's very humble about last week ; and quite calm again. At present he's being very hard upon himself, almost too hard."

" Then he *is* all right ? He sees it ? "

" He sees that you acted solely for his sake. Naturally nothing else would occur to him ; he has no notion of what you have done. Neither had I at the time."

" No. Of course not."

" He was wrong ; he is convinced of that now."

" Yes ? "

Brother Anselm considered again.

" You want to know what he said ? "

" Please."

" Remember what he still thinks about you. He said : ' Beauty is right. It means good-bye.' "

She paled ; but controlled herself.

" But you assumed he would take it that way ? " suggested the monk.

" Until I let him know. Yes, that was the horrible part."

Brother Anselm waited.

" I told him to write. Did he say he was going to ? "

" He said you had asked him."

Anxiety appeared. Then fear.

" But he will, won't he ? "

" He will write sometime, you may be certain."

" But why not now ? " she urged.   " Brother Anselm, what is it ? You know something."

She was frightened.

" I wish I could say I did know," he replied.   " There's something on his mind, and I can't quite make out what. I asked him to tell me, and he said : ' Not yet.' "

With an effort she mastered herself.

" Is it anything to do with me ? With the future ? "

" From his reply I should say it is to do with his future movements. If so, I suppose it would concern you."

She said nothing, but sat silent.

" I shouldn't have told you, perhaps," he said, half to himself.

She looked up.

" Why shouldn't I write to him myself ? I could now, surely ? "

Brother Anselm did not reply.

" What do you think ? "

" I'd sooner leave it to you. I might advise wrongly."

" Would you, if you were in my place ? "

" Quite honestly, no, I shouldn't. You see, you left it to him to take the next step."

" But it would put things right at once," she persisted.

Again he did not reply.

There was an engrossment about him. A look as if a light were slowly shedding itself upon a problem in his mind.

" Wouldn't it ? "

" I'm not sure. It depends on what—— Beauty, will you trust me ? "

It was a hint as well as a request. She was not to press him further. Her lips began quivering. . . .

" Will you trust me with Basil ? " he asked.

She looked up and found the monk's gaze fixed intently upon her. There was a quiet assurance in the grey eyes that brought her strength, a wisdom in them deeper than her own.

His chin was resting on his right hand. She saw the gap, and the stump of his middle finger.—And remembered.

"I love you both. You know that," he said simply.

She rose and stood before him, her eyes brimming. Then, in silence, took the big, rough hand away from his face and drew it to her lips. . . .

"Will you trust me with Basil ? "

She touched the stump.

"Yes, dear monk. I will."

§ 2

It was four o'clock as she entered the gates of Regent's Park on her way back.

Before she had left, Brother Anselm had told her that he was starting for Issano in two days' time. It had come as a blow. She had not realized it was to be so soon. He had given her the monastery address ; she was to write whenever she liked. Basil, she had learned, was writing to him after his return.

The good-bye had been sad.

She walked through the gardens, noticing little, deaf to the call of spring and the songs of birds. Still absorbed, she crossed Marylebone. Gaining the pavement on the further side, however, a row of newspaper placards against the railings caught her eye.—" Attack on immorality," " Licentious scheme exposed," " Famous public speaker hits out," were blazoned forth in turn.

She walked down Portland Place. Passing the Queen's Hall she stopped for a moment, a flood of memories surging up. A night nine months ago—Basil and herself standing in the entrance there, Brother Anselm coming out to meet the vast crowd's roar, his car moving slowly through the sea of heads. Basil had taken her back afterwards. It was the night their love had been born.

At Oxford Circus she noticed the same placards as

before, booming at the stream of passers-by. At the head of one was " Father —— " The sheet had curled up in the wind, obscuring the rest. Turning down Bond Street the same paper greeted her at the corner opposite. This time it brought her to a standstill.

" Father Thornton and grave public danger."

She was awake now, and thrilled. She crossed over quickly and bought a copy. The wind wrestled with her efforts to open the leaves. Refolding it she walked on and found harbour at Gunter's. Inside she ordered tea and then spread the paper out. Her search was brief. Across the top of the centre page a bold headline proclaimed : " Stirring appeal by Father Thornton." Beneath came a short paragraph in italics : " *Father Thornton, the Roman Catholic priest whose opposition to the late Julian Verrers aroused such public interest, has requested us, in common with a section of the Press, to publish the following letter. In view of its nature we have decided to do so. Readers will understand, however, that its publication in no way commits this paper. Our own comments on the matter will be found elsewhere.*—ED."

The letter itself, occupying a good part of the page, followed.

Beauty began to read.

" Sir,—During the course of the last year it has been my privilege to address the English public, by speech and in print, on certain moral questions connected with the proposals of the late Mr. Julian Verrers. May I be allowed in your columns to address them once more, perhaps for the last time ?

" With the death of Mr. Verrers I had hoped for the death of that for which he stood. I find, however, that a further attempt is now being made upon the moral sense of the public. I refer to a certain publication at present being circulated far and wide and, doubtless, read by thousands. It contains the two speeches made by Mr.

Verrers at the Queen's Hall last year, and also some
' Comments.' Since these ' Comments ' include a
peculiarly distasteful and misleading reference to my own
efforts in defence of Christian morality, I am compelled,
though unwillingly, to make some sort of reply.

" For the sake of those who are in ignorance of the
fact, may I first state that this publication and its dis-
tribution are the work of an organization whose existence
is nominally unknown, its *raison d'être* being the exter-
mination of Christianity and its method the destruction
of morality. The author himself is not an Englishman,
as might be imagined, but an apostate French Catholic—
a member of a group who, exotic though it may appear
to the English mind, are banded together under the
watchword : ' *Contra Fidem et Ecclesiam.*'

" As regards the publication itself, it is not my intention here to say anything in answer to the first part, *i.e.*
the two speeches of Mr. Verrers ; since my own reply to
them, given at the Queen's Hall last year, will shortly
appear in print.

" The ' Comments,' however, which comprise the
second part, call for immediate attention, if the appeal
which I make in this letter is to be effective.

" For the author's references to myself I have nothing
but contempt. He expresses ' admiration for the sincerity ' with which I plead my cause, ' appreciation for the
ability ' with which I conduct my arguments, and ' regard
for the simple candour ' of my speech. Lest any should
be misled, may I assure them that the purpose of this
apparent generosity is to produce an impression of im-
partiality on the minds of his readers, that it is introduced
calculatingly as the surest means of obtaining a hearing
from those I may have influenced, that the author's smooth
utterances throughout are the carefully chosen weapons of
an opponent who dare not openly attack. This man hates
passionately everything for which I stand.

" Neither let any be misled by the seemingly dispassionate line he takes to establish his thesis. This man loathes morality, but believes that his strength lies in concealing the fact.

" To ensure——"

Beauty moved the paper from the table, disturbed by a waitress with her tea. She laid it down, filled her cup and began to sip.

" That's damned fine ! "

The exclamation caused her to glance sideways. It had obviously been uttered by the man at the next table, who was in the act of folding an evening paper, embarrassed at having expressed himself aloud. He smiled apologetically as their eyes met. She recognized his paper and was inspired to dispense with conventions.

" You've been reading Father Thornton's letter, haven't you ? " she asked.

He had. And forthwith unburdened himself on the subject.

As she listened she found herself wondering how many thousands reading it to-night would be affected with a similar enthusiasm. " Will it do good ? " she asked as he slowed down. " I haven't read it all yet." The man helped himself to a cake. " It will go home," he answered. " He knows his public and doesn't pander to them. That's why he gets there. Have you heard Father Thornton ? "

She replied that she had.

" Do you like him ? "

" I do, very much," she answered. " Do you ? "

The man swallowed.

" I heard him at the Queen's Hall last year and went away cursing every word he'd said. I——" He hesitated doubtfully.

" Yes ? " she encouraged him.

" I was going to try for a divorce a week later, one of the stumped-up kind. And—well, I didn't. The case was withdrawn. Do you see ? My God, he went home ! "

The simple statement bore witness to the monk's power. It left her wondering. How many did he influence like this ?

In the library, after her return, she settled down to the rest of the letter, her table strewn with evening papers, all of which gave it the same prominence. It was the big thing of the day, as the leaders, most of them favourable, testified. She glanced at these hurriedly first. He certainly had the Press with him, as she was able to discover more evidently next morning, although it was the pragmatic rather than religious standpoint from which it judged his appeal.

She resumed from where " That's damned fine ! " had interrupted her at Gunter's—

" To ensure the reading of his ' Comments ' by the public, the author attaches them to the speeches of Mr. Verrers, to which they are but loosely related. He sees also an advantage in doing so. In contrast with the more provocative manner of Mr. Verrers his own milder tone will reassure. To put the unwary on their guard, may I aver that these ' Comments ' are all the more dangerous for the very way in which they are couched. Their subtle, insinuating *motif*, at first a suggestion, then a presumption, and finally a dogmatic statement of man's inability to control his passions, is carefully chosen to deaden the protest of the reader's higher faculties. The author knows well the value of the psychological factor ; the value of sounding one note, one idea, of repeating it, of steadily and increasingly insisting upon it, until it dominates the mind ; he emphasizes the passions of the body until they assume the appearance of irresistibly ruling man's whole being.

" The whole content of the ' Comments ' is the pressure of one idea—the futility of conscience, will, or moral law in face of the ' urgency of sex-instinct ' ; man is ' impelled by his nature beyond the bounds laid down by moralists, whether he will or no ' ; he is the ' victim of desire ' ; there can be ' no fixed channels for instinct, as is being slowly realized ' ; the ' removal of taboos ' is but a matter of time ; Christendom is powerless to stave off ' the coming reign of freedom awaiting human love.'

" Very good.

" Beyond the remark that ' moral laws cannot restrain, since, plainly, they are for ever being broken,' the author makes no attempt to offer any proof for his thesis. Relying on reiteration, his statements and ' facts,' all to the same effect, follow one another in endless array, producing an impression of overwhelming might before which morality must quail.

" What kind of answer shall I give ?

" A very simple one. It is this.

" These ' Comments ' constitute what is no less and no more than a clever and malicious piece of jugglery ; fifty pages of careful deception, of suppressed truth, of half-truth, and untruth.

" Shall I instance ?

" It is a suppression of truth to state that ' moral laws cannot restrain, since, plainly, they are for ever being broken,' whereas it is a truth to state that ' moral laws *can* restrain, since, plainly, they are being kept, as well as broken.' It is a half-truth to state that man is a ' victim of desire,' whereas it is a truth to state that ' some men are victims of disordered desire.' It is an untruth to state that ' man is impelled by his nature beyond the bounds laid down by moralists, whether he will or no,' whereas it is a truth to state that ' man is *not* impelled by his nature beyond the bounds laid down by moralists, unless his will is depraved.' Instances could be multiplied to show that ninety per cent. of the author's statements fall under these three categories.

" Do I make myself clear ?

" The ' Comments ' are a consummate attempt to capture the mind with a cataract of false ' facts ' ; to sweep away scruples with the suggestive and seductive notion that man is irresponsible, because unable, where his passions are concerned ; to strike conscience, free-will and moral law with poisoned arrows from behind. I say ' consummate attempt ' because the author hopes to circulate three million copies of the same. I say ' from behind ' because his method is to circulate, not sell.

" You, who have followed me so far, will expect some kind of refutation of his ' facts,' or rather ' fact ' ; for the whole may be reduced to one assumption—man's powerlessness to control himself. What sort of refutation do you expect ? An array of statements to counter his own ?

" No. One answer is enough to refute his fifty pages.

" And I would prefer that answer to come from you—the thousands to whom he is supplying his ' Comments'; you whom he would degrade to their level. In addition, I should expect that, if law can forbid expectoration, it would also forbid the vomiting of poisonous filth into your homes. This is not the first case of its kind.

" The answer ?

" It will be yours to these questions :

" Is there anyone among you, not sunk in lust, who would admit, ' My body is the master of my soul ' ? Is there any among you, not a coward, who would declare, ' I cannot keep the moral law ' ? Any, not a liar at heart, who believes ' man's passions must prevail ' ? Any, not an ignoramus, who would deny that men can control themselves, and do ? Any libertine, not an irresponsible, who could honestly avow, ' I cannot help myself,' or, not perjuring his soul, would kneel and say, ' You made me thus, O God ' ? Any Christian, not a hypocrite, who would deny the power of grace to conquer human frailty ?

" I will ask this of you, too :

" Is there a single husband, worthy of the name, who

would hand these ' Comments ' to his wife ; a single wife, worthy of the name, to her husband ? Is there a single father, not a contemptible cad, who would give them to his daughter ; a single mother, not lost to all shame and honour, to her son ? Is there a decent man or woman who will not destroy, or cast them on the fire ?

" The answer lies with you.

" With you, too, it lies to answer their concluding challenge : ' Julian Verrers is dead. His work will live ! '

" Do not look too lightly on that boast. The England of to-day is not the England I once knew. Will you deny the licence that is stalking in your midst ? The censored sensuality in your shows ? The cult of the unclean, the nude, the foul in what you see and read ? The divorces streaming through your courts ? And facilities ahead for more ? The exhibits in the windows of your shops ? The things your children learn ? The paganism now shadowing this nation's soul ?

" Do not laugh too lightly at that challenge.

" Julian Verrers' scheme was but to extend that which you tolerate now. The soil was here for his seed ; it is here still for its growth.

" ' His work will live ! ' Will that proud boast be proved—or shattered ?

" The answer lies with you.

                    " ANSELM THORNTON "

§ 3

It was the middle of April when Basil's letter came.

Three weeks she had waited. And then one morning it was lying with the others on her breakfast-table.

Yes. It was from Basil.

She began her breakfast. Once she glanced at it and then went on eating again. Half-way through she remembered to help herself to coffee. She drank it. Then, abruptly, left the meal unfinished. Gathering up the letters she crossed herself and went into her library.

Even now she did not open it, but laid it on her escritoire and began to read the others, forcing her attention to their contents. Then she placed these inside her writing-case and——

Her heart was thumping as she picked it up. Her fingers hesitated. " Don't be a fool ! " She looked at the writing of the address and the Esterton arms on the back. The colour left her face as she began to tear . . .

She sat there motionless.

The letter had fallen. It lay on the writing-case, straightened out as she had read it. After a while she passed her hand over her eyes in a dazed way. She noticed the letter where it had dropped. She took it up and read it a second time :

" DEAR BEAUTY,—I must apologize for not writing sooner. This letter will explain why I have delayed.

" First of all, I want to say how sorry I am that I turned up at the flat like that. I did it in a moment of weakness, as I know you will understand ; and, I think, did understand at the time. I was wrong, and I am very grateful to you for letting me see it ; because you did. You were wonderful to do it—I mean, to tell me straight that I ought not to ask you to marry me, as things are.

" I had a talk with Brother Anselm when he came down here to say good-bye, and he was very good to me.

" Now, Beauty, this is the thing that has happened.

" I saw that I should have to face things out. There was no chance of anything coming of our love. You said that I should not have to kill my love for you ; but

I don't think you realize. I couldn't go on just loving you and no more. Perhaps a woman can do that kind of thing, but a man can't. I began to see that I should have to face life without you.

"I had foreseen the possibility of this before, and had even thought about what I have now decided on. Ever since I met Brother Anselm, and especially since I became a Catholic, the idea of the religious life has attracted me. When things came to an end between us—for it was that the other day—the desire for the religious life became very strong. I waited for two weeks and then came to a decision, the result of which is that I am to try my vocation in a religious order. More than that I cannot tell you.

"It has been rather a heavy blow to my people ; because it means renouncing everything. I should have inherited, of course. But they are being very good over it.

"Now, Beauty, it *does* mean this—I've got to renounce our love as well. Perhaps love can't be killed, when it's like mine for you. I've just got to forget. There's absolutely nothing else to do.

"I want you to help me forget by not answering this letter. You understand, don't you ? And you understand why I am writing like this ? I simply do not trust myself for more.

"I shall always pray for you, that, somehow, in the end the grace of God will bring you back.

"Good-bye, Beauty.

"BASIL."

Slowly she laid the letter down. Her eyes rested on it for a while. Then she gazed in front of her. . . .

When she moved it was to take a sheet of writing-paper and her pen. She bent over and began to write : " My dearest Basil——" The pen slipped from her fingers. She sprang up. " No, you don't ! " The sheet was torn quickly in two, and crumpled. She did not sit down again, but stood there, motionless once more.

A shudder came.

She looked about vaguely. Her eyes fell on his photograph in its place on the mantelpiece. She went and stood before it. Then returned, picked up his letter again and ran her fingers along the edges uncertainly. She put it down.

Her hands dropped weakly on the desk. She bent her head, closing her eyes.

When at last she sat down, her lips were set.

She searched the row of pigeon-holes in front, found a key and unlocked a drawer to her right. From it she took a packet of letters, untied, and laid them out.

She took up one, and began to tear. Half-way through the sheet her fingers paused. Next moment she was blindly gathering them together, feeling for the drawer....

Then she buried her head in her arms, quivering. . . .

And so she stayed.

CHAPTER XXI

§ 1

H E stopped.
It was his first clear view of the Alps. He had reached Issano last night after dark and had only seen their shapes looming up.

This morning he had started from the hotel to walk, leaving orders for his baggage to follow. For ten minutes it was narrow streets and tall houses ; then a winding, climbing road enclosed in pines, with occasional glimpses of blue sky. After a mile of this the way had suddenly opened out, and they were there—the Alps.

They took his breath away.

All round and above him towered the heights, white sunlit monsters guarding the valleys below. He shaded his eyes to the glitter of their snows, marvelling at the mystery of the glistening peaks, the blue solitudes in which they soared, tremendous and aloof.

He had pictured them as cruel, because of Eric. Passionless was his impression as he watched. Somewhere amidst that vista of cold purity Eric had . . .

He went on.

The road climbed more steeply. On either side were meadows sweeping away to the lower slopes, radiant with Alpine flowers, smiling to the sun ; oxen grazing, white and solemn-eyed, ringing with the melody of their bells. He liked the haunting sound.

" I wonder——" He took a letter out of his pocket and examined it. " Nearly a mile after you leave the pines," he read, " you will find, to the right, a path up the meadows—soon after you get the first view of the monastery." He put it back.

The road became steeper still, a pitch now. The mountains ahead began to sink from view. After a steady climb they were rising again and, quite abruptly, the road flattened out to the level.

" Ah ! "

The monastery !

To the right, half a mile away on the edge of the valley basin, it stood—a grey pile defying the dark bastions of rock behind. The monastery of Issano ! His heart beat quickly.

He studied it, mouth open.

Then he hastened on, looking for the path to the right. It appeared shortly. He took it and was soon mounting steadily between banks of grass and every peeping colour. The monastery grew as he approached, so also his own excitement. He could see its lines now—the buttressed walls of the great church, the long length of the monastery front itself studded with innumerable stone-mullioned windows, crowned with a medley of roofs and chimneys, the whole rising triumphant from its rocky base and perched to the four winds of heaven. In front there appeared to be a stretch of gardens. To the right there were clumps of trees, towards which his path was winding.

He reached them at last, and some roughly-cut steps twisting up amongst the trunks. At the top he found himself on an open space of lawn in their midst, green velvet to his feet after the stony path.

He stood still, entranced by the beauty of the tree-encircled grove, the dancing shades and lights of spring foliage. There were birds on the wing and their songs in the sun, and, near by, a stream tinkling on its downward way. A sense of familiarity about the scene struck him. And then in a flash it came. This was the place Eric had so often described ; the haven of peace where his days up here had been spent.

A moisture gathered in his eyes.

He walked on, blinking it away, across the sward to an

opening in the trees leading from this Paradise. He met no angel guarding the entrance with a fiery sword, but a monk advancing with a shining scythe, who smiled and said : " Well, Basil ? " . . .

" Brother Anselm ! "

The monk unburdened himself of the scythe and laid it down. Basil stared in astonishment.

" My hat ! I—I hardly knew you."

Brother Anselm smiled again.

" But——" Basil stuck. He examined, open-mouthed, the person before him. Except for his habit, Brother Anselm might have been a farm-labourer. Beneath its weather-stained folds appeared a pair of heavy boots caked in earth. His hands were also caked. On his head was a wide-brimmed hat that once had been white straw.

" So you've found us. Come along."

Brother Anselm propped the scythe against a tree trunk.

" You got my letter at the hotel ? "

" Yes. Thanks very much."

The monk led the way down a short avenue. It ended at a wall with an archway cut through. They passed beneath it. On the other side appeared the gardens of the monastery, wide and open to the immense panorama across the valley and the soaring Alps. They passed some monks at work, digging. Basil observed wonderingly. One was wheeling a barrow of manure. They came to some outhouses on the right, then the great walls of the church and, at length, the monastery front itself, Basil wide-eyed all the way.

Brother Anselm led on. Beyond asking a question or two about his journey the monk had said nothing. At the main door half-way he stopped and said : " I have to leave you now. It's the Greater Silence. After *pranzo* we shall have half an hour together."

" But, wh—what——" stammered Basil.

" A brother will let you in, and fetch the guest-master."

said Brother Anselm. He pulled a chain. A bell clanged
cavernously inside. He went off.

Basil looked after his retreating form and then at the
door. It opened. A monk with an impassive face was
motioning him to enter. He did so. He was in a stone-
vaulted hall. A gesture indicated that he was to follow.
They passed down a corridor at the end of which his
guide bowed him into a room and left him. Inside, Basil
drew a long breath and waited.

After three minutes the door opened and another monk,
genial-looking this time, appeared. This would be the
guest-master, Basil concluded, and returned his bow. He
was evidently Italian. He expressed a hope in broken
English that the *signor* had had a " good journ*ee*," and
said he would show him to his *camera*.

Again he was led off.

More stone-vaulted corridors. They came to cloisters,
opening on the inside to a court in the centre of which a
fountain was playing. They crossed it, passing monks
who inclined slightly—to himself, Basil perceived, doing
likewise. They gained the far side and re-entered. More
corridors. He followed up a flight of stone stairs, then, at
the top, down passages pigeon-holed all along with doors,
each marked " *Fra* " somebody.

His *camera*.

The guest-master opened a door and stood aside for
him to enter. He found himself in a small room with
bare walls, a bed, and a table and chair in the centre.
Over the bed was a crucifix. In a corner was his baggage,
already arrived. The guest-master beamed, pointed to a
framed card on the table, announced that *pranzo* was at
twelve o'clock, and that he would come for him five
minutes before the hour, bowed and retired.

Left alone, Basil looked about.

He went to the window ; it faced the gardens and the
valley. He contemplated his baggage ; there was no
chest-of-drawers, only a cupboard in the wall. He

examined the framed card on the table. It was a time-table stating the hours of Masses, Office, and meals.

He began to unpack.

At two minutes to twelve, after another personally conducted tour, he was standing in the cloisters opposite the Refectory door. Outside a bell was issuing its summons.

It ceased as a deeper one thundered out midday.

At the last stroke he saw, across the court, figures moving in single file. They came all round the cloistered way, an interminable line of monks. As they turned the corner towards the Refectory, each in turn placed his fingers under a running tap let into the wall, wiped them on a towel and re-entered the line. They then stood with their backs to the outer court, waiting. Another figure came, walking by himself. The line inclined as he passed. The Abbot! Next moment Basil had dropped on one knee and was kissing the ring on a hand extended to him. He rose self-consciously. The Abbot motioned him towards the Refectory door; then to walk at his side, which he did, down a great hall with pointed roof and tiled floor between lengths of wooden tables with places laid. At the high table on a dais he was placed at the Abbot's right. They stood waiting while the line of monks continued to stream in, some hundred in all, he guessed.

Grace was sung in Latin.

Each went to his place. One of them appeared in a pulpit in the wall and began to read, also in Latin. Lay-brothers girded with white aprons moved about serving the meal, almost noiselessly. The clatter of knives and forks was subdued. A monk appeared, walking down the hall. When he reached the dais he knelt at its foot, with his head bowed. Basil, wondering, glanced at the Abbot.

He seemed not to notice. After a time the monk raised his head, watching the Abbot's face. At a sign he rose, bowed and went to his place.

It was some time before Basil discovered Brother Anselm in the dark-robed rows, all so alike. He was at the top of the table to his left, a few yards away, eating unconcernedly and listening to the voice from the pulpit, now reading in Italian. He found it difficult to realize that this *was* Brother Anselm. He watched him between mouthfuls. He was the same, and yet. . . . He was somehow merged in these hundred monks.

The meal ended.

The Abbot struck the table sharply with a wooden mallet. They rose and stood like an army to attention, hands hidden beneath scapulars. Grace was intoned again. The same long line wended its way from the Refectory through the cloisters to a door half-way round. Through it they passed into a church, a cathedral it seemed to Basil. He knelt at the back beside the Abbot, while the stream dispersed to its knees.

There was dead silence.

§ 2

" It was awfully decent of him to accept me," Basil was saying. He was sitting with Brother Anselm in the gardens.

After the visit in the church he had been taken to the Common Room for Recreation, where Brother Anselm had introduced him first to the Abbot and then to some of the monks. He had been rather overawed by the Abbot with his hooked nose and piercing eyes, and felt more at home with two of the monks who were English, to his surprise. They had talked in English while addressing him, but otherwise in Italian, obliged by the rule to do so ; it was on the Italian side of the Alps here. So one of them had informed him. His eyes had wandered about watching the rest, trying to discover their different nationalities. Some wore beards ; they were from the East on foreign missions, or going there, he learnt. There was the same quality about them all, a kind of self-suppression. He had experienced a curious sense of smallness in their midst.

Recreation had lasted for thirty minutes. After it Brother Anselm had taken him out of doors.

" It was decent, wasn't it ? " repeated Basil.

" The Abbot has not *accepted* you yet, Basil," replied the monk. " You are a *guest* for the first month."

Basil turned.

" Oh ? " he said slowly. " Oh ? . . . I see."

He digested the bald statement.

" Then, what happens—after that ? "

" Packing—generally."

Basil stared.

" How do you mean ? "

" Four weeks are enough, usually."

" Oh ? " said Basil again.

He thought.

" But why ? "

" Most men find they've made a mistake by then."

" What, they've no vocation ? "

" Exactly," said the monk.

Basil looked cheerfully at him. " I simply love it all. It's wonderful."

" One meal is not all," said Brother Anselm.

" No, of course not. But it sort of gives an idea."

" Does it ? "

Basil appeared flattened.

" The order of things is this," the monk pursued indifferently. " If a man still wishes to try his vocation at the end of four weeks, he may ask for admittance to the postulancy. If he *is* admitted and is successful as a postulant, then, after six months or so, he may seek admission to the novitiate. If he is accepted for the novitiate, then he enters for a period to be trained for the religious life. If, during that period he—— What's the matter ? "

Basil was looking aghast.

" But I thought one started straight off ? "

" Oh dear no," replied the monk.

The other was plainly crestfallen. His throat began to work.

" I'm sorry if you've had a wrong impression. Perhaps I should have told you this in my letter."

" But you said the Abbot was willing for me to try my vocation."

" Certainly. So he is. But he's not going to rush you into trying it. You may not even wish to try it."

" But I do."

" At the end of four weeks, I mean," said Brother Anselm. " Look here, Basil, there's something you don't quite understand and I'd better make it clear. An impulse for the religious life is not necessarily a sign of vocation ; especially when it comes at a crisis. There's something else too. You've only been a Catholic for— what, barely four months ? You've hardly found your feet yet."

Basil was silent.

" I'm going to ask you a question. Don't answer it if you'd rather not. Why didn't you tell me what was in your mind at Hendringham, that evening ? "

It embarrassed the boy. He answered, however.

" Because the idea had only occurred a day or two before. At least, seriously. I'd seen that—that it was the end of everything with Beauty. It came after that."

The monk waited.

So did Basil.

" And a fortnight later the idea had become a decision ? So you wrote off to me without further delay to say that you believed God was calling you to the religious life, and that you would like to try your vocation at Issano. The whole thing was decided in your own mind within two weeks ? "

" I'd felt an attraction for some time," said Basil.

" That's nothing. You were still hoping for—the other thing, until quite recently. Isn't that so ? "

" I was still hoping she'd——"

" Quite so. This is what I want to say, though. I wrote back that the Abbot was willing to try you, but that you would be wiser to wait. I then got a cable from you to say that you were starting immediately. You sent it off almost by return, the same day as you left, too. Isn't that right ? "

" Er—yes."

" I had no time to stop you. There was nothing left to do except send a letter down to the hotel for you when you arrived."

There was a shuffle of feet.

" I don't want to hurt, Basil. But haven't you been a bit precipitous ? "

No answer.

" Honestly ? "

Basil's throat was working again.

" What are you driving at ? " came rudely. " Do you want me to go back ? "

Brother Anselm became engrossed in the mountains in front.

" I'm in dead earnest. Don't you believe it, or what ? "

The monk suddenly laughed. " I'd like to spank you."

It brought Basil to his senses.

" I say, I'm awfully sorry. I really am."

Brother Anselm laid a big hand on his curls, pulled

him nearer, and regarded him. Then he looked away over the mountains again.

Basil did the same.

" So you want to be a monk ? "

He turned his head.

Basil nodded.

CHAPTER XXII

MAJOR BRANDRETH chuckled.
He contemplated the coffee-pot, and chuckled
again. He pushed his chair back and stuffed his hands
in his trousers pockets.

More chuckling.

He took a cigarette, struck a match, absently let it burn
down to his fingers, said " Damn ! " blew it out, struck
another and lit up.

After inhaling deeply he began to think—his eyes
resting upon a letter lying open on the breakfast-table,
the envelope of which bore an Italian postmark.

There was an intriguing smile on his face when at
length he rose and crossed the room. It was still there
as he entered his study next door. Inside he stood for
a moment eyeing the telephone. After placing the
morning's letters on his desk he lifted the receiver, gave
a number and waited. Then :

" Hullo ! That you, Beauty ? "

" Speaking," came back.

" Major Brandreth here. I say—going to be in this
morning ? Eh ? "

He listened.

" Dropping in on you, then. Eleven o'clock do ? . . .
Right."

He hung up the receiver.

Before tackling his correspondence he searched amongst
the litter on his desk and found a letter addressed to
himself in Beauty's handwriting. He had received it
some days ago. He drew it from the envelope and read :

"DEAR OLD MAJOR,—You're one of the very best. It was just the nicest thing you could have done to write to me like that. It helped me tremendously. I didn't know you knew. I suppose Brother Anselm must have told you.

"Perhaps some time I'll be able to talk about it; but at present I've got to face it out alone.

"You say our religion's a 'darned queer thing' to shut up men like Basil in monasteries. No, it isn't, dear old pagan, not if it's what he's for. Not if the good God wants him. I never deserved Basil. That's not just a thing to say. It's true. Do you remember: 'It is a far, far better thing I do, than I have ever done'? Well, I want to feel like that—in letting him go.

"But, oh, it hurts, terribly. I don't even know where he is. Major, I can't write about it. I can't.—Yours, BEAUTY."

The Major put the letter down, and blew his nose.

Then he smiled. "It's a darned, darned sight better thing *I* do, than I have ever done. . . . Hullo, cat!"

It was after ten when he left his flat. He walked from Bayswater through Hyde Park, and reached Curzon Street by eleven. At the Mansions he went up in the lift. Outside her door he stood for a moment, then pressed the button. . . .

He emerged at eleven-thirty, hugely pleased, by his face, and walked down the stairs. Outside on the pavement he looked about.

"Hi!" He gesticulated with his stick.

The taxi pulled up and wheeled round. "Oxford Street—Selfridge's." He jumped in. Once on the way he tugged viciously at the scrub of his moustache. "My

God, that girl's suffering hell ! " At Selfridge's he dismissed the taxi and entered the shop. He pushed his way through the swarm, apostrophizing the " damned fug," and reached the department of " Thomas Cook and Son."

Here over the counter he entered into consultation with an affable young man.

Returned to his flat he wrote a letter.

He wrote it slowly and with much care. He addressed it to : " Reverendo Fra Anselmo. Il Monastero, Issano sott'Alpi, Italia."

Then he helped himself to a liberal drink.

*   ●   ●   *   ●   ⁂

The same evening at Hendringham the last post brought a letter also bearing the Italian postmark.

Lady Esterton received it in the drawing-room. She laid down some crotchet-work on her lap, put on her glasses, opened it, drew out the sheet and began to read. At the end of the first page her eyebrows had lifted perceptibly, at the end of the second she was smiling ; by the signature on the third she had become visibly excited.

She gathered up the crotchet-work, dropped it, picked it up with trembling fingers, dumped it on her chair and fluttered out of the room.

She found Lord Esterton in his study, peering over the evening paper at her sudden entry.

" Guess whom this is from." She brandished the letter at him.

He put down the paper and conjectured : " Basil ? "

" No—Brother Anselm. But it's about Basil. Read it."

He took the letter and perused it line by line. His face, at first grave, began to relax. Soon it was beaming. When he had finished he looked up at Lady Esterton and exclaimed : " Thank God ! "

CHAPTER XXIII

§1

BROTHER ANSELM sat perfectly still.
Standing before him was Basil—struck dumb.

A dry sound came from his throat at last, and he found his tongue to ask hoarsely :

" Is that true ? "

" Quite true," the monk replied. " She returned to her religion over two months ago, at the end of February, to be exact."

He was met by a further incredulous stare.

" But it's impossible ! She'd have told me. You're wrong ; I'm certain of it. She said she hadn't."

" Are you sure of that ? " from the monk.

" She said a Catholic oughtn't to marry an apostate."

" Well ? "

" She said so."

" Certainly. But did she say that *she* was an apostate still ? " Basil paused.

" She never suggested anything else."

The monk moved round, facing him.

" You went to her that evening, believing her unchanged. You asked her to marry you, believing her still to be an apostate. That was why she did not enlighten you."

Comprehension was coming.

" If she had done so, the chance to retrieve yourself would have gone ; at any rate, in the way she wanted."

More comprehension, mingled with perplexity.

" But she could have written long before—before that evening."

" She had a reason for not doing so. She wished to prove herself before letting you know."

Doubt returned.

" How do you know all this ? "

" Beauty took me into her confidence."

" Oh ? "

A sudden resentment flashed into the boy's eyes.

" You deceived me, then."

Brother Anselm said quietly :

" Withdraw that, if you please, Basil."

Basil looked obstinate.

" At once ! " snapped out the monk.

In a moment he was hanging his head. " I'm sorry. I'm awfully sorry. I didn't mean it."

" Now listen, Basil. I was as ignorant as yourself, at Hendringham that night. You described what had happened, and I took for granted what you had taken for granted. I learned the truth next day, as a matter of fact. Beauty came and told me about herself."

He understood at length. At least—— The monk read the question in his face.

" Why didn't I tell you at once ? " Basil found the grey eyes fixed upon him. " Yes, Basil, and I even advised Beauty to wait. It lay with you to re-establish yourself first ; that was her stipulation. Then she was free to speak. There was something more. It only came to me while I was talking with her, what it was that was in your mind—that you were thinking of the religious life. It distinctly complicated matters. There was just the possibility of a genuine vocation. Do you see ? "

The force of facts was telling. Basil began to rub his finger about on the table that stood between them.

" Otherwise I should have acted differently. And, incidentally, I should never have asked the Abbot to let you come out here—in answer to your own request."

The rubbing went on. And then stopped suddenly.

" Why have you told me now—about Beauty ? "

Instead of replying the monk went to a locker in the wall, found something and came back.

" That's a letter she wrote to me, after she heard from you.   Read it, if you like."

Basil took it eagerly.

Brother Anselm watched as he read.   The light from the little window fell full upon his face. . . .

" Well ? "

The hand holding the letter had dropped.   Basil was standing, looking through the lattice.   He did not answer.

" It's as you'd wish, surely ?   You gave her to understand that everything was over ? "

Basil made as if to speak, but looked away instead.   He handed back the letter.   Brother Anselm replaced it in the locker, sat down at his table again, and suddenly became brisk.   He consulted a calendar.

" Now, let's see.   It's May the seventh. . . . You've been three weeks here.   You will be free to ask for admission to the postulancy to-day week."

A knock came at the door and a lay-brother entered with letters.   The monk took them.   The lay-brother retired.

" Now, I must get busy," said Brother Anselm.

He heard Basil's feet shift uncertainly and then move towards the door.   At the click of the handle he turned his head quickly and looked.

The boy's shoulders were drooping heavily.

The door closed.   The monk buried his chin in his hands and stared at the wall.   Then he stretched out a hand and fingered the crucifix that stood before him on the table.   He touched the Feet : " Don't let me make a mistake. . . ."

He stirred himself to examine the letters.   Amongst them he found one from Major Brandreth.

" Good ! "

§ 2

A scratching noise.

A match flared. The candle-flame hesitated, grew and revealed Basil leaning on his elbow, the match-stick in his fingers. Its red point vanished and he flung it on the floor.

He lay back in bed and listened. The swishing sound in the corridors outside continued, accompanied now by a low murmur. Once, in strained attention, he shuddered. It ceased. Feet shuffled. Doors closed quietly. Silence.

He had listened like this on other nights. Sometimes he had dropped straight off to sleep and not heard it. To-night he had, subconsciously, waited. On the first occasion the sound had baffled him completely, as well as alarmed. He had questioned Brother Anselm. " Taking the Discipline," the monk had informed him dryly ; it was scourging he had heard. The murmur was the *Miserere*.

He lay still for a few minutes and then threw back the bed-clothes and scrambled out of bed. Inside the cupboard he found a cigarette. There were half a dozen left, his last. As a postulant he would not be allowed to smoke.

He lit it at the candle and wandered to the window. It was open. He watched the distant shapes of the mountains, blowing clouds into the night without. The gardens lay in the moonlight, blue peacefulness above.

The cigarette became a butt-end. He threw it out and went back to bed. There was a puff at the candle, and darkness. After that the rustle of straw mattress.

An hour later the moon was streaming in. He was lying on his back with his hands behind his head, wide awake. Eleven o'clock boomed in the stillness from the monastery tower. At the last stroke he turned on to his side. Soon there came the sound of regular breathing.

It was a quarter to the midnight when a bell began to clang, distantly. The sound drew nearer. It ceased ;

then resumed closer still. It ceased again ; then came crashing along the corridors and past Basil's door.

He stirred. There was a grunt.

" Phew ! "

Then :

" Damn ! "

He raised himself wearily, lit his candle and rolled slowly out of bed. On the table in the middle of the room his clothes were dumped in a heap. He stripped off his pyjamas and began to dress. There was an impatient wrestle with twisted braces.

By three minutes to twelve he was in the corridor, tugging to straighten his coat. He followed the hooded figures making leisurely towards the head of the stairs at the far end, each carrying a lighted lanthorn—a silent stream of ghosts. At the bottom he followed again through the cloisters and out into the *cortile*. The night air struck cold. The stream congested at the sacristy door beyond. It flowed through. Basil climbed the narrow stairs leading to the tribune at the back of the church, the place from which guest aspirants could watch the Night Office. He entered through the door in the wall, closing it behind him, genuflected and knelt against the stone balustrade. It was flush with the wall-face, and the sensation was of kneeling in mid-air. There was darkness beneath and above, concealing the columns and roof of the immense nave. A glimmer of oil-lamps hanging in screened-off chapels faintly illuminated the aisles.

He waited.

A side door down below opened, pouring in a flood of light. There came through a double line of figures, each one with his lanthorn. The procession turned up the middle of the nave. They came on endlessly, a glittering river, flowing up the steps of the choir, wave upon wave, slowly dispersing to the stalls. There were scrapings as the monks fixed their lanthorns in position.

The Office began.

Every night for four weeks Basil had watched this scene—the blazing glory of the choir, the altar beyond, the mighty crucifix hanging high up in black outline. He had watched, absorbed. He had related himself to it in imagination, seeing himself amongst them there.

To-night he watched again, but in an unseeing kind of way.

As the sonorous chant swayed up and down, he moved restlessly from one knee to the other. At the first Lection he sat, lit the candle on a bracket by his head, and opened a breviary. It had been lent by Brother Anselm, and he had learned to follow the Latin in places. His head bent to it now. For a time he remained so. Then he was shifting restlessly once more.

At the end of the second Lection an impatient breath escaped him. He closed the book with a snap, laid it on the top of the balustrade, and folded his arms. . . .

It was over. The last lanthorn had disappeared into the sacristy.

He stayed staring into the darkness of the nave. After a while he moved as if to go ; but, instead, remained —his hands hanging at his side. Next he shook himself, muttering fiercely. His fingers began to clench and unclench. In the candlelight the veins on his forehead were standing out.

Then, all in a moment, he dropped on his knees, with his head pressed against the stone of the balustrade, his shoulders writhing. . . .

The sacristy door clicked.
In the flickering glow from the lamps the figure of

Brother Anselm passed down the side aisle. He glanced up at the tribune before vanishing into the blackness of the choir. There was some rustling.

And then quiet.

The head on the balustrade raised itself.

CHAPTER XXIV

§ I

THE Abbot had listened at first with an assumed severity, tapping spasmodically on the table with the butt of his pen as if in disapproval. With the unfolding of the case, however, the show of sternness had been laid aside and a very human twinkle come into his eyes.

"And when is it to be?" he had asked at the end.

"To-day, with your permission, Father Abbot."

"An act of charity does not require permission, Padre Anselmo."

* * * * * *

The lay-brother, whose duty it was to admit visitors, had a little room off the entrance-hall of the nature of a sentry-box. In this room was the only telephone in the monastery.

This morning about ten o'clock a tap came on his door and he opened it to Brother Anselm. On hearing that the monk wanted to use the telephone he withdrew into the hall. There, snatches of a one-sided conversation, at first in Italian and then in English, reached him through the half-open door.

The Italian preliminaries were apparently with the manager of the hotel down at Issano, who was questioned whether an English *signor* (name not caught) had arrived last night. He had, it seemed ; for the *signor* was to be informed, with *complimenti*, that his presence was required at the telephone.

There was a wait.

The lay-brother heard a chuckle of pleasure from Brother Anselm, and English noises. He knew very little English, but the sounds undoubtedly indicated delight. " Brick ! " was called out twice. The lay-brother wondered what " brick " was. Something was " Splendid ! " —three times. Then Brother Anselm was listening and saying, " Yes ? " occasionally ; next, engaging in a low and rapid conversation, the drift of which was entirely lost. The only further words conveying anything intelligible were : " Six o'clock, then."

A click told him that the receiver had been replaced. Brother Anselm emerged, smiling broadly to himself, pulled the lay-brother's nose, and went off down the corridor with great swinging strides.

The lay-brother looked after him with his mouth open.

＊　　＊　　＊　　＊　　＊　　＊

§ 2

" You didn't shave this morning, Basil."

Brother Anselm threw it over his shoulder and then drove in the spade with his foot. Basil's solemn countenance lightened a shade.

" I doubt if you brushed your hair."

He left the spade standing in the soil, wheeled round and surveyed him.

" Your general appearance is that of a fourth-rate tramp. Is that the only suit you've got ? "

Basil was looking astounded.

" But—aren't you going to answer me ? "

" Your vocation ? We've an hour yet. How long would it take to shave and put on a decent suit ? "

Basil was more astounded.

" What's the idea, exactly ? "

" The idea," said the monk, " is that an immaculate

young man who arrived here four weeks ago should reappear in half an hour's time. Now go ! "

" But——"

" Go, or——" Brother Anselm seized a pitchfork.

Basil went.

The monk watched him to the side door of the monastery, and through it.

Then he strode quickly across the gardens to the main entrance. Inside he tapped on the lay-brother's door and entered in response to " *Avanti.*" The door closed after him. Quite shortly it opened again and Brother Anselm came out, followed by the lay-brother, who was saying, " *Si, Reverendo* " repeatedly to some injunctions. They went outside and down the gravel drive that led to the gates. Half-way, Brother Anselm stopped and indicated the road beyond them, winding its way down to the left steeply with the valley. He pointed to a bend in it, at a distance. The lay-brother pointed after him, interrogatively. Brother Anselm pointed again, emphatically. The lay-brother pointed again, corroboratively. Brother Anselm seemed satisfied. The lay-brother walked on towards the gates. Brother Anselm walked back towards the monastery.

He crossed the gardens to the right and went through the archway in the enclosure wall. On the other side he was in what Basil and he referred to as " Eric's place." Here he surveyed for a minute.

Then he returned to the gardens and resumed his digging.

Shortly after half-past five Basil reappeared along the path to where Brother Anselm was working.

The monk turned a last sod, drove his spade in the earth and inspected him. He was well groomed now, with a polished head of curls and face smoothly shaved.

A smartly cut tweed suit adorned his person, and brown shoes that had been carefully cleaned.

" You'll do," said the monk. " Come along."

He led the way to a seat further on, at the extreme point of the gardens from the monastery.

In front of the seat, to its left, stood a shrub obstructing the view. Basil dropped into the other corner, to the right. Brother Anselm took him firmly by the shoulders and plumped him to the left, proceeding to occupy the right himself, from where the meadows could be seen running down to the road below. To Basil's momentary surprise at this behaviour he replied with an enigmatical smile.

" So you want to know what I think ? " he began. " Before I give you my answer, will you tell me this ? Do you wish to ask the Abbot for admission to the postulancy ? You are free to do so to-day."

Basil crimsoned painfully.

The monk waited, drumming a tune with his fingers on the wood of the seat. His eyes were on the road.

" Well ? "

There was a scrape from the boy's throat. He shifted his position. The monk folded his arms beneath his scapular and studied his sandals.

Gloomy silence.

" What's the trouble, Basil ? "

Basil suddenly sprang to his feet :

" Oh, I'm a damned coward ! I'm a damned coward ! "

It was choked out.

" I hate myself ! "

He stamped angrily away, and then stood there glaring and biting his lips.

" You'll think me an absolute fool ! "

" No, I shan't," said Brother Anselm.

He sat still, giving him time. Basil began pacing up and down. When he had succeeded in controlling himself, it was to blurt out :

" I didn't know it was like this."

" Tell me," encouraged the monk gently.

Basil swallowed.

He began jerkily. He continued more easily as he found Brother Anselm listening with entire sympathy.

It took him five minutes.

" You don't mind, do you ? " he finished with, apologetically.

" Not a bit," replied Brother Anselm. " Now, sit down."

Basil did so.

" You've said very much what other men have said at the end of a few weeks. It merely comes to this. The natural man in you is revolting against what seems inhuman. Certain things appear almost brutal, the scourging and so on. It could scarcely be otherwise. You're not a coward."

" But *you*——"

" I'm a monk. The religious life is my vocation. You're not a coward, Basil. You couldn't be a coward if you tried. This is not a question of cowardice, but natural repugnance."

A gleam of relief was appearing.

" Does it mean I haven't a vocation, then ? "

" Repugnance is nothing to go by. I hated it all, at first," said the monk.

Basil was silent.

" *By itself* repugnance is nothing."

The deliberate emphasis brought the crimson surging back. The grey eyes fixed him mercilessly for a moment, and then became intent on the road below. From a distance came the sound of a car, audible in the stillness of the valley.

" I will answer your question."

Basil braced himself.

" In a few minutes' time."

He looked surprised.

" Meanwhile—have you heard from your people lately ? "

Basil was more surprised. He answered, however :

" I had a letter from the Mater this morning."

The note of the car was increasing with its approach.
Brother Anselm edged, carelessly, to the extreme end of
the seat.

" Are they all right ? "

" Oh yes."

The purr of the engine came strongly round the bend
of the road. Basil became aware of it.

" Visitors ? " he asked disinterestedly.

" Probably," replied the monk, equally disinterestedly.
The note of the engine lowered and ceased. The car had
evidently stopped.

" The Mater's more cheerful," Basil volunteered.

Brother Anselm did not seem to hear. His eyes were
narrowed, as if watching something.

" Sorry," he said. " The Mater—what ? "

" She's more cheerful, I think."

" Good ! "

Six o'clock rang out from the clock in the tower,
followed by the chime of the Angelus. They stood and
said it together. Basil dropped into his former position
on the seat and contemplated the shrub before him.
Brother Anselm sauntered leisurely to the low wall in
front, from beneath which the meadows fell away on
their downward sweep. He shaded his eyes from the
sun and observed the path on the left which climbed up
from the road through the long grass, as if following
some object. With his back still to Basil, and for no
apparent reason, he began remarking on the mountains.
Basil responded with " Ums " and grew restless.

Brother Anselm turned round at length.

There was a mysterious smile on his face. He came
nearer and took stock of a gap beyond the shrub, through

which the path could be seen entering the trees that sheltered " Eric's place." Next, he strolled round and occupied the gap with his large person, arms akimbo.

" What *are* you doing ? " asked Basil.

Brother Anselm was still smiling.

" You asked me about your vocation."

" Yes."

" And you want my answer ? "

" Very much."

" You will find it over there." The monk indicated " Eric's place."

Basil stared.

" Sorry. I don't quite see."

Brother Anselm pointed towards the archway in the enclosure wall.

" That's the way."

Basil stood up. He looked in the direction and then back at the monk.

" Is this a joke ? "

Brother Anselm came across and linked his arm. " Come along."

He led him in bewilderment across the garden. At the archway he stopped. Without saying anything he stood aside. Basil turned enquiringly. The monk was motioning him to pass through. He took a step forward, hesitated and glanced. . . .

" Go on ! " said Brother Anselm roughly, in a queer voice. His face was averted.

Basil did so, and passed through the archway. On the other side he turned round.

Brother Anselm had left him.

§ 3

Basil stuck his hands in his pockets, mystified.

He wondered perplexedly why Brother Anselm had

gone—and why he had looked like that. There had been something strange about him. He had never seen him like . . . Yes, he had. Brother Anselm had looked like that when Eric was . . . He had not wanted him to see his face. " Go on ! " His voice had gone all shaky. . . . But he had been smiling just before. . . .

Basil looked about.

He went slowly down the avenue that led to the grove amidst the trees, puzzling.

Why here ?

It was the place he had come to frequently during the last four weeks—to dream at first ; then to struggle with himself. To-day, early, he had paced up and down this path, calling himself a coward. Brother Anselm had shattered the notion with one sentence just now, and lifted an immense weight from his soul. The monk had answered his self-accusation, but not his question.

Was he to decide it for himself ? Here ?

He paused half-way down the avenue. But Brother Anselm had said : " *My* answer." He went forward slowly. The trees parted more widely, opening out to encircle " Eric's place."

On the fringe of the green sward in its midst he paused again, held by the strange spell of its peace, the deep stillness. From beyond came the tinkle of the stream. He could hear in the distance the clink of spades—the monks at work in the gardens. From the tree-tops came the wind's whisperings. Above them the evening glow.

Whether some movement attracted his attention or whether it was intuition, he never knew ; but there was a sudden sense of not being alone here. He looked around. Something met his eye, at the side where the path from the meadows entered. Next moment he saw it was a white dress. A girl was standing there beneath the foliage twenty yards away, a ray of sunlight striking her uncovered head. She moved. She was coming towards him. . . .

He stared. His heart began to thump. He tried to speak, but could not. Only when she was before him, the cry came hoarsely :

"Beauty !" . . .

"It is *you*, Basil ?"

Even now, as he heard her voice, it seemed impossible. He came a step nearer, as if to assure himself.

They stood there, a yard apart.

Her colour was returning ; she had been as white as her dress at the recognition. The truth of her slowly took possession. . . .

"How did you find out ?"

She answered in a maze :

"I didn't know you were here. I don't understand."

"But . . . Somebody told you ?"

"Basil, I was told nothing."

He was baffled, utterly.

"How did you get here ?"

She pointed towards the meadows :

"The Major sent me up. He's gone round by the road."

"The Major ?"

He put his hand to his forehead.

"We're at Issano. He brought me with him."

He stared.

"But—what's the idea ?"

"He wouldn't tell me."

The hand dropped.

He remained with his lips pursed in concentration. His eyes wandered over the green sward, about the trees, to the avenue, at the far end of which the enclosure wall could be seen, and the archway. . . .

Suddenly he started.

His head turned and his eyes met hers.

" Beauty ? " . . .

He whispered it wonderingly. The tense expression was relaxing.

A smile came.

" Beauty ! "

She watched his face.

" Oh, Beauty ! Can't you see ? "

She shook her head.

" I know nothing. I didn't know you were here."

" Oh, my dear ! " he cried.

He was drinking her in now. She was no longer an incredible vision, but a glorious reality whose significance had burst upon him. His look became radiant with the joy of what he understood—and she did not.

" Help me, Basil," she was saying.

He answered :

" It was Brother Anselm."

And then he told her the thing he had just guessed.

●　　　●　　　●　　　●　　　●　　　●

She knew now.

And why the monk had sent for her. She had turned away, the colour glowing in her cheeks.

Basil had come to a halt.

He was watching her, shyly—the golden head bent down, the slim form poised tremblingly, the loveliness and all the wonder of her that he had striven to drive from his life. He did not move—held by the spell of her nearness.

She turned round.

Without speaking, she laid her hands upon his shoulders. For a while her eyes looked steadily into his. Then tears came, blinding them both. When he could see again, there was something in those blue wells of purity that brought the fire flaming through his being and left him shaking under her touch.

Her arms closed round his neck and she drew his head down. . . .

      o   *   *   *   *   *

They had been sitting there on the grass for some time, holding hands like two children. The hush of evening had fallen.

" It's so silent. What is this place ? "

" It's Eric's place," he whispered. And explained.

She looked about, in awe.

" His Paradise. . . ."

The sun's rays were slanting through the trees, patching the sward with gold. The gap opposite, where the pathway entered, was all white glory from the distant Alps.

" Oh, Basil, I'm glad it was here."

She nestled her head on his shoulder until his cheek was against her hair.

They were still for a time.

" You dear, dear monk," she murmured.

Basil moved.

" But, I'm not a monk."

" I meant Brother Anselm," she said.

THE MASTERFUL MONK is the best-known of Father Dudley's books and introduces the main character of several of his novels — Brother Anselm Thornton, the monk himself.

THE MASTERFUL MONK is also Father Dudley's answer to the present-day attack on man's moral nature. It is the romance of Beauty Dethier, a society girl, and Basil Esterton, a handsome and intelligent young man. The main theme of the story is the antagonism between Father Anselm Thornton, the champion of Catholicism, and the free-thinker Julian Verrers who is the spokesman of certain materialistic scientists, philosophers and leaders of thought. Father Anselm saves Beauty from the sinister influence of Verrers and plays an exciting role in saving Basil's life.

There is no over-moralising in the telling of this story. Rather, incident is flung upon incident and climax upon climax to unfold the theme and force the moral issue.